Flowers from Afghanistan

Suzy Parish

Flowers from Afghanistan
COPYRIGHT 2018 by Suzy Parish

All scripture quotations, unless otherwise indicated, are taken from the Holy Bible, New International Version(R), NIV(R), Copyright 1973, 1978, 1984, 2011 by Biblica, Inc.™ Used by permission of Zondervan. All rights reserved worldwide. www.zondervan.com

Cover Design by *Nicola Martinez*
Cover photo courtesy of *Stacy Defourneaux Photography*
Green Beans Coffee used with permission of Green Beans Coffee Company
Zarbul Masalha: 151 Afghan Dari Proverbs by Captain Edward Zellem used with permission of Captain Edward ZellemNo Dogs Get Left Behind used with permission of Save the Pups, Inc

Harbourlight Books, a division of Pelican Ventures, LLC
www.pelicanbookgroup.com PO Box 1738 *Aztec, NM * 87410
Harbourlight Books sail and mast colophon is a trademark of Pelican Ventures, LLC

Publishing History
First Harbourlight Edition, 2018
Paperback Edition ISBN 978-1-5223-0044-1
Hardcover Edition ISBN 978-1-5223-0116-5
Electronic Edition ISBN 978-1-5223-0042-7
Published in the United States of America

Dedication

In 2011, my husband, Investigator Chet Williams, set out on assignment to train Afghan nationals in police techniques. His e-mails painted vivid sights and sounds that inspired me to write Flowers from Afghanistan. The attack scenes are very close to what my husband experienced. The story of Mac's running shoes is an actual event.

Chet, you were the eyes and ears necessary for this book. You are the one who described starry nights in Afghanistan and made me fall in love with children like Bashir.

I love you, babe, for your sacrifice for your country and your family.

For the lights of my life; my husband Chet, our children; Stacy, Christi, Ashley, and our grandchildren, Simon, Jack, and Cora.

For Jesus Christ, The Light of the World.

1

Huntsville, Alabama-2010

"Little Mac, where are you?"

Giggles came from behind an old sheet draped over our breakfast nook table, a makeshift tent. I pretended to look behind the sofa. "Are you behind the couch?"

More giggles.

"Are you under the coffee table?" I crawled on my belly, looking in the 3-inch space between the coffee table and floor. "Nope. I don't see you."

Infectious laughter.

I crawled over to the table, slowly, slowly, calling his name until–"Gotcha!" I threw the sheet back and grabbed him in my arms, tumbling and tickling him until his laughter bounced off the walls.

"I thought I heard my two favorite guys!" Sophie came in from the kitchen, pulling an oven glove off her hand and laying the mitt on the table. The yeasty smell of warm bread breezed in her wake. "I'm having photos made from your going away party. The sergeant's words about you were very touching. I hadn't heard stories about a few of those calls you were on. How was the office party today?"

"Good. Chief even came by to wish me luck."

"Luck. I hope you have more than luck. I'm praying for God's protection."

I shook my head. "Don't start in on me about God-stuff again."

Sophie turned away. "Dinner's ready."

"I promised the guys I'd bring Little Mac by the barbershop to visit and get a haircut."

"Wait until tomorrow. You'll have more time," Sophie said.

If I'd listened to her, things would be different.

I ignored her request and scooped him off the floor, dressed him in khaki shorts, a blue T-shirt, and red sneakers. My little man was going for a haircut at the same barbershop all my fellow police officers on first shift frequented. "We won't be long," I said.

"If you won't listen to me, then at least take a picture of us before you go. I'll miss these curls." She wound her finger around a bit of his strawberry blond bangs and kissed his forehead. Sophie hugged Little Mac into her lap.

He squirmed.

"Hand him his pinwheel. That always settles him down."

I found my son's favorite toy on the end table and handed it down to Sophie, trying to center their faces on my phone. "Say, Pumpernickel!" The name of that bread always made Little Mac laugh.

"Pump-a-ni-coo," he repeated in his squeaky voice. Little Mac's face spread into another of his infectious grins. The dimple on his left cheek deepened as he spun the pinwheel. The blue blades threw glints of light onto the floor and ceiling. He clutched the plastic toy to his chest like it was a treasure.

I bought it for him when Sophie was still carrying him in her womb. I was amazed it survived two years of his rough play. He graduated to toy cars and building sets, but the pinwheel was still his favorite. I snapped a picture, a light flashed, illuminating the room. They were frozen in time on my phone. I'd won the argument but wasted precious time. The barbershop was only four blocks away, but it closed in thirty minutes. I scooped Little Mac from Sophie's lap.

"Babe?"

I stopped mid-step at the door.

"Drive careful. It looks like a storm is on its way."

"Will do," I said, blowing Sophie an air kiss. I hurried outside carrying Little Mac, letting the screen door slam behind me. Lightning flashed in the west. I pulled away in a cloud of dust.

Little Mac kicked his feet against the back of my double cab truck seat, in time to his favorite song.

I sang along, though Sophie wouldn't have called it singing. I put on my turn signal and stopped at the red light. When I hit my brake, my cell phone slid across the front seat. I grabbed it, and as I did, a text message flashed. My breath caught. It was the name of a first shift dispatcher who'd sent me on most of my calls. *I thought I'd made it clear when she approached me at my going-away party. I wasn't interested in any relationship outside my marriage.* I fumbled with the button to erase the message.

The light turned green.

I hit the gas. How did she have the guts to text–

Out of the corner of my eye, a flash.

The loud bang of two vehicles colliding reverberated in my head, then grinding metal on metal. Airbags deployed.

I coughed and blinked to clear my eyes of the white cloud that filled the truck.

Smoke? Are we on fire? No, it's powder from air bags.

The truck stopped spinning. I tore myself from the seatbelt, grabbed my pocket knife and cut Little Mac free from his car seat harness. "Hold on, son!"

Red lights flashed. No siren. No traffic sounds. Only the fear-filled bass of my heart and my own ragged breaths. It seemed to take forever to reach the ambulance. I tucked Little Mac's small body against my chest. Focus. A few more feet. I ran until I threatened to push my lungs and legs past their limit of endurance. I handed my two-year-old son off to the waiting paramedic and jumped in the back of the ambulance with them.

Later all 1 could recall was his hand, so tiny, grasping my sleeve as if he were trying to do his part, too.

2

Huntsville, Alabama-2011

Sophie hovered around me like those moths that fling themselves against the lights in ball fields. "I still don't understand how you can leave for Afghanistan. It's only been a year since…"

I continued to sort my equipment into piles to pack. Socks, underwear, T-shirts. A plastic bag held my body building supplements.

Sophie paced around my gear in the living room, her hands fluttering, clenching and unclenching.

When I was a boy, I'd pick up those little moths, thinking I could save them. Instead, handling them rubbed the powder off their wings until they could no longer fly. I had to get away before I did the same thing to Sophie. "It'll pay off the medical bills. Contract work as a police trainer is not the same as being military."

Her face crumpled.

I dropped the pile of T-shirts I was packing and drew her into my arms, carefully so I wouldn't rub off the imaginary powder. I cradled her face in my hands, made her look at me. "We can do this."

She was not buying it. She wrenched out of my arms. Redness crept up her neck, colored her cheeks. Who was I kidding? Sophie was no fragile moth. She was an iron butterfly.

"Is that all you have to say? We can do this?

Where is the 'we' Mac? Because all I see right now is the 'you.' You signed up for this mission. You know what I'm doing? I'm packing our little boy's things and cleaning a room that will never be used by him again."

I could make order out of my clothes, but I had no answer for Sophie. Shame kept my gaze from seeking hers. I continued to pack. I was aware of Sophie's voice in the background, but I wasn't focused on what she was saying. In my head, I saw Little Mac's curly hair covered in blood.

"Mac? Did you hear what I said?"

I shook my head to erase the image of Little Mac in my arms, his warmth pressed against my chest. "What?"

"I'd like to escape, too. You aren't the only one struggling. I'll never watch Little Mac play baseball, never see him go to prom. Now I don't have dreams. I barely sleep."

I twisted my face away, turned toward the wall so she wouldn't see I was in torment. If there really was a hell, I was already there. I wasn't escaping. I was serving a self-imposed sentence for killing our son.

Sophie's foot brushed against my backpack, and it toppled over. The bright blue fins of the pinwheel protruded from the side pocket. "You're taking Little Mac's pinwheel?"

"It helps me feel close to him."

She didn't have an answer for that. She took a deep breath, and her shoulders relaxed. Was she finally accepting my departure?

When I picked up my running shoes, her forehead wrinkled in frustration.

She changed the subject. "Where are your boots?"

"My boots?"

"You know, the ones they issued you?"

"Oh, I don't get those until I hit Arkansas. It's where we'll do our initial training, and our gear will be issued."

Her face clouded for a moment, and then a thoughtful look replaced frustration.

"What?" I asked.

She smiled and shook her head. Her blond hair swung across her face, and she flipped it away. She leaned over and hugged me. I guessed the cloudburst was over for the time being.

"I'm not mad, but it'll be lonely here. I know you feel you need to go, and I'll be happy once those bills are paid. Maybe then we can heal." She studied me intently, eyes full of hope. She twined her fingers through my red hair. It'd taken months to grow out, and I looked more like a surfer dude than an investigator. Sophie's finger twirled a bit of hair at my temple.

"You won't get all this cut off, will you? I love your hair long."

"No. Contractors aren't held to the same standards as active military."

Sophie's hands moved to my shoulders. She leaned against me as if she were trying to hold on to us as a couple, as if she were savoring the moment. Instead of comforting me, the action made me nervous.

"You know I wouldn't go unless I had no other choice." My heart beat rapidly. Was I convincing Sophie? Did she suspect I was responsible for Little Mac's death? I had to get away where I could sort the nightmare in my head. That was why I chose Afghanistan. I couldn't think of any place more unlike Huntsville's rolling green mountains and parks full of families.

Sophie shook my shoulders. "Mac? Did you hear what I just said? Hand me your running shoes. They'll have to do."

I handed her my shoes and went back to work, stuffing items in my duffle bag.

A few minutes later Sophie returned with a mysterious smile on her lips. She dropped the shoes in my lap.

I'd learned when Sophie got an idea in her head it was best to comply, forget the argument, and file the questions.

I should have paid more attention to those running shoes.

3

Kandahar, Afghanistan-2011

My running shoes were white when I left Huntsville. I looked down, studied them. Tan against the plywood floor of the tent. I doubted they'd ever look the same again. I was no longer the same man who spoke vows to Sophie. I felt as filthy inside as my shoes looked. During the day Afghanistan took me away from the pain of causing Little Mac's death. Nights were different. At night every black thought shrieked in my dreams.

A knock at my tent door made me jump. I hadn't been in camp very long, and any unexpected noise made me jittery.

Travis, another of the police trainers, pushed his way into my room. From my seat on my gorilla box locker, his lanky runner's frame loomed over me.

"Hey, I noticed you're using that thing for a chair."

"Yeah, well, the room was advertised as unfurnished."

Travis chuckled. "Come on." He led me down the hallway into a small area we used as a snack room. It was sparsely furnished with a shelf, coffeepot, and college dorm fridge.

Another of the instructors at the camp, one new to me, poured himself a mug of black coffee. The scorched odor of day old coffee overtook the small area. "What are you two up to?" He shook his head as if he were correcting unruly students.

"Shelf building detail. You up for it?" Travis asked.

"What? Did you destroy yours again?"

Travis ignored the remark and nudged me toward the coffee-drinking dude. "Mac, this is Glenn Thurman. He's an instructor at camp, but his unofficial position is procurement, at least in this tent."

I stuck out my hand, and Glenn's engulfed it. Broad shouldered and square all over, he gripped like a vise. I tried not to let on, but it felt as if he was breaking my fingers. It was a challenge. I looked him in the eyes and didn't break contact. "Nice to meet you."

"Glenn's the old man around camp. Thirty-eight," Travis said.

Glenn grimaced. He released my hand and brushed shaggy brown hair out of his eyes. The haircut made him look younger than his years. But he appeared to be a guy who'd gotten into one too many fist fights with life and lost. "So, we have shelves to build?"

"Yep," I said.

Glenn swigged his coffee then winced. "Burned my tongue. Always do that." He sauntered down the narrow, dark hallway, balancing his coffee mug. He stopped at the room across the hall from mine and shoved the door open. Glenn sat his cup down on a vintage keyhole desk. The top had swirls of chestnut stain, and it was decorated with bronze drawer pulls. He turned to us. "Wipe your feet."

Travis obediently backed up and wiped his feet on a small mat.

What kind of pull did this Glenn guy have around

here?

The room was the same size as mine, but the similarity ended there. I bent down and ran my hand across a handmade, red and gold wool rug, framed in red diamond shapes. "This is incredible. Feels like velvet."

Glenn was on his belly, dragging boards from under the cot.

"Where'd you get all this?" I asked.

The dense carpet muffled Glenn's voice. He felt around under the bedframe. "This is my home. I don't have a wife to go back to like you guys, so I make the best of where I am." He straightened and pulled more two-by-fours from under the bed. "Travis and I go on scouting missions to the dump. Occasionally, we come up with excellent finds."

"The rug?"

"No, not that. That was a birthday gift to me. Top-of-the-line. Made by the locals." A twitchy, sad smile pulled at the corners of his mouth.

I couldn't tell if he was proud of his bounty or wished he had a wife back in the States.

He motioned to me. "Grab that hammer and nails."

The construction crew had a new member. We walked barely three feet across the hall and into my room.

Glenn grunted disapprovingly when he saw the gorilla box and my books and other items piled on the floor. Embarrassment made heat creep up my neck. Back home, Sophie made fun of me for being compulsively organized. She wouldn't recognize the mess I was living in now.

"Hey, watch it. You daydreaming? I need help

here," Glenn said.

His voice made me jump. It resounded like rusted hinges on an ancient barn door. I stepped back as a board sailed near my head, narrowly missed my chin. Either the caffeine kicked in, or Glenn savored the challenge of making a desk out of all this chaos. Flinging boards here, nails there, he handed me a two-by-four. "We've got to get you up to speed. Be right back." A few seconds later, he was back with a short handsaw. "Travis, hold the end of this board across the gorilla box. We're making a man's desk."

I marked off lines with a tape measure and Glenn made the first cut.

Travis steadied the board as the metal teeth of the saw bit into soft pine.

An hour later, we stood back and admired our work.

"You might have the nicest room in the tent." Travis ran his hand across the plywood desk. "Wanna trade?"

Glenn gathered his tools. He stepped back with satisfaction in his eyes. "Not bad, only he needs a chair, and I know where we can get one."

"Where?" Travis asked.

"I took a jog around camp today and noticed three broken computer chairs on the trash pile. With a little luck, we may be able to get one good one from the parts," Glenn said.

The sun sank behind the cold mountains of the lower Hindu Kush to the west of camp.

I remembered a small flashlight I kept in my gorilla box. I dug it out and flicked the switch. On, off, on. "I'm game if you two are."

4

"Watch it," Travis said.

I jumped.

"There are camel spiders out here, man. They're as big as my hand."

"Do they bite?"

"Heck yeah. They can near take your finger off." He squinted into the dark. "And don't think you can outrun them. Ten miles per hour, top speed. The things are like gazelles on crack."

"I'll be careful."

Travis needed a vacation.

I swept the flashlight side to side as we picked our way in darkness down the wide gravel path that surrounded the camp. The night air was shredded by jets flying so low I felt as if I could reach up and touch them. I shivered from excitement rather than the coolness of the desert air, which was welcome, compared to the sizzling high that day: one hundred fourteen.

Sitting at a desk and standing behind lecterns all day left my legs eager to stretch out on a walk. I squinted, taking in the scenery, and trying to remember the way in case Glenn decided to pull another trash run. There wasn't much in the way of landmarks, just rows and rows of cement walls engulfed in darkness. They closed in on me until my gaze found the night sky.

Travis plowed into my back.

"Hey." Travis bounced off. "Watch where you're going."

I didn't reply. I was too busy taking in the expanse of a night sky that opened before me. I tipped my head back, like a parched man under a spigot. The sky was blue-black, flecked with silver. Like the lapis lazuli stones indigenous to the region. The moon was so bright I could see the crags on its face. I didn't want to leave the spot. The scene drew me in like a sleeping bag on a frosty night.

Travis followed my gaze. "I remember the first time I saw the night sky here. I did the same thing. Just stared. Back home, city lights obscure the stars."

I didn't answer. My mind was back at another night, black as this. Only there were no stars to give hope.

"Here it is. Come on," Glenn called impatiently from five yards ahead.

I reluctantly moved forward.

He was backlit by the orange glow of the burn pit, an area enclosed on three sides by twenty-foot-high blackened cement walls. It burned day and night, smoke constantly spiraling up from embers. The wreckage was piled next to the pit, waiting to be thrown in. Small pockets of flame eerily threw shadows on the soot-covered walls.

I instinctively covered my nose as acrid smoke blew in my face.

Travis sneezed.

Glenn was already dismantling a chair. "No sense in carrying back more than we need. Pull off the good parts and leave the rest." He pulled a pair of pliers from the cotton laundry sack and tossed the tool high in the air in an arc toward me. "Heads up."

I made a grab for it, but it spiraled over my head and plowed into a mound of rags.

A high-pitched squeal of something in torment erupted from the pile.

Three of us who endured daily explosions jumped at the sound of innocence.

For a moment, I hesitated. My brain was whirring. Years of training kicked in. I stuck my flashlight between my teeth and moved toward the sound, dreading what I would find. I swept the filthy mound with my foot, probing for whatever had made that cry. Ashes coiled up reducing the effectiveness of the flashlight. On the fourth search, my foot bumped a mass, about the size of a loaf of bread, and as soft. A shiver ran up my back, but I steeled myself. Working in law enforcement for seven years taught me to stuff my feelings down. I gently pulled aside filthy rags.

Next to my boot, curled in a ball, was a black and gray mottled puppy. His littermates lay close beside him, but they hadn't fared as well. At least their suffering was over.

I gently probed the puppy with my hand, and it wiggled. Its pink tongue protruded over white baby teeth. The animal's chest heaved in and out with great effort.

Travis called low behind me. "What is it?" He didn't approach, but hung back.

I bent down and gathered the animal in my arms. "Glenn, hand me that bag."

Glenn moved hesitantly forward, all bravado went out of his walk. He handed me the olive-green bag.

I swaddled the animal in it like an infant. I cradled him against my chest and walked him back toward the gravel path.

The still-frightened wheeze of his breath echoed against the night air.

Travis finally seemed to make up his mind about the situation. He moved closer and lifted the cloth now swaddled in my arms. He did a sharp, ragged intake when he saw fur. "Oh." Travis wiped sweat from his face in apparent relief. "I was afraid it was a baby."

I ran my hand across the ashy fur. "How did this puppy get here?"

Glenn gathered his tools. "Locals. Dogfighting's a huge sport over here. In litters, only the best are kept for fighting. Runts are usually left to die or are killed." He continued to sift the ashes for chair parts. "Afghanistan's a harsh place, for man and beast." Glenn gathered as many pieces as he could hold. "Travis, get the rest. Make sure we don't leave anything behind." He turned to me. "Come on. Let's go put your chair together."

I was more than ready to leave that place. I handed my flashlight to Travis and followed the weaving glow that guided our steps. I could feel the drumming of the puppy's heart beating against the palm of my hand. Down inside me, stirrings of hope flickered like the light against those cement walls. Life could spring from ashes. I lowered my mouth next to the grimy ears and spoke soothingly, quietly so the guys couldn't hear me, "You'll grow up big and strong." I paused to think for a moment. "Phoenix."

We burst into my room and dumped chair parts on the floor in a heap.

"I need a chair base." Glenn sat on the plywood flooring and held out his hand.

Travis fished chair parts aside and laid them out like instruments to a surgeon. "Here." Travis handed

Glenn a chrome base.

"It's missing a wheel."

"Wait." I set the puppy down on the floor and dug through the pile of dirty parts. "I know I saw a loose one a minute ago." My hand closed around a smooth, plastic wheel. "Here it is." I handed it over to Glenn, and as I bent low, the puppy slipped beside me and licked my face. My mouth drew up into an involuntary grin. I waved him off, got up, and filled a plastic bowl with water.

He gingerly lapped until the bowl was empty, then waddled over. Just getting him hydrated seemed to make a huge difference. His belly began to swell out.

Glenn sat cross-legged, the chair base in his lap. He mumbled at me as he held a screw in the corner of his mouth. "So, what brings you to this godforsaken country?"

"He gets straight to the point, doesn't he?" I glanced over Glenn's head at Travis.

Glenn grunted. "People come here as contractors for three reasons. Financial trouble, hiding from a predicament in their life, or they're idealists, think they'll change the world." He paused. "So, which one is it for you?"

I studied the dark creases in Glenn's face. "I've got some bills to pay, and I wanted to be part of something bigger. I'm not so sure this country is forsaken."

"Idealist!" Glenn looked smug. "An idealist who also sees the opportunity to get ahead. Now, are you quite sure you're not also hiding?"

I tried to hold it at bay, but a shiver ran up my spine. I pulled back.

The room was uncomfortably empty of conversation.

Mine Resistant Ambush Protected vehicles backup warnings screeched outside the tent and broke into the stillness.

Travis leaned in closer.

Glenn snapped a wheel into place and rolled the base of the chair in little circles on the floor, waiting for an answer. He toyed with me the same way he played with the seat.

I wasn't so sure I even liked this Glenn character. I wasn't hiding, was I? No, I was here to pay off bills from the hospital. I made sure no one here knew the real me. They only saw me as Mac the trainer, the guy who was always on time. They only saw the part of me I allowed them to see. I stuffed my pain down into an imaginary box and chained it safely away. I didn't owe him or anyone else an explanation. I stared back, unflinching. Glenn looked away, and I breathed out a sigh of relief.

"Hand me that seat so I can attach it to this post." He pointed to a raggedy computer seat, stuffing exploding from the seams. It would do. I handed the part to Glenn, and he snapped it in place, removed the screw from his mouth, and tightened it on the post.

"Which one are you?" The words jumped out of my mouth before I had time to stop them. Let him have a go at his own little game.

Glenn grinned as if he'd just received what he'd been waiting for all along.

"I am unabashedly here for the money. I make no apologies. I seek no absolution for my sin. You see, I was an officer for the great state of Georgia. There I took an oath that I would protect the rights, lives, and property of all citizens. That I would uphold the honor of the police profession, with my life if need be. My partner did just that. He paid with his life. After that, all the honor in the world wouldn't have been enough to redeem his life. I decided if I was to be shot at, I might as well make money while doing so." Glenn smiled with satisfaction and punched the computer chair seat. "Done. Give it a spin."

I rolled the chair up to my desk and sat gingerly. "This is great."

"Beats a gorilla box, doesn't it?" Travis gathered tools from the floor and handed them to Glenn.

Glenn bowed and waved his hand dramatically. "And now, I take my leave. Enjoy the chair. No assembly charge. Welcome to Camp Paradise."

"Camp Paradise?"

A sarcastic grin spread across Glenn's face. "My name for this place. Because it is anything but."

I stood and grabbed Glenn's hand. "Thanks."

Phoenix sniffed Glenn's pants cuff expectantly.

Glenn carefully stepped around the puppy, ignoring him. The door closed behind the man.

I shook my head. "Wow, talk about jaded."

"He's not as bad as he seems. He's had it pretty hard. The same year his partner was shot, his wife died."

"Of what?"

"Cancer."

Travis moved to the door. "I'm outta here, too. Enjoy the chair."

I nodded as he closed the door, but I couldn't speak. *What if that had been Sophie?* I set the puppy down and settled into my new chair. I glanced at my watch and wondered what time it was in Sophie's world. Ten thirty Friday night in Afghanistan meant one in the afternoon in Huntsville. Maybe Sophie was on her computer. I scooted closer to my desk and powered up the Internet. I was happy to try out my new setup. The thumbnail picture of Sophie appeared, and I clicked on the green video button. I could hear her in the background even before the video pulled up.

"Mac?"

"I'm here."

Strained silence. We both sat stiffly.

Her hair fell across her face, and she brushed it impatiently out of the way.

That small act, so familiar, sent a rush of longing through me. I began to second-guess my reasons for being in Afghanistan.

"I need you to come home." Sophie pressed her lips together.

My heart rabbit-thumped against my ribs, remembering Glenn's wife. "Is something wrong?"

Sophie shuffled in her seat. "I didn't sign on for this. I told you when we dated, I never wanted to be a military wife. I've lost Little Mac and now you."

The words hit me like a blow to the stomach. By coming to Afghanistan, I'd closed a door. Only I hadn't meant that door to be Sophie. My hand tightened on the edge of my laptop. She seemed so distant, walled in by the constraints of my computer screen. I mumbled about paying bills. She probably suspected I was hiding. Just like Glenn. "I've got to go to bed. It's late."

It was just an excuse to end this painful exchange, and we both knew it. We signed off our computers simultaneously.

My hand fell to my side, and the warm fuzz of Phoenix's head bumped against my palm. How could he trust a man again after being discarded like trash? I picked him up and held his mottled, furry body to my chest. He relaxed against me, and his breathing became smooth and regular. His tenderness opened the last floodgate in my chest, and sobs I'd wrestled with since the funeral clenched my stomach. Was this what my life had become? Sophie in Huntsville, her heart broken and me in a country full of people who would kill me at the first chance? There was a time I would have done anything to comfort Sophie the way I was holding Phoenix, but now, there was nothing left of me to give.

Moisture stirred up the rancid odor of trash and decay in Phoenix's fur. We wouldn't make it as roommates if he smelled like that. I grabbed my shower bag, lifted Phoenix into the crook of my arm and headed to the Conex boxes. It wouldn't be too busy that late. Rows of tan and gray metal rectangles came into view. Conex boxes were shipping containers outfitted for use as showers and latrines. Up the wooden ramp, I trudged, stopping to readjust my handhold on the puppy to keep him from slipping out of my arms.

Glenn stomped out of the doorway, his towel slung over his shoulder. His spiked hair gave him the appearance of a porcupine. "Cleaning up your buddy?"

"Oh, yeah. Phoenix smells like a polecat." I grabbed the puppy tightly to stop his squirming.

"What's that?" Glenn asked.

"Being a Southerner, you don't know what a polecat is?" What was the deal with him? He was from Georgia, but he did his best to stamp down any trace of a Southern accent. I got the feeling he was ashamed of his roots. "Polecat is slang for a skunk."

"Aptly named."

I stuck my head in the doorway to see if I had the place to myself. I didn't want to be chasing a puppy around a group of showering soldiers. The place was empty. Gray water from backed up shower stalls overflowed and covered the floor. I shifted Phoenix to keep him from jumping down into the scum. "Looks like things are pretty backed up here. Is the pump truck coming soon?"

"Estimated sometime tomorrow. Not soon enough for me."

"I hear that."

Glenn focused on the struggling dog in my arms. "Combat shower. Limit five minutes, McCann."

"You really think I want to stand in this swamp more than five?" I scooted around Glenn. Once inside I let Phoenix down, trapped him in the shower stall with my foot whenever he tried to escape. I threw off my clothes, and we both took a quick scrub down with my body wash. It was a fight all the way. "You're not one for soap and water, huh? If you're going home with me, you'll have to learn to like clean." I frowned even as I spoke the words.

How would I get Phoenix home? I needed to ship him out, and it had to happen soon. They euthanized strays here. Rabies was rampant, and the only means to protect the soldiers was to control the animal population. Phoenix appeared healthy for now, but I didn't want to endanger him and the lives of the guys I worked with.

I dried him off and stopped at the latrine before heading back to the tent. As I rounded the corner, a dark form, about the size of my hand, leaped across the path. I gripped Phoenix a bit tighter and squinted into the shadows. I couldn't make out what it was, but the thought nagged at my mind that it could have been a camel spider. Travis had been talking about them earlier that night. Newbies were tortured with tales of camel spiders in their sleeping bags or jumping down on unsuspecting, showering soldiers.

It was only a quarter mile to the Conex boxes from my tent, but I didn't relish the thought of running across those arachnids at night. With each story I heard, the spiders grew larger. The current story was eight inches across. The one fact I had been able to corroborate was their speed. According to Travis, they ran as fast as ten miles an hour. That was quick enough. I didn't want to encounter one on a late-night trip to the latrine.

5

I wedged the tip of my knife into the pine wood bench, carefully carved Mac McCann, Huntsville, Alabama. Afghanistan sun sizzled on my neck. Sunscreen was for sissies. Sitting back, I admired my work. I was official. It was a tradition for WinCorp contractors to carve their names into the rugged bench. For some, it was the only proof they'd ever been in Afghanistan. Others left a larger mark on the country. I intended to be the latter.

Travis rustled the pages of yet another of the self-help books his wife constantly sent him. His nose was practically glued to the page.

Curious, I waved my hand in front of his face. He was oblivious. Not sound officer survival technique. I wound my finger back and gave the cover a good thump, almost hit Travis in the lip.

"Hey!"

"What're you reading?"

Travis flipped the cover around and stared at it as if to remind himself of the title. "Book Tricia sent me about cops and family relationships."

I ground my boot toe into the dusty tan gravel. "If Sophie sent me any books like that it would only mean one thing. She thinks she'll change me."

Travis studied the far "T" wall, a cement reinforced barrier that encircled the camp. "I don't know. It's making me think. I even sent Tricia an e-mail apologizing for her birthdays I've missed. I have to try harder, maybe send some flowers."

His earnestness almost disarmed me. I wished I could go back to that place in time where my relationship with Sophie could be fixed solely by a bouquet of flowers. But flowers were for funeral homes. Memories of the musty smell of a room overflowing with flowers filled my head. My temples pounded. My polo shirt clung to me like a sweaty second skin, and a dark tunnel of panic threatened to close in on me. Panic attacks were becoming a daily occurrence.

Now it was my turn to contemplate the "T" wall. The cement blast protector shimmered in the heat. Chunks were missing in sections. Circular reminders of the impact of past rocket propelled grenades. "Flowers aren't all they're cracked up to be." I rose from the bench, turned sharply on my heels, and headed for the tent. Each crunch of gravel under my boots was a declaration. I shoved through the gritty door of our tent and stomped down the dark, narrow hallway to my room, such as it was.

Seven by seven feet, if you rounded up. My cot hugged one canvas wall. If my arm happened to flop over the side of the mattress at night, the enemy would be able to spot me from the bulge. At least I wasn't sleeping on the ground underneath some MRAP like many of my buddies. I settled down at my desk and fired up my laptop. Stupid, slow connection.

A white U.S. Postal box poked out from under my cot and I retrieved it while waiting for the Internet to load. Sophie's care package from home. I dug around in the box. My hand closed on the smooth stick of a grape sucker. She remembered. The wrapper crinkled under my fingers, and I shoved the lollipop in the corner of my mouth. Artificial tang puckered my lips. I rolled the candy around, savoring it.

A video game was loading on my computer when Travis burst through my door. "Hey, I'm sorry if I upset you. I wasn't making a comment on you and Sophie."

"Look, you didn't upset me, but I work hard. That's how I show her I love her," I said. "We're over here in tents, share a shower house with five hundred other men, toilets that back up every other day. Has the irony escaped you that the scum we used to arrest back home had it better in jail than we do here?" I leaned back, head pounding. "Flowers," I said, slowly, squeezing my eyes shut to prevent the vision of the funeral home from returning, "are empty gestures. I'm paying off our bills. What more does she want?" I opened my eyes.

Travis had retreated to the doorway. He propped hands on either side of the frame. "That's the question I used to ask. On my last leave, Tricia had to stay with her mother for a few days. I began to see how hollow that house felt when there was only one person there. My arguments about how useless gifts and flowers were seemed weak compared to Tricia's faithfulness."

I twisted around, showed Travis my back. Eyes burned. I reached down and fumbled with the care package. "Want some candy?"

Travis exhaled and moved across the room. "Sure." He stuffed the pop in the pocket of his BDUs. "Thanks. While we're on the subject of wives, do you realize every time you want to avoid confrontation you escape to that computer?"

OK, that was it. Did this guy think he was my shrink? I leveled my gaze at him with a look that said,

"Back off." Evidently, he was not reading me because he forged on.

"Yes, you do. You're always playing that game."

I chewed the last of the candy down to the stick and pitched it toward the wastebasket next to Travis. "Now you're starting to sound like Sophie."

Travis dodged the stick, and it plunked into the can. "We all have our escapes but if I were Sophie and you did that to me, well, no wonder she's not happy with you."

When the door closed, I reached for my care package, unwrapped another pop, and started a new game.

6

Dust touched everything, even the morning colors of the sky. It was wild and beautiful. The sun was a searing, orange haze.

I slid my sunglasses on, which I'd bought cheap off a fellow worker returning home. With people coming and going constantly there was always a fair amount of trade going on for equipment. One could find pretty much anything one needed if the word got out. When I made my way to Travis's door, he was just locking up. Rumbling in my stomach reminded me I hadn't eaten since lunch the day before except for that granola bar I'd scarfed down just before sleep. I couldn't wait for Travis, so I walked down the gravel path to where a line was already forming outside the dining facility.

Travis eventually caught up. "Hey," he called from behind me in line. "Meet me under LSU."

I grabbed my tray and slid it down to where they were dishing hot eggs off the griddle.

Risaldo motioned to me with his spatula. His starched white garrison hat bobbed as he nodded a greeting.

"Three over easy," I said.

"No can do. I have to cook eggs well."

"What's with the well-done business?" I asked Reynolds who was ahead of me in line.

He shook his head.

"Salmonella. They're afraid of food poisoning."

"Breakfast is the only meal I look forward to around here."

Reynolds' mouth turned up in a wry grin. "You won't look forward to breakfast anymore if you end up with your keister parked on a toilet for three days."

Risaldo impatiently tapped the spatula on the griddle. "Come on, man. The line's backing up behind you."

"Point taken. Give me three over well then, and two scrambled." Phoenix would appreciate eggs, too.

Glenn had already settled in under the purple and gold LSU Tiger banner where we usually congregated. The dining facility was decorated throughout with college and professional football flags. Anything they did to make it seem like home helped.

"Morning." I slid my tray down the table and settled into a chair.

"Morning." Glenn took a long drink of orange juice and set his cup down heavily. He had dark circles under his eyes. Looked like his razor was broken, too.

"How's your new boarder?"

"He didn't sleep much, kept whining, so I'll make sure he has enough to eat today. I think he was hungry last night."

"Yeah, I heard him. Those plywood walls aren't soundproof, you know." Glenn rested his hand on his knee and leaned in closer. "I'd be very cautious if I were you. Animals are not allowed in the tents."

My abs tightened. Fingers gripped the bumpy cardboard tray. "I'm aware."

"Look, it's no skin off my nose if you want to keep that hairy little poop bag in your room. I'm just saying, there are those who would love to have you strung up over something as inconsequential as that." Glenn nodded in the direction of a short, sandy-haired figure across the room.

He ate alone, hunched over his tray. He reminded me of turkey vultures back home, crouching over road kill.

"That's Lieutenant Stockton. He's got the room between Travis and me," Glenn said. "And he treats contractors like garbage you would scrape off your shoe. Best stay clear of him."

"I'll keep the puppy quiet."

Glenn shrugged. "Good luck."

I spooned scrambled eggs into a disposable container then started working on those fried eggs before they got cold.

Travis stared from the bowl to me and back again.

"Planning a mid-morning snack?"

"For Phoenix."

"Is that what you call him?"

"Yeah, what do you think?"

"I like it. Fits him. Out of the ashes and all that."

Glenn made no effort to conceal his amusement.

I pushed my chair back and moved across the room to the dessert stand. Sophie would have a fit if she knew I had ice cream for breakfast, but the way I figured it, whatever comforts we got that reminded us of home was worth it. I was pouring a stream of caramel over my concoction when out of the corner of my eye I caught a flash of blue.

A blast echoed off the wall.

It happened so quickly my instincts lagged.

People around me dove to the floor, plastic chairs bounced against table legs. The metallic clatter of weapons resounded in unison.

I drew my M9 and rolled to the floor with the rest

of the soldiers.

Risaldo tumbled to the floor under a stack of serving containers.

A supply line had split loose and flailed madly around the room, hissing like a cobra.

Relief coursed through me like a wave. I thought I had prepared myself for coming here. It would be ludicrous to think I'd be a year in Afghanistan and never come under attack. Still, when the confusion and noise were upon me, it was quite a different thing. I was secretly relieved it was a supply hose rather than the Taliban. I holstered my weapon and crawled across the floor, wrestled the writhing hose into submission. "What happened?" I asked Risaldo, as he scurried around on the floor, gathering scattered utensils.

"I tripped and hit a supply line. Can't seem to stay out of trouble." He grabbed a metal spoon from under the counter just as the boots of the kitchen supervisor entered my field of vision. They planted themselves before me, and my eyes traveled up into his bloodshot eyes. He flexed his husky arms in agitation.

He glanced from me to Risaldo.

Risaldo continued to gather the utensils and pans he'd dropped. He didn't deserve to be called out in front of a room of soldiers. His only sin was being in the wrong place at the wrong time.

"Hey," I yelled over the hissing of air that whistled from the black hose.

The supervisor turned his glare on me.

"Looks like a pressurized line busted loose off some equipment."

The supervisor nodded his head, seeming content with my assessment. He exited to the rear of the kitchen, and within a minute the hissing stopped. The hose sagged to the floor.

Risaldo stood and wiped his hands on a towel. "I told them that clamp was loose."

"Sorry for the interruption. No one's been injured."

All around us, soldiers scrambled up off the floor, emerged from behind serving displays, and began eating as if nothing happened.

I think that shook me more than the explosion. Danger was so commonplace, soldiers returned to eating quickly. I wondered if I would become so hardened.

Risaldo extended his hand to me, teeth flashed in a broad smile. "Hey, thanks, man. I owe you. I'll have to think of some way to repay you."

"I'm sure I'll think of an option." I studied his hand-stitched cowboy boots.

Risaldo's eyes traveled to his own feet. "No way, these are Italian leather. Ordered them from Austin. Took me three months to receive them."

"What size are they?"

"Elevens, but they aren't negotiable."

"Say the next attack is for real, and you don't make it. I get your boots?"

Risaldo looked stricken.

"Just kidding. Besides, they're the wrong size," I said.

Risaldo relaxed and clapped me on the back. "Thanks, man."

I navigated my way across the room and wiped my spilled ice cream off the floor.

Glenn gathered his empty tray from the table. "It's been fun, boys, but I have to go. See you in class."

"I'm outta here, too." Fresh air would do me good.

My hands shook from adrenaline. I pushed the exit door open, discarded my trash in the recycling barrels, and headed toward my tent.

The minute I pushed the main door open I heard Phoenix's high-pitched bark. It echoed off the plywood-lined walls and down the hallway. I needed to find a way to keep him quiet. I unlocked my door and pushed it open. The puppy ran circles around my feet. I shooed him into the room and closed the door. "Little man, I'm glad to see you, too. Look what I brought you." I pulled the container out of my pocket and fed bits of cold scrambled egg to the ravenous puppy. His needle-like teeth scraped my fingers as he nuzzled rubbery eggs from my hand. "I won't let you starve. Those days are over."

Phoenix licked the last bit of eggs from my hand.

It was then I noticed the destruction he had wreaked on my room. I must have left a bag of pops out because the paper was chewed off every pop. Some were barely touched, and some were chewed down. Even the sticks were missing, except for a stub here and there.

I'd prepare for an epic case of diarrhea in the puppy. I ruffled the fur on Phoenix's neck. At least he smelled like soap instead of sour burn pit. I swept up the mess, Phoenix at my heels. He tried to play tug of war with the frayed ends of the straw broom, and the sight made me draw in a deep breath and laugh. I pulled the door shut and caught up with Travis walking briskly down the hallway. "New students today?"

"Yeah. Glenn's walking them in from the front gate." Travis scratched at his beard. "No telling how many are Taliban."

The thought was sobering. Unconsciously, I patted the side pockets on my vest, the gear we called our kit. "You carrying extra magazines?"

Travis nodded. "Taliban manage to slip through the screening process into some of the classes, though the students are all vetted. We know it. I'm not sure what the higherups believe." He cast a sideways glance at me. "We're the ones who'll get a bullet to the head if we turn our backs on students at the firing range." He paused and studied my face as if sizing me up.

I knew the look. I'd seen it on many of my partners' faces back home at the precinct. He wanted to see if he could depend on me to watch his back.

"So, keep one eye on the material you're teaching and another on the students at all times."

I started to crack a joke to relieve the tension, but when I looked into Travis's usually happy face, fine lines of strain crept around his mouth and eyes. That drained the last bit of mischief out of any comment I wanted to make. A somber purposefulness settled over me.

Travis paused at the door to the academy. "It'll be a long day. The first day always is. We have to translate everything, not only into Pashto, but also Dari. It usually takes twice as long to get everything across."

I didn't want to start a full week of teaching off on a wrong note. I fumbled around in my mind for anything positive to say. I turned the handle to the door but stopped. A recent conversation I'd had sprang to mind, one that made sacrifices here a little more bearable. "Travis, you want to hear a neat story?"

He paused before entering the building. "What?"

I cracked the door open and watched our newest

students file into the classroom. They were chatting excitedly. They wanted to be here. Just outside the gate, their families were in danger every day. IEDs threatened even a trip to the local market to buy vegetables. These men were doing what they could, all they could, to secure peace in a fragile country. I always studied my students. It was a long-term habit I picked up when I was a Field Training Officer in Huntsville. Tried to find out what new recruits enjoyed, what I could do better to keep their attention. "Two days ago, I asked a student what his favorite class was. Can you guess what he said?"

Travis took the bait. The worry lines smoothed out on his face as he pondered my question. "Dynamic Entry? Range?"

I could feel the grin that broke out on my face. "Nope. He said 'Literacy.'"

"Literacy?" Travis sounded incredulous.

"Yeah, so I asked through the interpreter, 'Why Literacy?' and you know what the guy said? He said, 'Because I learned to write my father's name.'" I delivered the punch line with deep satisfaction. We were making a difference.

Travis whistled low through his teeth. He got it.

7

"Man, I need a haircut," I said.

Travis bobbed his head to my right.

I moved my head to the left. Then I realized he was using my sunglasses as a mirror. The man always worried about how he looked. It was funny when one realized there was no one here to impress, just a bunch of stinking guys. I guess he was staying in practice for when he went home on leave to see Tricia.

"Come on. Let's check the barbershop and see how long the wait is." Travis ambled ahead of me down the gravel path.

The sky was pale blue. The intimidating frame of the Hindu Kush Mountains loomed in the distance. Even in summer, veins of snow cut through the mountain top, carving sharp valleys. Back home what we called mountains were hills compared to the hulking white-capped giants that bordered Kandahar.

We pushed the door to the barbershop open, and I stopped short. The line for haircuts already stretched wall to wall, and there were only two barbers. At eight by fourteen feet, the barbershop didn't take many people to fill, and it was at capacity that day.

I know Sophie liked my hair long, but it would grow again once I returned home.

Travis jammed in behind me and wedged the door shut. He glanced around the room and waved his hand toward the barber on the left. "That's Gul Hadi. Best barber here. Try and get in his line if you can."

A dark-haired rascal tapped a soccer ball noisily against the wall.

Travis followed my line of vision and nodded toward the boy. "And that is four-year-old Bashir, Gul's son. Gul's been bringing him to work since the kid was old enough to walk."

Bashir pushed his straight, licorice-colored hair out of his eyes. He kicked the ball mightily with his spindly brown leg.

My skin prickled when he paused and looked up at me. His eyes were green. Like my son's.

A sergeant in line next to me called to the boy in Dari. The little guy tucked the ball under his arm and trotted over. His even, white teeth shone brightly against nut colored skin. He grinned even wider when the soldier pulled a package of red licorice from his cargo pants and placed them in the boy's outstretched hand.

Travis frowned. "You'll spoil that kid." But I could tell by the tone of his voice he heartily approved.

The soldier chuckled softly. "I'd give him that and a whole lot more if I could."

Travis leaned toward me. "Let me introduce you. McCann, this is Sergeant Thorstad. The sergeant is responsible for most of the cavities in the teeth of local children."

I extended my hand toward the guy. "Nice to meet you."

Thorstad took my hand and pumped it enthusiastically. "Same here."

"Next."

Gul Hadi pointed a black plastic comb in my direction. I was just about to settle into the leather barber's seat when Lieutenant Stockton rushed into the room.

He slid into the chair before I could claim it. He avoided my eyes, jabbed his finger at Gul. "You work me in, right? I have a meeting in thirty minutes with Colonel Smith, and I need to look sharp."

Gul looked at me, almost pleading. I thought maybe he wanted this guy gone as much as I did. But I nodded my head resignedly at Stockton. "Go ahead." I squirmed inside. I should have said no. Why did this dirt bag think he could bust line for a haircut? Because guys like me let him. I mocked myself by answering my question. I settled back against the wall next to Sergeant Thorstad and began my wait.

Thorstad flipped wordlessly through a tattered three-year-old issue of an outdoor sportsman's magazine. Any magazine more provocative than that was banned.

Gul worked his magic quickly.

Lieutenant Stockton counted out two seventy-five in change. He slapped it into Gul's hand for a three-dollar haircut.

I was embarrassed he was one of us.

With that, Stockton moved up and out of the chair. "Keep the change." He left as quickly as he came.

Gul muttered under his breath. *"Az khers mui kandan."*

Thorstad burst into laughter and clapped the rolled magazine against his thigh.

"What's so funny?" I asked.

"He said 'Pulling hair from a bear.'"

"What does that mean?"

"It means," Sergeant Thorstad's eye twitched from laughter, "getting something from greedy people is as hard as pulling hairs from a bear."

My throat vibrated with laughter as I lowered myself into Gul's chair. It was hard to stop laughing long enough for him to begin trimming, but I reminded myself I'd get a lopsided cut if I didn't sit still. I shoved my feet down onto the footrest and straightened the cape as Gul floated it across me. He snapped it behind my neck with the air of an artist about to begin his project. I never knew what to do with my hands in a cape. I didn't like the helpless feeling of having them hidden. My M-9 rested reassuringly against my thigh. I wondered how many guys had sat in this same seat, getting ready to go home on leave. I wondered how many never made it. I shook my head in disbelief. I'd make it back.

"How do you want it?" Gul twirled his scissors in a semicircle around my head like a wild-west gunslinger. For a moment, I wondered if he would accidentally put my eye out with the things, but he spun the scissors with precision. He'd been at this a while.

"Just a trim."

Gul started in enthusiastically chopping at my hair. It cascaded in clumps to the floor.

In the mirror, I could see that I did need a trim after all.

Bashir moved about the room, tapping a worn soccer ball.

I shifted my gaze to avoid watching him. I went to Afghanistan to get away from children, anything that would remind me of Little Mac.

"You like a little shorter?" Gul's bloodshot eyes and bushy eyebrows came into view and blocked the little guy from my sight.

"Yeah, that's fine."

He spun the chair around, and an electric razor buzzed loudly next to my ear.

I could no longer hide in the mirror.

Gul's son rolled his soccer ball to the wall and squatted next to it. His intense eyes seemed to take in every face in the room. Probably looking for more candy. At last, they rested on me.

I quickly turned my head down, studied the cracked rubber mat beneath my chair. Maybe if I ignored him, he'd find another subject of interest.

Gul was still trimming. He took my chin and angled it back up so he could continue his work.

I couldn't escape Bashir's gaze.

Menthol rolled up in waves of steam, mixed with the greasy smell of hair cream and the body odor of four GIs just back from the field. My stomach knotted into a tight ball, and my mouth went sour. It felt like Bashir could read my soul.

The cement floor rushed up at me, and voices jumbled off the plaster walls, tinny and harsh. Sweat ran down my back and plastered my shirt to me, increasing the claustrophobia. I took a few deep breaths. Tried to calm down so Gul wouldn't notice.

The last time I nearly lost it was the day we held Little Mac's visitation at the funeral home. A long line of people had shown up to express their condolences. The people stretched down between the polished pews of the funeral home. The line wound its way around the corner and out of sight down the hallway.

I wiped my clammy hands down my black suit in between shaking people's hands, hoping they wouldn't notice me sweating. Visitors in line dressed in muted colors or black. Their faces blended into the same sallow color. I knew most by name.

They were officers with the police department and had brought their spouses to pay respects. Even the chief was there. He put on his best politically correct face and extended his hand to me, though he and I rarely saw eye-to-eye. "Sorry to hear about your loss."

My loss? Wasn't Little Mac tucked in his bed at home, waiting with the sitter for Sophie and I to kiss him good night? But that was the dream. It only took a glance to my side to see the casket covered in flowers.

Only three days before, Sophie had been wiping grape jelly off Little Mac's ruddy cheeks. He tried to wiggle out of her grasp, protesting. He never did like his face washed much. Then she picked up his tiny metal patrol cars from the hallway, fussing that she'd probably slip on one in the dark and break a bone.

The funny thing was, after the fact, I wouldn't have cared if cars were scattered all over the house.

After what seemed hours at the funeral home the line finally emptied out. The funeral home director walked the pews, collecting papers and trash left behind by visitors.

I could tell he was stalling, trying to give us as much time as we needed.

After a few harried glances at his watch, he finally addressed Sophie and me. "It's time to lock up. I'm sorry."

My gaze roamed over the mahogany box.

Sophie was looking at the coffin, too. She glanced from the funeral director to the casket and back again to me.

"Mac, go home and get our sleeping bag. It's in the hall closet next to the emergency lantern. As a matter of fact, bring me the light, too, and some water bottles and the bag of cheese crackers. He loves cheese crackers."

"What do you want the sleeping bag for?"

Sophie wrinkled her forehead as if she was frustrated with having to explain. "I'm staying here tonight, of course."

"Do you think that's a good idea?" I glanced around at the growing shadows with doubt. "They'll lock up. Let's go home." I didn't want to stay in that place one minute longer than I had to. Our little guy certainly wasn't there. He wouldn't have chosen that place to play. He liked sunlit parks and metal slides that he could catapult himself down into my arms. I reached for Sophie to guide her to the exit, but she wrenched out of my grasp.

"I want to stay with my baby."

My heart seized in my chest. "Sophie," I lowered my voice. "This is a little insane. Come home with me."

"Bring me the sleeping bag, Mac. Please. I'm not asking much." Her voice lowered to a whisper.

Sophie crossed her arms over her chest and gave me a look I'd seen so many times. Once I got that look, the game was over, and I'd do whatever she asked. "OK, but this isn't right," I muttered as I walked down the rows of pews.

The funeral home director approached her gently. "Mrs. McCann, we need to close up for the night."

I turned. Maybe the director could help Sophie understand this was a bad idea. I glanced back at Sophie, but she stood with her arms crossed.

"I've made arrangements. My husband is bringing a sleeping bag for me. I'm staying here tonight," Sophie said.

The man looked confused and glanced back and forth from Sophie to me.

I held my hands up in surrender.

His eyes creased. "I'll be right back." He appeared in a moment, one of the HPD honor guards in tow. Two at a time had stood guard next to Little Mac's coffin.

The guard nodded at Sophie. "Mrs. McCann, I would consider it an honor to stay here with you tonight and make sure everything is secure."

Sophie smiled for the first time since the accident. "I'd love that."

The guard solemnly took up his position at the head of the coffin. His uniform was crisp, white braided rope over one shoulder, black hat with a patent leather brim. Shoes polished like mirrors. He stared straight ahead.

That used to be me when I was in the Honor Guard. How many funerals had I attended? How many times had I been the one with the perfect uniform, the unreadable expression on my face? Only this time, I was the one on the other side. I turned and exited the building. My presence was only making Sophie more upset. The only thing I could do for her that night was follow through with her request and spend the night alone in a cold, king-sized bed.

The once packed parking lot had emptied of vehicles, except for a couple of employees' cars and the patrol car driven by the honor guard.

I unlocked my vehicle, got in the car, leaned against the steering wheel, and put my head on my hands, wrung out. I stood by Sophie at the viewing. I shook hands. I'd done everything asked of me, but I was a wooden man. My heart was hollowed out and buried in a little mahogany coffin.

A cold drizzle began. I glanced up through the

rain-streaked windshield and pled. "Sophie talks to you. If you're up there, give me something. Show me a star. Just one star, God."

I wiped the fogged windshield with the palm of my hand and strained to see through smeared glass, but no stars shone that night. The black sky above me was as empty as the void in my chest. It was just as well. I didn't deserve starlight.

I started up the car, drove home, and collected the things Sophie wanted. The house was so still, as still as the viewing area back at the funeral home. I walked in total darkness to the kitchen for a drink of water, and when I opened the refrigerator door, light washed over me, making me blink. Casserole dishes lined the wall in the fridge. In the South, the balm for grief is fried chicken, potato casserole, and banana pudding. Sophie's uncle must have let our friends in the house.

Back at the funeral home, I knocked on the locked door, and the manager let me in. He studied me in a sad, pitying way. I was sure he'd already seen his share of grief. But the way he looked at me and nodded his head toward Sophie let me know. He understood this was killing me.

I crept quietly to Sophie, set the sleeping bag, lantern, and cheese crackers down, still hoping she'd change her mind. "I brought your pillow, too."

"Thanks."

I shuffled my feet on the cold tile floor, like an outcast. I pleaded silently. *Come home. I need you just as much as you need me. I need your warmth beside me tonight.* But the words came out clipped. "You don't have to stay here, you know."

"Yes, I do. Don't worry about me. Go on home, and I'll see you tomorrow." She paused and searched my face as if seeing me for the first time that day. Her voice softened. "You have dark circles under your eyes. Please go home and get some sleep. Tomorrow will be a long day." She turned her back to me and unrolled the sleeping bag. She didn't want to go home with me. She just wanted to stay there all night, next to her little man.

I swallowed, but my mouth was dry. There was nothing to go down. I shuffled to the door and glanced over my shoulder in time to see Sophie crawl into the nylon cocoon.

She waved me off, a signal that meant, "Don't fuss over me. I'll be OK."

But I stood at the back of the funeral home, hidden by flowers on a wire stand. I stood guard over my wife until I saw her face relax and her hand slide down and rest across her chest. Quietly, I walked to the front, by Little Mac's casket.

The officer stared straight ahead.

I bent to his side, close to his ear so I wouldn't wake Sophie. "Take care of her."

He gave a slight nod, never breaking his protective stance. He understood. We cared for our own.

Sophie wanted to stay there alone, a mother's vigil.

Bone crushing guilt prevented me from arguing. I'd try to go on. I'd provide for Sophie financially, but I had nothing else to give. Time as I knew it ended the day he died. I'd be forever trapped in my pickup, trying to stop the bleeding.

8

The tickle of horsehair and the smell of talcum powder jolted me back to the barbershop. Gul swiped my neck with the round brush, covered every inch with powder, and swept it off with a professional air. He nodded his satisfaction in the mirror. I peeled off the barber's cape, laid it across the chair, and handed him a ten. Maybe that would make up for Stockton's stinginess.

"Keep the change." I was already out the door as Gul's "Thank you, sir" echoed off the walls. I felt the gaze of Gul's son follow me.

I headed for the nearest place to sit down, which happened to be the hangout of all caffeine addicts in camp. Green Beans Coffee had a little stand-alone structure with a walk-up order window. Their coffee gave us a comforting taste of home. Nearby a group of Adirondack chairs were scattered haphazardly. Seats worn smooth from the rump of every coffee hound in camp made a welcome place to congregate under a tarp-covered patio. Shade from the tarp spelled relief from the searing Afghanistan sun. I pretended to study the menu to give myself time to regain my composure.

Troops milled past me.

I didn't want them to see some newcomer having a panic attack.

A small bell on the door of the video shop next door chimed each time it was opened and closed. MRAPs roared past on the crackling gravel. None of that noise stood a chance against my raspy breaths and pounding heart. I never wanted to see that kid again.

"Help you, sir?" A thin man with a Malaysian accent leaned across the counter of Green Beans.

I studied the menu for real. "Yeah, give me a tall mocha frappe." I slid my bills across the counter and grabbed the plastic cup, threw the straw aside, and removed the clear dome top. I chugged the iced coffee until my temples throbbed from the cold. In the middle of a swig, my back got a hard thump from someone's palm. I coughed and spun around as Travis barreled into me.

"There you are. I wondered if you would wait on me." He reached for his wallet.

I waved his money aside. "This one's on me. You bought last time."

Travis leaned toward the counter. "Tall espresso." He tapped his foot nervously.

I recognized that mannerism. "You think you need caffeine? You look pretty wired to me."

He ignored my question and gasped. "Man, you got your head shaved, didn't you?"

The wind felt a little cooler on my scalp than normal. I leaned around Travis and gazed at my reflection in Green Bean's window. I had a head of stubble, nothing more. Gul had gotten a little happy with the clippers, and I'd been too distracted to notice. The corners of my mouth twitched then pulled into a broad smile. From deep inside, a belly laugh rolled up. It felt good to laugh. It felt good to be alive. I headed back to my tent, nursing what was left of my coffee. I stopped at the barrel outside our tent and pitched in the empty cup.

Sophie loved coffee. Her collection of mugs took up more space in our kitchen than our iced tea glasses.

I wondered what she was doing right then.

Three thirty Afghanistan time. Subtract nine and one-half hours. That would make it six in the morning in Huntsville. Sophie was probably just rolling out of bed. I could almost smell the pot of Café de Catalina.

The thumbnail video of Sophie popped up when I signed on my computer. She clamped a thin hand over her mouth and giggled when she saw me. That wasn't the reaction I expected. After all our arguments about my being here, it sure was good to see her smile.

"What have you done to your hair?" She leaned closer to the screen as if that would actually bring us closer together. Her eyes opened wide. Sea glass green, Destin beach at high tide.

Seeing her made me want to run wild with her again, the way we did the week of our honeymoon. Two crazy kids splashing down a beach at midnight. Some part of her had always been a parcel of me, a missing component that, by a great act of benevolence, fate had returned.

Sophie had a way about her that made me feel I'd always known her...I thought back to the day she became mine. We were sitting in my new truck. Red, short-bed, V8 with 4-wheel drive, a graduation gift from my parents. I'd driven her all over town that day and ended up stopping for hamburgers and onion rings at the local fast food drive-up. She talked nonstop, but I still don't remember a word she'd said. The setting sun made a halo around her head. Her green eyes were wide, pulling me in. The curve of her lips.

I brought her there to give her my going-away speech. I was joining the Army, and she deserved someone better than me. She didn't deserve to wait on some Army grunt.

But that little spot of ketchup was on her cheek, and when I wiped it away, my hand didn't stop. I curled my fingers into the back of her hair, wondering how it could be so soft and perfect, and I did what I'd been dying to do all spring. I brought her face to mine and pressed my lips to hers.

My breath reeked from onions, but I didn't care. And wonder of wonders, she relaxed into me and kissed me back. My ears roared like the sound of breakers at the beach. I pulled back, ashamed of my lack of self-control. Kissing her wasn't part of the plan.

Sophie curled into my arm. "I guess this makes it official."

"What?"

"Us. It makes us official."

"That depends." Onion rings churned in my stomach.

"On?"

"On whether you can wait for me to finish basic training."

She unwrapped herself from my arm, like removing last year's worn jacket. "What did you go and do?"

I straightened the rearview mirror. "Joined the Army." I was afraid to look at her, afraid to see disappointment, or worse, nothing.

She pulled my jacket around her shoulders as if she were chilled, glanced at the leather sleeves, the felt front with the orange letter G embroidered on the front. She pulled off my prized jacket and laid it in my lap. "Why did you kiss me if you're leaving?"

I twisted around in the seat so I could see her better. "Wait for me, Soph. I know other guys want to date you, and we've only been seeing each other a month..." My heart willed the answer, but uncertainty clouded her eyes.

She reached across and played with the sleeve of my jacket, examining the lining as if the answer lay stitched in secret code. "I never wanted to date a military guy. My dad died serving in the military. You know that?"

"Just wait for me through Basic Training. Give me that much. When I come home on leave, if you still feel the same, we'll call it quits."

Sophie took my jacket and slipped it back over her shoulders. "Only until the end of Basic." Her teasing voice faltered just a little.

I wrapped my arms around her. My right index finger traced letters on her back.

"What are you writing?"

My self-conscious laugh echoed off the windshield. "It's a secr—"

"Incoming! Incoming!" The warning horn echoed off my tent walls, tearing my glazed eyes and numb thoughts from the windshield of the past. I jumped, stiffened for a moment, moved to my feet, and leaned toward the computer monitor.

Sophie's eyes searched the room. "What's happening?"

I grabbed my stuff. "Gonna find out."

"Be careful."

"Gotta go." I closed my laptop.

Guys piled into the hallway. Everyone pulled on his gear. Travis ran out the door. Two minutes later he reappeared, slowly dragged his feet in the gravel, helmet in hand.

"It was a false alarm?"

"Yeah, an initial sweep of the area revealed no breach of the perimeter. Someone in the tower accidentally hit the button to the new system. I guess they weren't familiar with it yet."

I wandered back into my room, shook off the adrenaline rush and hung my stuff back on the wall. I slumped down on my bed, grabbed a flavored sports drink and took a big gulp. Lifting the laptop's cover, I found Sophie was still online. I hit the video button, and her face came into view.

She turned away, trying to hide her swollen eyes and runny nose.

My heart pinched, a pain that betrayed my outward calm. *Give me a year. I'll fix all of this, and we can pick up the pieces and go on.* My throat constricted at the desperate but unspoken words.

She dabbed at her mascara-ringed eyes. "You had to get offline so fast, and the thing said 'incoming.'"

"It was nothing. Someone hit the wrong button." I tried to laugh, but it came off as a nervous cough.

"All I could think about was how awful our last video call was, and if anything happened to you, I couldn't stand myself." Sophie wadded the tissue into a little ball, gripped it tight in her fist. She leaned closer to the monitor.

Despite the intensity of the moment, I had an eerie disconnected feeling. While Sophie spoke, I soaked up her face and mannerisms. How much time did I spend back home paying this close attention to her? Her words vibrated from the monitor, words that brought me back to the present.

"I'm sorry for being so short-tempered with you. I've been frustrated a lot lately, furious at God for allowing Little Mac to die. Angry, even at Little Mac, for leaving."

"Don't apologize, Sophie. I never meant to hurt you, and I have. I've probably hurt you worse than anyone in my life, and I don't deserve you." Would she accept my words and let us heal?

Time would prove this.

How I wished I could bend time to my will.

9

The nerve-jangling beep of the alarm clock thrust me into consciousness. I rolled over and smacked the clock until I was sure it was dead and scrubbed my hands with the ever-present bottle of hand sanitizer. I hated the sharp alcohol odor of the stuff. I banged on Travis's door as I passed. "Come on. Breakfast."

I heard him scrambling around behind the door. I was so hungry I kept walking. He'd catch up eventually. The greasy smell of bacon and the mellow aroma of coffee welcomed me to the DFAC. I grabbed a tray loaded with eggs and an extra biscuit and slid into my usual seat.

"Your turn to pick up Afghan Uniformed Police students." Glenn took a swig of coffee, a wicked gleam in his eyes. He took extreme pleasure in seeing me gobble down my breakfast.

Eggs steamed on my plate. So much for enjoying them. I cut into the fried eggs with the side of my fork and shoveled them into my mouth. Chewing rapidly, I washed the whole thing down with a half pint of chocolate milk. I folded the bacon into a napkin and tucked into my pants pocket, a snack for Phoenix. As I stood, Stockton passed behind me. Out of the corner of my eye, I noticed him looking at our group. He hesitated for a moment as if waiting to be invited to sit down.

Glenn pushed a forkful of eggs into his mouth and looked away.

Travis jumped to his feet. "Want some company picking up those students?"

"Sure," I said, glancing over my shoulder at Stockton.

He turned slowly and sat at the next row of tables by himself. Part of me felt sorry for him. I had dealt with his type before. Seemed there was always one in every workplace. Some know-it-all who wanted to be respected by their peers. They never saw that the thing they craved most they were throwing away with both hands.

I dumped my trash and hurried to the door.

Travis was hot on my heels.

"You sure left the DFAC in a rush," I said.

"Stockton. No one wants to be around him. He's nothing but trouble." Travis spit on the gravel at our feet. "I can't stand even to breathe the same air he does."

We hiked down to the gate to pick up the students. Camp Paradise was humming.

"It feels good to be part of something bigger than myself," I said.

"I forgot to tell you. Yesterday we got some good news. Some of our students from the last graduating class put their training to use."

"What happened?" I yelled over the grinding engine noise of a Buffalo vehicle powering past me. It threw dirt into the air, covering me with yet another layer of grime.

"Our graduates apprehended a couple of local criminals, using the techniques we taught them."

Warm pride flooded my chest.

On the other side of the gate, students milled around, anxious to get started. Dressed in native garb, they would change into uniforms once inside the camp. To travel outside the gate in a police uniform with no weapon would be to invite trouble. Taliban were none too happy we were training local police to keep order in the country once ISAF troops pulled out.

I approached the sergeant. "McCann here to pick up AUP students."

An MRAP passed, and all I could see was the man's mouth moving.

I cupped my hands around my mouth and shouted, "What?"

Sergeant shouted above the roar of the vehicle. "I said, we've got a guy with hashish on him. Found it on him when we were checking them in this morning."

"A student?"

"Yes."

A growl of frustration escaped my lips. "Can't things go smoothly just this once?" I shouted back above the noise. "We've briefed the students about drugs. They know it's not acceptable."

The sergeant nodded. "I know. We found it concealed inside a flap in his wallet."

I kicked at a big chunk of gravel. The MRAP finally pulled through the gate, and we were able to talk at a tolerable level. "Look, we told them plainly the rules of the academy and what we expect of them."

He put a hand up. "I'll get the supervisor. Let me see what I can do." He turned to walk away. "Sorry about this."

"Don't apologize. What can you do?"

Twenty minutes later, I stood, watching the sun climb higher in the sky. A trickle of sweat rolled down between my shoulder blades. I wiped my damp forehead with the back of my hand. The sergeant was talking on the phone to the immediate supervisor.

Travis had been waiting patiently to the side, but even he'd had enough. He ambled over. "What's taking so long?"

"They found hashish on a student. I'm trying to have him removed so we can continue to class."

The sergeant motioned to me. He hung up the phone and pointed to the offending student. "We'll get his information, remove him from camp, and place him on a permanent no-entry watch."

Tension drained out of my shoulders. "Thanks, Sergeant."

"Just doing my job."

"All right, let's get these guys checked in before we lose any more time." Travis turned to the interpreter and let him know we'd be moving on to class.

The sergeant glanced past me. His face tightened. "Looks like we have someone else coming to give their two cents."

"There a problem here?" The whiny voice was unmistakable.

I spun on my heel. "No worries, Lieutenant. Just picking up AUP students."

Travis whipped his head around, and he studied Stockton.

I couldn't tell if he wanted to punch him or was going to be sick.

Stockton's forehead wrinkled. "I heard a student was put on no-entry watch."

"That's right," Travis said. "We had a student with hashish on him."

I didn't say a word, just kept my eyes fixed on the gate. I hoped Stockton would give up and go away.

"Sergeant!" Stockton would keep shaking things until he caused a problem.

The sergeant stopped beside us. "Yes, sir?"

I ground my teeth until my jaw ached. The morning was turning into a circus.

"Get your supervisor on the phone," Stockton snapped. "I have seventy-one students on the roster and seventy-one will show up for class."

I stepped closer to Stockton and lowered my voice, allowing him to save face. "Look, we got two different stories from this guy. First, he said he found it on a prisoner and was turning it in. Then he changed his story and said another officer gave it to him to be destroyed."

Stockton sneered. "I don't care if he said aliens dropped it from the mother ship. I want him re-instated."

I met Stockton's eyes. "When we brief students, we tell them, very clearly, what we expect of them. These students have been told they'll be expelled from the academy and sent back to their posts if they violate the rules."

Stockton turned sideways to me. "I'm up for promotion," he whispered in a menacing tone. "I will have my quota. I will not have some contractor come along and tell me how to do my job."

"I thought we were doing this for the Afghan people."

"What?" Stockton thundered.

"This training is valuable," I said, trying to keep my voice even.

Stockton raised his voice another few decibels. Passing soldiers slowed down to look, probably wondering what was going on. "Valuable? Look around you. What do you see? I'll tell you what I see. Sand and more sand. Roads so dangerous you can't drive them without risk of being blown sky-high by an IED, and Taliban rule by fear. Do you honestly think your effort will improve anything in this country?" The sneer on his face went all the way to his soul.

I stepped closer and pushed the limits of his personal space. I wished he'd take a swing at me, and I'd have a valid reason to bloody his face. "I'm not naive enough to believe I can rewrite a country's history. Things were bad before we came, and they'll likely be bad when we pull out. There's one thing I know. What I do matters to the students and interpreters. Rasool has a wife and three boys to support. Nazarullah is married. Ahmed is engaged. How will they provide for their families if we don't give them the tools? Don't you get it? The world doesn't revolve around Lieutenant Stockton. Your biggest problem is a promotion? How'd you like to try and raise a family under these conditions?" I had just moved my name from Stockton's annoying list to the side that said 'enemy,' but I didn't care. I gave it my parting shot. "Most of these guys have never even been through a police academy. They'll likely never get another chance to take any classes once we leave their country. Don't you think we owe it to them to hold Kandahar Training Center to a high standard? Something they can be proud of accomplishing?"

Stockton stopped listening. He stalked over to the sergeant's station.

Travis sidled up. "What did you say to him?"

"That we owed it to the students to enforce our rules." I ground my fist into my empty hand, wishing it could have been Stockton's face. Any sympathy I felt toward him at breakfast had vanished like wisps of morning clouds, burned away by the desert sun.

"Release that student to attend class and get me Colonel Smith on the phone," Stockton ordered. He turned and directed a heated glare my way.

I lost this round. Would there be any wins with Stockton? I called to Rasool, our interpreter. "Tell the students to gather their things. We're heading to class."

Rasool paused. He looked confused. "And the one they found with hashish?"

I was sickened by the words coming out of my mouth. "Him, too," I said.

Rasool frowned at me for a moment, but he gathered the students for the walk to the academy.

As we traveled down the gravel path, I mulled over the morning's events. The decision went against everything I stood for. We could make a difference in Afghanistan, given the time and resources. First, we needed to build a model based on truth and integrity. How could I instill trust among students who knew I just broke the academy rules by allowing that student in? This spiraled out of control and it wasn't the first time academy rules had been undermined. The only thing I had control over were my own actions. In light of that, reluctantly, I knew what I had to do.

Once the students were seated, I turned the class over to Travis.

"I'm going to step down as a trainer."

Travis's face fell. "What?"

"We won't have any level of respect from the students once they find out we broke our own rules. I'll be worthless as an instructor," I said. "How does anyone accomplish anything here with this kind of inconsistency?"

"Can't you just let it slide this once? This is nothing new. Stockton comes up with a new problem every week. We're just trying to survive him being here."

"Let it slide? Are you kidding me? I thought I knew you better than that, or at least I thought your work ethic was better than that."

"Is one student really worth fighting over? How about your job? What will you tell Sophie?"

"Will Sophie be happy to hear I'm coming home? Of course, but what would she say if she found out I stayed and compromised my values? I know what she'd tell me to do." I shook my head, gathered the materials, and handed them to Travis. I addressed the class. "Today Mr. Blackburn will go over first-aid techniques with you."

Travis exchanged places with me.

"I'll stay and help you finish today's lesson, but then I'm going back to our tent to submit a letter of resignation," I spoke so only Travis could hear.

His gaze burned into my side, disappointment in his stare.

At lunch, I skipped the DFAC and instead sat alone at my computer.

I began my letter.

This morning at 0730 hrs. I was at the front gate escorting students to the classroom when the guards found hashish on one of the students.

I was about to give up everything I'd come there to accomplish, but if I stayed, I'd be giving up something even more valuable. My integrity. We had to be seen as truthful by our students. We should be setting the example, and we'd failed.

My fingers clicked keys on the keyboard. I finished the narrative of the day's events and closed my letter.

I have pride in the police profession and feel that we are not making a difference in this mission if we allow the rules to go unpunished. If the Afghan people, especially the police, are to take over this country, then they should be held to certain standards. Because of this incident, I have decided to resign my position with WinCorp. I have never quit anything before in my life. It's a hard decision to make, but I do not feel I can remain here.

Sincerely,

Mac McCann, Police Trainer

My fingers hovered over the "Enter" key. I glanced around the tent. I hadn't even unpacked all my gear yet. I was only beginning to have an impact on the students. I'd be leaving Travis and Glenn, and I hadn't found camaraderie like that since I was in the Army.

The locals wanted to be allowed to raise their families and make a decent living. They wanted a stable country in which to raise their children. With that thought, Bashir's green eyes haunted me. What kind of future would he have if no one stepped in? So many thoughts crowded my mind. I took a deep breath and clicked "Send."

Had I just become the most recent in a long line of people who failed the boy?

10

Sophie wouldn't be waiting as long as she thought for me to come home, but she didn't know that yet.

Another day marked off the calendar with a black slash, and I still hadn't told her I'd resigned. No sense in doing it until my travel orders came through. I think I was in denial. Telling Sophie would make it real.

Phoenix squeezed in under my legs, tongue hanging out. He planted his paws on me and tried to climb into my lap. He was growing so fast.

"How will I get you home?" I ruffled the fur on his neck. There was no way I would leave him. If I couldn't do anything positive for the Afghans, at least I'd rescue my dog. He had worked his way into a permanent place in my heart. Every day I expected to be called into Colonel Mark Smith's office to explain why I had a dog. I knew better than to think the little guy was quiet during the times I was absent from the tent.

Travis wouldn't say anything, and I was sure Glenn had my back, though reluctantly. Then there was Stockton, only two doors down. I'd been warned by Glenn that Stockton would pitch a fit and have Phoenix thrown out. Certainly, our standoff at the front gate had cemented his animosity toward me.

I got up, poured some water in a bowl for Phoenix, and headed out the door. I quickly slipped my sunglasses on. A good, long walk before morning classes was what I needed. A walk and a plan. I always thought better on my feet than behind a desk. I turned down the same gravel drive we walked the night we found Phoenix. Smoke curled in the distance. The sharp stench of burned trash stung my eyes and nose. Ashes rose from the pit on a thermal wave and glittered in the bright sunlight.

In the grand scheme of things, whether I stayed or not probably wouldn't matter much to the people of Afghanistan. But it mattered to me. Maybe I had been too hasty in submitting my resignation. I didn't want to lay down in defeat. I had to find a way to stay. I made my way back to the tent and pushed open the front door. It was strangely silent. Usually, Phoenix barked when he heard my footsteps. How much longer could I hide him? Time was running out for him, too. I opened the door to my room and stopped abruptly.

Someone had been there.

Phoenix sat in the center of the room contentedly chewing a tan and white athletic sock. I wrestled the sock from between his little needle teeth and turned it over in my hands. "Caribe" was stitched into the toe. I didn't own any socks like that.

I'd only been gone thirty minutes. Travis must have slid the sock under my door to keep the puppy quiet for me. He always had something up his sleeve. Another thing I'd miss, having friends who'd cover my back.

I grinned and flipped the ragged sock in the air. Phoenix leaped after it and bounced off my mattress.

My laughter echoed off the walls.

~*~

"Since you're going back to the academy, could

you escort Gul to the barbershop?" The sergeant at the front gate consulted his clipboard.

Crowded in with the students, Gul Hadi waited patiently at the gate with his son, Bashir. I was silent and stared at the father and son who stood so expectantly. At the sight of Bashir's small frame and hopeful eyes, I remembered the feelings of panic I'd had in the barbershop and anxiously hoped they didn't return. "Sure," I said with more confidence than I felt.

Gul, Bashir, and I started off down the gravel road.

Students fell into step behind us.

Gul ambled beside me. He was dressed in traditional Afghan garb, a knee length shirt, and baggy pants. He'd change into his work clothes, a tan polo shirt, and blue jeans once he entered the barbershop.

The view was not so great of the city from that gate, but on my early morning jogs, I'd pass another gate and peer outside, anxious to take in whatever sights of the city I could glimpse from my protected position. We spent weeks inside these walls without venturing outside, almost like being in prison, only it was for our own protection. The only time we saw the outside was on transfers or to go home on leave.

That morning I'd seen a parade of locals. One particular motorbike sported an entire family. The littlest guy looked as if he was six months old, dressed in a western-looking, red shirt and dark pants. He had a seat on a handlebar contraption. The older brother had what appeared to be the preferred place, in front of his daddy's lap and right over the gas tank, his head covered in a white ball cap. Next came the father, sitting on the motorbike seat, wearing a blue western T-shirt, tan cargo pants, and sneakers. Last was the woman, whom I guessed to be the mother, sitting on what looked like the luggage carrier. She was swathed in midnight blue fabric from head to toe. I marveled at her composure, balanced on a swaying bike.

I glanced over at Gul.

What was his life like outside these walls? He seemed to sense my curiosity and contemplated me for a moment.

"Gul, how far do you live from here?"

"About five kilometers." A smile creased his face. "How far do you live from here?"

I chuckled and tried to do the math in my head. "About thirteen thousand kilometers."

He studied my feet. "Your boots wear well." He said after a moment and grinned.

"Likewise, your sandals."

I enjoyed the game. Gul was about my age, and it was fun to match wits with him. We looked as diverse as two individuals could be, but wordplay rubbed out the edges of our differences until we appeared simply as men. People who wanted nothing more than to be left alone to live, provide for their families, go home to their wives, and a hot meal at night.

Gul Hadi nodded and then added in Dari, "*Kafsh-e kohna dar beyaabaan neamat ast.*" He waited, knowing I'd take the bait.

I walked past another two buildings and finally broke. "OK, what does it mean?" I asked.

Gul Hadi smiled, revealing even, white teeth. "It means 'Old sandals in the desert are a blessing.' Even if something is old, it is a benefit if it works and meets your needs."

"Well put," I said.

"Toss it up for me, please?" Bashir held his worn soccer ball out toward me. Bashir's command of

English was admirable. I was embarrassed at how poor my Dari was compared to his English. I imagined hanging around GIs all day gave him lots of practice. I didn't know how Gul managed to keep the boy from growing up too fast in this place, but evidently, the barber had pulled it off. There was an innocent trust in Bashir that was a short commodity in a place where families had to dodge roadside bombs just to get to market.

"He wants you to toss the ball straight up in the air to show you his newest soccer skill. It is an honor for him to ask you, Mr. McCann."

I threw the ball in an arc. Bashir ran under it and played the ball with his forehead when it descended. The ball rebounded, and he ran to retrieve it.

"Well done." I clapped.

"He practices his soccer every day," Gul said, with pride. "And his English on anyone who will speak with him."

An MRAP sped around the corner, engine roaring and dust billowing out from under the mountainous tires.

Gul called to Bashir, yelled at him to get to the side of the path, but the boy did not respond.

The ball rolled closer to the road. Bashir was hyper-focused on his prized possession. His gaze never left the soccer ball.

Gul and I took off running, tried to catch up to Bashir and pull him to safety, but the distance was too far. There was no way we would reach him in time. Gul's anguished cries tore into my heart. I shouted until I was out of breath.

Sophie would have said her God showed up because at the very last minute, Bashir's gaze turned, and he saw the vehicle bearing down on him. He grabbed the ball, somehow trapped it in his arms, and made a dash for the chain-link fence. He bounced into the mesh just in time, out of the way of the speeding vehicle. The MRAP thundered past, coating us in a cloud of chalky dust.

Gul ran up, took the boy roughly by the arm, and gave him a protracted scolding.

I couldn't blame him. My bones shook. I reached the two and handed Gul a bottle of water from my backpack.

He spoke in Dari to Bashir, who obediently took a drink. Two small tears ran silently from the boy's eyes, washing away the dust that clung to him.

Gul patted down the boy's frame and made sure he was whole. Then he took the soccer ball and tucked it under his own arm.

We started silently down the path.

After a few tense moments of silence, Gul turned to me. "A proverb." His voice shook.

I stared at him questioningly. "You want me to give you a proverb?"

We both needed a diversion.

"Yes, now you." His voice wavered, and his hand was wrapped tightly around the hand of his son.

I must come up with a witty saying to match his. I walked on for another ten feet or so, contemplating. Above us, a mottled sparrow dipped and rolled in the heat-thinned Kandahar air. I pointed. "A bird in the hand is worth two in the bush."

Gul appeared genuinely surprised and delighted by my proverb. He dropped Bashir's hand and clapped enthusiastically. His body seemed to relax, and he took a deep breath. "We have a saying, '*Yak teer, wa doo neshaan.'* It means, 'one shot and two targets.'"

A small bridge, those proverbs, but large enough for us to meet on. I took a deep breath and delivered Gul and Bashir to the front door of the barbershop.

Gul gratefully shooed Bashir on inside the building and stopped to wave a hand at me. Bashir was nothing more than a rascal, not a ghost from my past.

"Have a good day," I said.

"And you also." Gul disappeared behind the smudged glass.

I watched the glass door slowly close until Gul's face was replaced by my own reflection. Our cultures intersected, there in that unusual place. I expected to go to Afghanistan to work, to help build a viable government, yes, those things. But now I was drawn to people who were not my own. Each day I caught a glimpse of their struggles, hopes, and dreams.

11

I stopped in the hallway to brush the dirt off my clothes. I was late for class due to our battle with the MRAP. I opened the door slightly and looked in the classroom.

"I'd like to introduce our guest speaker today, J. Samuel Reynolds." Travis waved Reynolds over to the lectern.

The more I interacted with our students, the more I enjoyed their company. They had quick wits and they easily conjured up smiles. They especially loved seeing themselves on camera. The days I carried mine to class, slung around my neck on a canvas strap, they'd crowded around, each vying for his turn to have a picture made. It surprised me. In the age of smart phones, they found a picture so novel. I decided it wasn't the technology that entertained them; it was posing for a photo. I paused at the door to our classroom, maybe for the last time, and glanced at my watch. All this introspection wouldn't get our class going. The thought that this could be one of my last classes seared my conscience. I shoved the classroom door open a little more forcefully than necessary.

Travis jumped when the door bounced against the wall.

I gave him what I hoped was a reassuring nod and slinked back against the wall so as not to interrupt the proceedings any further.

The speaker crossed the room. I recognized him

from the breakfast line in DFAC Saturday.

Travis held his hand up for silence, and the students complied.

Reynolds strode up to the podium and took over. "I'm here to instruct you on IEDs, the protocol for their detection and disposal." He nodded.

Travis turned on the overhead. The fan whirred to life. He then took his place beside me, leaning against the wall. He flipped off the light switch so the images would be clearer on the mustard-colored wall.

"What's up with you today?" he whispered sharply out of the side of his mouth.

"I'm angry. That's all. I'll get over it." I let the words slide out from between clenched teeth.

"At what?" Travis asked.

"A system that forced me to choose between integrity and a student head count. At the man who rigidly enforced those rules."

"Stockton?"

"Yeah. I love my job more each morning that I roll out of my bunk. Thanks to Stockton it doesn't look as though there will be many more days of that."

"I know. Stockton's been a burr under everyone's saddle here. Even before you came to camp."

"I'm mad at myself, too. I fell right into a trap. Glenn warned me."

"He did," Travis whispered.

A knock at the door interrupted Reynolds's speech on how to detect wires in the roadway.

The class was momentarily distracted.

I jumped to the door and cracked it open.

Sergeant Thorstad's six-foot-two frame loomed in the doorway.

"What's up?" I asked.

"Good. You're the one I was looking for. Come with me." Thorstad pulled the door open wider.

I could feel the question from Travis even without turning around. But I didn't have the answer either. I exited as quickly as I could to let the students refocus.

Reynolds cleared his throat and returned to his material.

"Colonel Mark Smith wants to see you in his office," Thorstad said.

"What's it about?"

"Haven't a clue. I was only instructed to get you."

It was never a good thing to be called to the colonel's office. My stomach twisted.

Our boots echoed off the hard tile floor as we made our way down the hallway.

I automatically swung my sunglasses down off my head to cover my eyes from the blast of light that was sure to hit us as we exited the building. We swung the door open to frenzied activity, a sharp contrast to the echoing classroom.

Four-wheelers steered their way down the gravel path that looped through camp. The constant rumble of generators and roars of diesel engines from MRAPs and Buffaloes made conversation difficult. So I didn't try. I studied Thorstad as he marched ahead of me with those ground-eating strides of his. I admired his style. He was younger than me but already seemed so self-assured. He was completing his third tour in Afghanistan and had the war-weary countenance to prove it. Still, I admired his sense of purpose. The irony was that I wouldn't complete an entire tour before returning home.

I glanced up at the deep blue, cloudless sky, visible above the green, sniper-fabric covered fences that surrounded our academy. The razor wire was a reminder not everyone wanted a stable police force in Kandahar. Taliban would just as soon see police fail or come under their corrupt control. We provided the means for our students to take freedom into their own hands. Freedom. My mind turned to the problem of Phoenix's freedom as well. Getting him home nagged me. I'd be shipping out soon. Colonel had read my e-mail.

Maybe Phoenix was one of the reasons I was being called to Colonel Smith's office. Stockton not only prompted my resignation, but he also threw me under the bus concerning Phoenix.

We entered the building housing Colonel Smith's office, and I paused at his door. I quickly straightened my polo shirt and pushed my sunglasses back on top of my head before rapping on the hollow wood door with what I hoped sounded like confidence.

"Come in." Colonel Smith's voice vibrated through the door.

"Good morning, Colonel."

He rose from his chair and extended his hand. "Please, take a seat."

My scalp tingled and my chest grew tight. I was never one for beating around the bush. Just give it to me quick, like pulling off a bandage. I sat awkwardly on the edge of the scratched wooden seating.

"Let me get straight to the point. I understand you turned in a letter of resignation." He clasped his hands behind his neck and leaned back.

I exhaled. It wasn't about Phoenix. It was preliminaries for releasing me. "Yes, sir."

"I was perplexed when your letter came across my desk, McCann." He leaned forward and toyed with a pencil-high American flag mounted on a wooden dowel. He straightened the flag, aligning it with a similar-sized black, red, and green Afghan flag mounted on an identical wooden dowel next to it. Seemingly satisfied with their placement, he leaned back, looked me in the eyes, and searched my face for a reaction to his statement. "I've been impressed with your professionalism since you came to camp. I interviewed your superiors and received nothing but glowing reviews from them. That was why, when you requested to leave, I felt I needed to personally investigate the situation."

I didn't know what he was getting at, but I nodded my head. At least, he'd had enough faith in me to do an investigation. At least, I could carry that home with me.

"Sergeant Wisler was interviewed, and it was determined you were following academy protocol."

That was good, at least the truth was out, and I could go home with my head high.

"Yes, sir. I feel we owe it to the students to hold KTC to a high standard."

Colonel Smith relaxed back in his chair. "I couldn't agree with you more. As a result of that investigation, Lieutenant Stockton has been reprimanded, and the student in question has been expelled. The reason I called you to my office is to ask you to withdraw your letter. I hope you'll stay on with us. I'm trying to build a team based on integrity, and I like the work you do." He leaned across the desk waiting for a reply.

Happiness welled up in me, and I jumped to my feet and extended my hand. "Thank you, sir."

Colonel Smith stood, grasped my hand, and shook it firmly. "Then I will consider the matter closed.

Welcome back to Kandahar Training Center."

"Thank you, sir," I said again, not knowing what other words should come from my mouth. Thank you seemed inadequate for a second chance to prove myself, to show Sophie I loved her by paying off our bills, to pay my penance for Little Mac. I tried to exit the building with dignity, but I wanted to run unshackled like Bashir, I wanted to bellow at the top of my lungs like a wild man. *I'm back, Camp Paradise.*

12

"McCann." The soldier waved a small package in the air.

I pushed my way to the front of the crowd and eagerly took the white USPS box. Sophie's handwriting flowed on the outside. Back at the tent, my mouth watered at the thought of what she'd shipped.

Travis tried to push his way into my room. "Did Sophie send you something?"

I slammed the door in his face. He knew my wife only sent heavenly stuff. With one deft swipe of my knife, I sliced the tape along the side of the box. A bag of pops spilled out and what looked like two pounds of lime jelly beans, my favorite. And a box of homemade cinnamon rolls. All that treasure didn't hold any value compared to what I sought. I dumped the rest of the contents on my bed, shuffled through the pile. My hand wrapped around an envelope. Sophie did things old school. I peeled open the envelope, and an aroma of blackberries and woods filled my nose. I didn't read the card. I'd save it for tonight when I wasn't being bothered by Travis. I shoved it under my pillow.

"OK, come on in, but you owe me. And don't try and pay with that junk your wife sends." I opened the door.

Travis barreled in.

Thorstad and his gang of munchkins popped into my head. "Do you know where I can get hold of Thorstad?"

"Who?" Travis mumbled through a mouthful of crumbs.

"Thorstad. I want to give him some of this candy to hand out to the kids."

Travis swallowed. "He hangs out at the barbershop a lot."

I grabbed the bag of pops, but not before removing a grape one and laying it on my desk. I headed out the door and down the hallway.

"You want me to come with you?" Travis called after me.

"No, stay here. Watch Phoenix."

~*~

I pushed the door to the barbershop open and searched for Thorstad's trademark six-foot-two frame. He wasn't there.

But little Bashir was. His gaze immediately took in the one thing all kids zero in on. His face beamed when he saw the candy bag. He kicked his soccer ball over to me and stopped expectantly. Thorstad trained him well. "May I have some candy, sir?"

Gul was in his element, cutting a customer's hair and chatting away.

He didn't even know I was there. I felt as though I should at least ask his permission before doling out candy and ruining his kid's appetite. I cleared my throat.

Gul glanced over, took in the scene, and began to scold Bashir.

"If it's OK, I'd like to give him some candy."

Gul studied me for a moment, and then his face broke out into a grin. Gul was known around camp for being very protective of his son. I wondered if I had made it into the inner circle yet. "Yes, yes, Mr. McCann. Candy is fine. Not too much, OK?"

"OK." I dug around in the bag and pulled out three pops, grape, cherry, and chocolate.

Bashir held his breath.

He took the pops from me, breathed out a puff of air, and then smiled as if he'd just won the lottery. "Thank you, Mr. McCann."

"Call me Mac," I said.

"Thank you, Mr. Mac." Bashir smiled, his eyes lit up. He unwrapped a pop and stuck it inside his mouth where it made a lopsided bulge.

I now knew why Thorstad was hooked. Just seeing Bashir happy from such a simple thing was as satisfying as any accomplishment I'd had that week. Bashir tugged at my heart, but there was something else. I didn't want to admit it. I was jealous of Gul Hadi. I glanced at him again, as he made conversation with his customer. Though I had material things, he seemed at that moment to be a much richer man.

Bashir tugged at my sleeve. "Mr. Mac?"

I glanced at my watch. I needed to relieve Travis from dog sitting. Hopefully, I could save the rest of Sophie's cinnamon rolls. "I have to get back to my tent, I have some things to take care of."

Bashir's face fell. He shifted the pop from one side of his mouth to the other.

He took my hand and determinedly pulled me toward the door, kicking his soccer ball ahead of him. He chattered excitedly in Dari to Gul.

I dug my heels in. "Whoa there. What are you up to?"

Bashir looked at me with pleading eyes. "I want to

kick my soccer ball with you. The field is just this way. Please, sir."

I was no soccer champ. Baseball was my sport, but Bashir's sincerity shattered my objections.

Gul glanced over his shoulder and spoke sternly in Dari to Bashir, and then he turned to me. "It is up to you, Mr. McCann. If you wish, the soccer field is just across the patio. Please keep him away from the gravel path." Worry creased his forehead for a moment. He was remembering the MRAP.

Bashir tugged again at my hand and pushed against the closed door, rattling it.

A deep sigh made its way up my sternum, but it was a sigh of release.

Bashir was so thrilled to have someone to play with that he galloped across the patio. When we reached the ground of the soccer field, he directed me with a wave of his hand. "You stand there, Mr. Mac, those two tires, my goal. I kick to you."

"I defend this goal?" I pretended not to understand.

Bashir laughed with boyhood abandon. "Of course you defend the goal, the tires. Don't you know how to play soccer?"

I hung my head in mock dismay. "No, Bashir. I've never played that sport in my life."

He picked his ball up off the ground and trotted over to me, wonder spread over his face. "What do you play in America?"

I dug around in my backpack, found my wallet. Flipped the pictures out. Inside was a picture of me as a boy, about Bashir's age. I was dressed in a blue striped, little league baseball uniform. "Laurel Little League" was stitched across the front. I showed the picture to Bashir. "This was me when I was your age. I played baseball."

He rubbed the picture with his finger and pointed to a tall man with dark hair at my elbow. "Who is this man?"

"My dad. He was a coach."

Bashir glanced at the mitt on my hand in the photograph. "What is this?" The boy was full of questions.

My heart tugged. I had so many advantages as a child. If only I could give those opportunities to Bashir. "A mitt, to catch the ball."

His eyes glittered with mischief. "Here is my head, to bounce the ball." He tossed the ball into the air and bounced it off the top of his noggin. It landed a few feet from us. He ran after it, and with a quick swipe of his foot rushed the ball between the makeshift goal. "You are not a good goalie." He laughed.

I backed up, placed myself between Bashir and the goal, and tossed him the ball. "Try that again," I yelled above the screech of a jet that raked the sky above camp.

He rushed the goal, shuffled the ball back and forth between his feet. With one last effort, he kicked the ball with all his might toward me, but I was ready. I smacked the ball back at him. It bounded in an arc and disappeared over his head.

He stopped in his tracks. "You are good soccer player, not bad." He grinned at me.

I lost track of time. Sport worked its healing powers on a lonely little boy in a war zone and a man who'd lost his way. We played together until the sun rolled down behind the mountains that bordered Kandahar. "That's enough for today. I need to get you back to your dad."

He picked up his ball, tucked it under his arm, and we walked back to the barbershop together. For the first time in a while, I left my heart unguarded. Bashir managed to breach a place I was running from. I opened the door to the barbershop, and Gul was sweeping up.

"You walk us through the front gate?"

I glanced at my watch. I needed to get back and feed Phoenix, but I nodded my head.

Gul inspected the two of us. "Was he a good boy?"

"Champion. You've done well, Gul."

"I beat him at soccer, Baba." Bashir beamed.

"That is not polite, to brag what you have done. It is fine to win, but it is better to be silent." Gul shook his head disapprovingly at Bashir.

"Hold my hand," Bashir ordered and grabbed my fingers in his small hand.

Gul locked up shop, and we headed toward the front gate.

It felt good to hold Bashir's hand protectively, to feel his footsteps fall in line with mine. I delivered the pair to the gate and watched as Gul's strong back swayed next to Bashir's tiny frame. They headed into the city to return to a culture I had no part of, to face dangers the average American couldn't begin to comprehend.

~*~

"What's that you're reading?"

Travis stood in the middle of my room, a perplexed look on his face, a sheet of paper in his hands. I glanced over his shoulder at the article. It was a printout of an Internet page. "No Dog Gets Left Behind," the banner read, and under it, a picture of a mixed-breed dog with a woebegone look on his face. I stashed the bag of pops in my gorilla box.

"I don't know. I went to the latrine, and when I came back, this was shoved under your door."

"I told you to stay and watch Phoenix."

Travis held his hands in the air in exasperation.

He passed the page, and I read the article. Seemed the organization helped soldiers ship rescued dogs home to the states. Exactly what I needed. There were contact e-mails and a snail mail address. "I'll get on this quick. They may be able to help get Phoenix home. Who do you think did it?"

Travis sat on the bed and rubbed his temples. "I don't know. That's what I was wondering when you came in the door. It has to be Glenn. We're trying to hide him from everyone else."

"Glenn never struck me as caring too much about Phoenix."

"Glenn's hard to read, but it's still my best bet he did this. If you ask him about it though, he'll deny it. He's always going around here doing stuff for other people without them knowing."

I sat down at my computer and zipped off an e-mail immediately to the head of the organization. "I had a close call with Colonel Smith, but it's only a matter of time before my next visit to his office really is about the dog. Here. Read this, and tell me what you think."

Travis studied the screen from his perch on the edge of my bed. He had Phoenix's head cradled in his lap. "Yeah, I'd attach a photo, too."

I inserted the saddest photo I could find of

Phoenix. It was the day we rescued him. He was still covered in ashes.

"If they turn this down, they have wooden hearts."

Travis scratched Phoenix's neck. "You're going home, boy."

Travis's proclamation gave me joy and sadness at the same time. Phoenix provided me comfort on late nights when explosions seemed too close, and when a seven-by-seven-foot room seemed as empty as the darkest cave. "I hope you're right."

I thought about sending Sophie a quick note to let her know her package arrived just fine. I could also let her know a little guy named Bashir loved those pops. Maybe she'd send more. I pulled my inbox back up. I already had a message from Sophie. "Travis, I've got an e-mail from Sophie I'd rather read alone. I'll see you tomorrow at breakfast."

"Oh, yeah, sure." Travis scratched Phoenix's ears one last time. "Let me know when you hear back from that organization."

"I will." I heard the door to my tent close. I was too focused on reading Sophie's e-mail.

Mac,

It's been pretty quiet around here since you've gone. I've had a lot of time to think. It's been hard having both the men in my life gone. But something I read made me feel better. When I read it, I realized for the first time I have something in common with King David. We both lost sons, and we'll both see them again.

I bet he's up there right now, holding his son.

Below were lines she'd highlighted. Bible verses.

I hadn't read the Bible since Vacation Bible School. I was eight. The room was stuffy, and the teacher seemed as though she'd rather be anywhere else than with a roomful of kids. She handed out verses on slips of paper we were supposed to memorize. The only thing I enjoyed was the felt board. When she left the room, I'd re-arrange the animals. Made the giraffe pilot Noah's Ark. Noah swam behind.

Those weren't little kid's stories Sophie sent.

I wasn't even sure I wanted to read it. I settled deeper into my chair and mouthed the words.

"David got up from the floor, washed his face, and combed his hair, put on a fresh change of clothes, then went into the sanctuary and worshiped. Then he came home and asked for something to eat. They set it before him, and he ate. His servants asked him, 'What's going on with you? While the child was alive, you fasted and wept and stayed up all night. Now that he's dead, you get up and eat.

"'While the child was alive,' he said, 'I fasted and wept, thinking God might have mercy on me and the child would live. But now that he's dead why fast? Can I bring him back now? I can go to him, but he can't come to me.'"

My chest tightened. Did she think that would make me feel better? I'd never see our son again. I hit delete.

13

"Tall mocha frappe." I trudged over to the canopy-covered patio and slumped into an Adirondack chair. Classes were over, and the next day the academy would be closed. I was ready for a break.

Teaching was fun, seeing the guys learn new skills, cutting up with them between classes. But a threat hung over our heads of attack from outside or even being betrayed by one of our own students. An emotional drain.

How did Travis and Glenn do it year in and year out?

At least I could finish out my tour thanks to Colonel Smith. I was grateful for that. I needed caffeine. I made a Green Bean's Coffee run and settled in at one of the tables.

A cup plunked down in front of my eyes. The uncharacteristically boyish face of Glenn Thurman grinned at me.

"What's that sugary stuff you're drinking, with that little frou-frou whipped cream on top?" His eyes crinkled, and he looked smug. A thin line of mustache was beginning to become more pronounced across his lip. He was entering Travis's beard contest after all.

"Mocha frappe."

"Coffee for infants." Glenn threw his head back and chugged from his cup. "You need some real coffee."

"And that would be?"

"Espresso, four shots. Makes you beat your chest and triumph over your enemies." Glenn took another swig, and then set his cup down. He studied me. "I heard about your run-in with Stockton." Surprisingly, his tone wasn't accusing. He almost seemed saddened by my luck, or lack of.

I stirred the whipped cream into my coffee with the straw. Of all the topics he could choose, Glenn was a master at picking the one I most wanted to avoid, but his sudden hint of understanding made me lower my guard. "I'm still trying to decompress from that little altercation." I reluctantly gave Glenn the information he wanted. "I can't understand why Stockton feels the need to cause trouble. We could accomplish the same thing without the drama. I just want to be left alone to do my job, that's all."

"I told you to steer clear of him." His brows bent down, and the old look of a principal shadowed his face again.

"I know, and I did, but he was like a bulldog. Wouldn't give it a rest. I turned in my letter of resignation, but the colonel fixed things for me."

"Stockton's an odd bird, but the colonel's a good man. I hear he even drinks espresso." Glenn's grin spread. "So, McCann, you're officially one of us." He studied me with renewed interest as if I were an organism, trapped under the lens of his microscope.

The old uneasiness returned. Would Glenn keep treating me like a greenhorn?

"Tell me about your hometown."

I tapped my cup on the table to mix the ice, swirled the straw around. "Huntsville, Alabama."

Glenn's face puckered. Being from Savannah, I thought I'd have an ally in him, but Glenn liked to hide his southern roots from everyone.

"I know what you're thinking," I said. "Cotton farmers. I thought that too when my parents moved us down from Maryland. Even though I was young, I still thought of the South as backward." A red-hot poker seared its way up my neck at the thought. I had been as judgmental as the people I now dealt with.

"What changed your perspective?" Glenn was actually leaning in, interest gleaming in his eyes.

"Huntsville was primarily known for agriculture, but then Redstone Arsenal opened its gates and welcomed some of the greatest rocket scientists on earth. Ever heard of Werner Von Braun?"

"Well." Glenn scrunched up his forehead, thinking.

For once I had him at a loss for words. "He and his team developed the Saturn V rocket." I prompted.

"Oh, yeah. I remember studying that in school. That was the one that took a man to the moon."

"Yeah, and Huntsville was responsible for much of the technology. We're full of engineers in that town. You can't throw a rock without hitting one. That's why when I landed in Afghanistan it was such a shock to find many of my students had trouble reading and writing." I took a long sip. Most of my coffee was gone, and I was stuck with chunks of ice.

Glenn turned his head, surveying the camp. From where we sat we could see the sniper-fabric covered fence that surrounded the academy, Green Bean's stand, Abdul's Jewelry and Gemstone Shop, and the barbershop. Behind us, the mountains rose up like some giant animal on its haunches.

Glenn took another swig of his coffee then offered up his story. "When I got here, it was the farthest thing

I'd ever encountered from home. I'm a history buff. Thought I knew about Afghanistan. What I thought I knew was actually romanticized history: Marco Polo and travel on the Silk Road, elementary school tales of treasure and adventure. What I found was a place destroyed from so many different occupations. Buildings were built, bombed, then abandoned. Schools are inadequate or nonexistent." He turned and pointed past the rutted soccer field. "Over there is what's left of the old fruit orchard. This used to be a cannery. It was productive. That cement pool behind us is where they washed and processed the fruit."

"Didn't know that."

"If you go down the path that runs alongside the pool, there are rose bushes, miraculous things, growing in the middle of dust and death. The Afghan guards keep them up, trim them, and give them water when it gets too dry. It's ironic."

"Ironic?"

"In the middle of this struggle to survive, man's spirit still craves beauty."

I stabbed at the ice chunks in my cup, tried to break them up so I could get one last sip through the straw. I had no reply for Glenn. This was the first time he'd let down his guard enough to talk.

Glenn swirled his coffee cup. He drew a long drink then set the cup down. "I'm on my third tour here. Been stationed in J-bad and Kandahar. Everywhere it's the same story. Not enough education available."

I tried to suck down the last bit of coffee, but it was useless. I only ended up making an annoying slurping sound. When I glanced across the top of my cup, I noticed Gul Hadi and Bashir over at the next table.

Bashir darted back and forth, in perpetual motion. Now and then, he tilted his face up for a sip of his daddy's drink. Bashir took a second from his wanderings, and his eyes lit up when he saw me.

My hand automatically went to my cargo pockets, patting them down. I didn't have a single pop on me. I needed to be better prepared next time. Thorstad would fail me if I were in his public relations class.

Bashir ran up, stood at attention, and smiled.

I held my hands out to show him they were empty. "Sorry. No candy today."

Gul called to Bashir, and he obediently ran to his father's side.

"Thorstad always has candy stashed away in his pockets," I said quietly, more to myself than to Glenn.

"He has a good heart, but he needs to keep his eyes open," Glenn said.

"What do you mean?"

"Blue on Green attacks are escalating. It's gotten worse each year I've been here."

"Blue on Green. There are fears that the Taliban are infiltrating the Afghan National Army and police force," I said. "Travis warned me about that." Another irony. I couldn't believe we had to protect ourselves from our own students.

Bashir galloped around the patio, reminding me of something I wanted to ask Glenn, but I didn't know how. I didn't even know if I should. I glanced over at him.

He stared into his empty coffee cup; his eyes looked distant.

I took a deep breath and pressed my question. "You mentioned when we were gathering parts to make my chair that you don't have a wife."

Almost imperceptibly, Glenn reached across his left hand. His fingers scratched nervously at his naked ring finger. "That is correct."

"Travis said you'd lost her."

Lines deepened on his forehead. His brows pulled together. It was the most transparent I'd seen Glenn since I met him. "She died four years ago. That's what set me on this journey."

"If you don't mind my asking, what caused her death?"

"I'm sure if Travis mentioned it, he also told you she died of cancer." Glenn's voice had a warning edge to it.

But I pressed on. I had to know. "How have you been able to handle it?"

Glenn studied me as if I was just another criminal he'd arrested. The implication came too close to the truth. Maybe I was no better than most of the people I put behind bars. "So you are running. I suspected as much the first time I met you. Well, don't worry. I won't try and dig up your dirty little secret. I'm long past wanting to know about other people's lives, other people's misery. I have enough of my own ghosts to keep me company at night."

I tossed my empty cup in the trash barrel. Points if it were a basketball rim and not a metal oil drum. "Sometimes, I wake up at night and feel like I can't breathe. I have this mind-crushing fear that I'll never be able to get past it." Words tumbled over each other. I sounded like the druggies I used to arrest, the ones who were desperate to get clean. "I need to know how you go on." I hadn't meant to sound as if I was pleading, but I was. I desperately wanted to go home a whole man. Travis had no frame of reference to help me. Glenn was the only one I knew who had been through a profound tragedy. Would he have an answer to guide me?

Glenn gazed at the tarp that threw a blanket of shade on our table. He studied the canvas intently. His hand rested on the wooden table, fingers tapping out a beat, and he hummed a tune. The song nagged at me. Glenn's voice cut into my thoughts. "We were married six years. Lauren was always the one who could make me laugh," Glenn spoke, not so much to me. He seemed to be thinking of his late wife. "The first time we had company over for dinner, she made stew. It simmered all day. Onions, tomatoes, and chunks of beef."

My mouth watered. I wished myself back home in our little house on Wells Street, with Sophie's meal on our table.

"We were hungry," Glenn continued. "We opened the pot and dished out stew. What I didn't know was Lauren put in three times the amount of pepper." Glenn rubbed his red-rimmed eyes. His laughter hinted of his mourning. "We tried so hard to eat that stew, but it wasn't edible. Finally, we gave up and ordered pizza. Lauren was mortified. She'd embarrassed herself in front of her guests, and she'd tried so hard to have everything perfect." Glenn looked across the patio, gaze scanning the cloud-covered mountains in the distance. "Lauren spoiled me."

He gathered himself and flipped his empty cup at the trash barrel. It bounced off the rim and landed in the dirt. "You ask how I go on? I'm afraid I don't have an answer for you. I'm not so sure I have gone on. I'm out here in this most desolate of places, like you, hiding. Your strength, and your Achilles heel, are that you hope in second chances. Sometimes life doesn't give you a second chance. As I said, Afghanistan's a harsh place. The world's a harsh place. Do me a favor and don't let yourself follow my path. Try to find something bright and shining to believe in, before your faith in humanity dies." He turned and stalked away toward our tent. Swirling in the dry air in his wake, I caught words of the song that nagged at me. It was about being a wanderer.

Was I becoming Glenn?

14

"Are you able to walk us to the gate? My workday is over," Gul called across Green Bean's patio to me.

I nodded reluctantly. I didn't have the heart to turn Gul down.

Gul stood and noisily threw his cup away. He took Bashir by the hand and led him over to me. Normally, I'd be up for a visit. Gul was my window into Afghanistan. Our morning walks had become routine. I actually volunteered to do the walk-in of the students each day just so I'd be able to trade small talk with Gul. I loved talking to him about customs and hearing his wit. He was like-minded.

But not today. I needed time alone to think about Glenn's words, only it didn't look as if I'd get that solitude. Gul had already changed into his civilian clothes. We picked our way over the loose gravel, headed in the direction of the front gate. Gul glanced at Bashir. He gave him instructions in Dari, waved his hand forward. He wanted Bashir out of earshot.

The little guy kicked the ball into the air, bounced it off his knee, then trapped it when it hit the ground. He gladly ran on ahead of us. Our slow walking and talking inhibited his play.

Gul stopped short. He turned to face me. The seriousness of his expression startled me. *"Yak roz dee-dee doost, degar roz dee-dee baraadar.* This means, the first day we are friends, the next day we are brothers." Gul's eyes reflected blue like the sky. There was no darkness in them, unlike the gloom in many of my students' eyes. "You are my brother?" he asked.

"Yes, we are brothers," I said, slowly emphasizing each syllable, and I meant every word.

That made Bashir my nephew. That was appropriate. He'd already carved a home in my heart.

Gul glanced around to be sure no one was close enough to listen in on our conversation. He resumed a leisurely walk, his clothing swaying with each stride. He walked, hands clasped across his olive vest in thought. Perched on his head was a beige prayer cap, embroidered with cream-colored leaf designs. His wiry brows bunched together. Thirty years old, he looked much older than his years.

I matched his steps, waiting patiently. After all our mornings together, I knew he'd speak when he was ready.

Gul cleared his throat, a raspy dry sound. He slowed to a weary step as if the effort of what he was about to say drained his momentum. He studied the ground and said nothing.

Vehicles growled across gravel in the background. A helicopter in the distance beat the air with a bass drone.

"I need your help. I am asking that you help protect Bashir."

"From what?"

"From shadow men."

"Who are these shadow men?"

"You see them in the marketplace, looking for the boys? Searching for the most beautiful. Some police units have what they call a 'chai boy.'"

"A 'chai boy?'" My stomach tightened.

"A boy who looks after the police commander. He makes the food, cleans the house." He looked away and his voice faltered. He wasn't telling me everything.

"And?"

"He gives sex."

Gul's voice dropped to a whisper, but I heard it. It echoed as loud in my brain as artillery rounds. My temples shot tight with blood, and I felt my face burn with hate. Hate for scum who would do that to a child. I stopped abruptly. I watched young Bashir innocently kick the ball ahead of us. A protective cobra coiled in me, one that would spit death at anyone wanting to hurt him.

Gul paused, looked at me, and called in Dari for Bashir to wait on us. He turned to me as we neared the gate. "That is why I bring him to work with me. I want a better life for him. I want him to go to college. I want him to become a doctor."

"But how could he possibly end up as a chai boy if you watch him so closely?"

"Because he is a beautiful boy. That can be dangerous in Afghanistan. The boys are in danger from men who want to lure them into becoming chai boys."

Bashir's long lashes and high cheekbones made him a target. I'd seen the men Gul spoke of, on mornings when I went to the gate to collect our students. I'd seen the shadow men. I vowed in my heart to do anything I could to help Bashir. "I will protect him."

"Thank you, Mac." For the first time during our walk, Gul relaxed.

Bashir ran ahead of us, his innocence a rare treasure to be guarded.

~*~

"Did you get my e-mail, the one about King David?"

"I got it." The last thing I wanted to have was a theological discussion.

Sophie leaned into the screen, fresh-faced. Probably just got out of the shower. Her hair was still damp and curled up at the ends. Too many nights sleeping alone was beginning to take its toll on me. Part of me had been glad when I thought I was going home. I shuffled uncomfortably in my computer chair. The spell was broken.

She breathed across her coffee cup and took a sip. "What did you think?" She was feeling things out, fishing around to see if I would take the bait.

But I didn't want the hook. And I didn't want her God. "'I will go to him, but he will not come to me?' I don't find that comforting. What it said to me was I'll never play cars with him again. What that meant to me, Sophie, is that I'll never have my TV buddy again." My answer wasn't what she wanted.

A frown pulled at the corners of her mouth, and her eyes seemed to darken. Sophie tried for years to get me to believe the way she did, but it didn't click with me. The God she talked about seemed distant. I couldn't see how He could be concerned with the details of my life.

"Thinking I'll see him again is the only thing that keeps me from going crazy. Heaven is real to me, but that doesn't take away the pain." She paused and took a ragged breath. "Nothing takes away the pain."

The tent felt hot and even more closed in than normal. I reached across my desk and snapped the switch on a small plastic fan. The blades hummed and pushed stagnant air toward my face.

Sophie shook her head. "Do you know what I have to endure while you're gone?"

I shuffled in my seat and flipped an ink pen end to end over my fingers. This conversation wasn't getting any better.

"Look at me," Sophie said. "Well-meaning people tell me not to grieve at all, that God 'needed another angel.' The God I know doesn't need anything because He created it all. He certainly doesn't need my little boy. I'm hurting just as much as you are, Mac. At least you're away from it. I can't escape. Our friends don't know how to handle me anymore, so they stay away. Even our friends with children have stopped inviting me to dinner. It's as if they think losing a child is contagious." She leaned closer to the screen. "He died from a car accident, not an epidemic."

I kicked my foot back and forth under the chair, like a pendulum. "I'm so busy here, I don't have time to sit and think about things."

"You don't think about losing Little Mac?" Her voice pitched high and squeaky.

I glanced away from her piercing stare. "Of course I think about it. I just choose not to dwell on it." My head started to pound. Lying to Sophie was becoming routine. I thought about Little Mac every waking moment. Afghanistan had not cured me.

"Well, I wonder about that woman who ran the red light and hit you. I'm not sure what I'd do if I saw her in public. I was thinking about the accident report the other day. I never saw a copy."

"Stop torturing yourself about details. We've got to move on." The harshness of my voice surprised me. That didn't sound like me at all. Words were out of my mouth before I could stop them, and I regretted them. Not only had I'd read the Bible verse she sent, but I'd also read the entire chapter. King David sent a man to the front lines in battle and withdrew his soldiers so the man would be killed. The man he had killed was the husband of a woman David had made pregnant. King David lied about the relationship and then caused the man's death. I couldn't get it out of my head how similar that was to my situation. I refused to lose Little Mac, and Sophie, too.

Sophie had gone quiet. We stared at each other. I looked over her head. The laptop must have been sitting on the kitchen table. The red antique kitchen clock ticked loudly, emboldening the silence that tried to grab us. Over Sophie's shoulder, the window above the kitchen sink was opened slightly. The lace curtains swayed gently as a breeze made its way through the window. Curtains she'd washed and hung that belonged to her mother, even though I'd argued she should buy herself new ones. She held onto things, that girl I loved. She collected souvenirs and memories. And wounds.

15

"All right. This here's your enemy." I tapped Ace on the back, and they laughed. I wanted the guys to know how to handle themselves when they were under fire. None of these men had been trained in any type of combat scenario.

Ace, as we nicknamed him, was our top student, and he was the first to volunteer for every exercise. He advanced quickly and had the pride to match.

"Your goal is to hide out in these mock buildings. You must have your weapon drawn and pointed like this." I pulled Ace's weapon from his hands and assumed a stance, weapon pointed down the alley.

"If he sees you or your weapon sticking out from a building or a wall, he will call out, and you will be dead." When I said dead, the students laughed again. This was nothing but a big game of hide and seek. "So, make sure you're not seen by your enemy, Ace."

I positioned him with his back turned to the guys, told him to stay until I returned. Then I took the other students one by one and hid them in doorways, against walls, under vehicles.

I came back to Ace and turned him around. "Go."

He took off at a lope, stopped here and there to call out "dead" students. They loved it. But there was only one problem. Students were having so much fun being "dead" they were starting to reveal themselves deliberately so they could be called out and return to the lineup.

Pretty soon, I was faced with a whole classroom of "dead" students. "OK. Let's do this scenario over again, but I'll show you where you're going wrong."

This time I took my camera with me. Each time a student showed the end of his barrel or the tip of his hat, I took a picture, called him on it, and showed him the shot. He could automatically see where he'd gone wrong. Besides, those guys were camera hogs. The next go-round, they were doing much better, and they even took pride in not being "dead."

After class, I walked back to my tent and put my stuff away. I was satisfied with the day's work and felt like an integral part of Camp Paradise. Even my physical ability had improved. The walk was less strenuous, and I wasn't as exhausted as when I'd first got there. I'd been working out at the gym every day, and I was proud of my abs. I glanced in the scratched mirror taped to the wall above my desk. Weak yellow light from my desk lamp burned my already gritty-from-lack-of-sleep eyes. I grabbed a bottle of eye drops off the shelf and rinsed my eyes with a stream of liquid. I hardly recognized myself from the man I was a few months ago. I ran my hand across the unruly reddish beard that sprung up across my face. Back home HPD standards allowed only a well-groomed mustache.

In Afghanistan, beards were honored as the sign of an elder. I felt the beard made me look more mature. My reddish-blond hair had grown out since Gul's massive attack on it. It was nearly collar length. I didn't intend on getting a haircut anytime soon. I was tired of rules. I let my hair do as it wanted, let the beard claim my face.

Miles of daily walking made me lean, more like

the soldier who'd married Sophie seven years before.

Travis knocked on my door. "Dinner?"

"I should skip it tonight. What's on the menu?"

"Mongolian Grill."

I groaned. Mongolian grill was my favorite. Huge strips of marinated beef seared over a hot grill with peppers and onions topped off with hot fried rice. One thing for sure, they fed us well at Camp Paradise. My stomach rumbled at the thought. "All right, you talked me into it. I'll add a few more minutes to my cardio tomorrow." I grabbed my stuff, put it away, walked out the door, and down the path with Travis. "I've meant to ask, are you extending when this tour is over?"

Travis trudged along for a moment. "Why do you ask?"

"I heard you talking about finances to Glenn one night. Just wondering."

Travis dragged his boots in the gravel. "I'm on my fourth deployment right now. If I go back, it'll be for a fifth."

"Wow."

"I have mixed feelings. Right now the job situation is tight back in the States. If I got out, I'd be making a third of what I'm making here and still getting shot at. You know the hazards of law enforcement. So I guess my motivation for getting out would be to have more time with Tricia. But If I go back home, number one, I need to find a job because they didn't hold my old one for me, and number two, I'd probably be working so much overtime I'd never see Tricia anyway."

I was beginning to see his point.

"What are you doing?" he asked.

"I'm only doing one tour. I need to get back and

spend time with Sophie."

Travis sauntered along, his forehead a mass of worry lines.

"My department, as soon as you're out of sight, you're out of mind."

"Hate to hear that."

We charged into the line, grabbed our trays, and loaded them up.

I sat my tray down, pulled up a chair, and soon Glenn joined us.

Thorstad showed up a few minutes later. It was awhile since we'd all been at the same table together.

"I have news from home," Thorstad said.

"What's up?"

"My little girl just graduated kindergarten." Thorstad was the Pied Piper of Camp Paradise, and he never mentioned his own child?

"Congratulations." Travis nodded. Did everyone at this table know but me?

"I didn't know you had a daughter." As soon as the words were out of my mouth, I regretted them.

Everyone stared.

Thorstad became interested in stirring the rice on his plate. He made a mound of rice and mashed it with his fork. "I don't talk about her much. I'm not allowed to see her." Thorstad's voice was flat.

I waited for further explanation, but none came.

Glenn started up a conversation about how the Gamecocks blasted the Tennessee Volunteers, and Thorstad relaxed as if he were grateful.

I made a mental note to never ask him about her again.

After dinner, I followed Travis out back, and we dumped our drink bottles into the recycle bin. We trudged back to the tent. I couldn't get the picture out of my mind of Thorstad, the gentle giant, not being able to see his child. So when we got back to the tent, I quizzed Travis on it.

He followed me into my room and took a seat at my computer chair.

I paced back and forth in the small space. "Why can't Thorstad see his little girl?"

Travis sighed. "I knew you'd ask."

"Well, don't you think it's kinda sad?"

"Of course."

"His ex-wife moved out of state, took his little girl with her. The new state has different visitation laws. Maybe that was why she moved there. Because Thorstad had been in-country only a certain number of days, his custody and visitation rights were revoked."

"Are you kidding me?"

"I wish I were. They said he voluntarily and willingly joined the military, and his deployment to Afghanistan constituted intentional abandonment."

"Of all the men I know in this camp, and, don't be offended, Thorstad is the most qualified to be a dad. Why is it that people who genuinely want children are deprived of them, and the ones who abuse kids seem to have no problem getting them?" This time it wasn't Little Mac's face that floated in front of my eyes. I saw a brown-skinned Bashir, his green eyes alive with mischief. In my mind, I saw men crouching in the shadows. Despite Gul's protective measures, those men would do their best to exploit Bashir's innocence.

Travis stared at me, his brow wrinkled. "Is this about you and Sophie? Are you two trying to have a kid?"

"No, we already." I stopped myself. Travis and I

were friends at camp, but still, I couldn't bring myself to talk about my son. "I mean, we can't have children right now."

Travis's face smoothed out in compassion. He stumbled over his words. "I'm sorry to hear that, man. Trish and I, well, Trish, decided that we don't want children yet. They require so much, and I just don't have it in me to try and parent a child right now. I have to focus on my job here, and Trish has her classes to keep up with."

"That's why Thorstad hands out candy and is so good with the kids," I interrupted.

Travis never missed a beat. He nodded. "Of course it is. He misses his little girl. Handing out goodies to the local kids is his way of taking care of the need he has to be a dad."

I sat down on my cot. "None of this makes sense. Glenn, who is a great guy, is a bachelor because he can't meet anyone here. Now Thorstad. It almost seems that if he tried to be some kind of reprobate father he would not have been punished any worse than he has been."

"It doesn't make any sense to me either," Travis said. "I'm just thankful Trish and I have a good marriage."

"You work harder on your relationship than anyone at camp. Every time I turn around, you're pushing another self-help book into my hands."

"Which reminds me, I just got a new one at the last mail call. Give me a minute, and I'll find it for you." He rose from my wobbly excuse of a chair.

I waved him off. "No, thank you. I was just going to check and see if Sophie is on the computer tonight. No more relationship books for me right now."

"All right, but it's supposed to be a good one." He said over his shoulder as he closed the door to my room.

I slid into my chair and pulled up the live video to Sophie on the computer. At first, the picture went through, sharp and clear, almost like being back in our kitchen. Just as I was about to say hello the image froze. Sophie's face was contorted into a gruesome mask of digitized images. The feed shut down, made an echoing plunk, like when a rock dropped down a deep well. It was the sound of something lost.

I thought of all the loss in that country. Glenn, without a wife, sad and jaded. Thorstad, being denied fatherhood and filling the void by handing out candy to the locals. I thought about Little Mac. It all felt like a dark, inescapable well. I rebooted the computer, and it worked. Sophie answered on the first ring.

"Hello, babe."

"Hello, Sophie." I was thankful to see her. I didn't know why it was awkward, but it felt as if each time we got on live video it was a new date.

"Mac, I was packing up some more things the other day. I was thinking about God, wondering where He was when our baby died. My whole childhood, I heard the story of how my dad died in a crash. It wasn't until I met the woman who held him as he died, that I saw God's hand in it. I blamed God for so many years for taking my father. If God sent someone to be with my dad in the last moments of his life, wouldn't He be with our son?"

God knew all along it would be me holding Little Mac? My temples pulsed. I heard my own heartbeat in my ears.

We were interrupted by the atmosphere-ripping

screech of a low-flying jet. The roar rattled my shelves and thundered through the tent canvas.

I was glad for the interruption. It gave me time to think.

As soon as we could talk again, Sophie continued softly, "The other day when we were talking, I heard an explosion go off outside your camp. Your situation hasn't changed, but you know what has changed, Mac?" She leaned in toward the computer screen. "I always looked to you to protect me, to make things all right. Since you've been gone, I have to depend on God. At first, I thought He was too distant to care about me, but the more I trusted Him, the more I found Him to be there. It's kind of hard to describe. I'm still alone, but I have peace."

"He hasn't shown up for me. Where was He the day Little Mac died?"

"I ask Him that, too, Mac, every day."

"Then how can you trust a God who would allow our son to die?" I didn't tell her what I really meant. I couldn't believe in this God because then I would be accountable for what I did.

We said good night and signed off.

Turning off that computer and losing Sophie's presence felt like losing the only remaining stability in my life. The day had been long, and I was tired. I hated to admit that this had not been the adventure I thought it would be. I questioned the wisdom of going to Afghanistan, but all I knew was I had to work those things out in my mind. I had to go home as a whole man for Sophie, but I had no idea how to accomplish that. Before I turned out my light, I slid down under the covers and pulled them over my face. Maybe if I lay still and made time for God, He'd show up.

But all I heard was the stuffy sound of my own nose. There was no voice from God, and I felt like that confused kid back in Sunday school, always the last to understand Bible verses. I drifted off to a fitful sleep.

The next time I was aware, sounds of camp intruded on my morning. Vehicles raced down the gravel drive on the other side of the T-wall and threw up a racket of diesel engines and grinding from the weight of their tires. Pieces of conversation blasted over the noise of vehicles. Men marched to the DFAC for breakfast.

Meanwhile, inside the tent, Travis was shouting above the racket to his wife about bills. I was concerned about him lately. Things were coming unraveled in tent 29. When I first arrived at camp, he peppered me with self-help ideas and lectured me on the importance of keeping a healthy relationship with my wife. He hadn't spoken to me about his own wife lately.

I rolled out of my cot and dressed in clean khaki pants and polo shirt, my usual uniform. As I pulled on my pants, my hands automatically searched the pockets.

Sophie always packed notes for me to find. One time I'd been away fourteen days working security in Mobile during Hurricane Katrina. I put on my boots that first morning and found something balled up in the toe. I'd pulled out a folded piece of pink paper with Sophie's flowing handwriting. It said she wanted me to be safe and know she loved me.

There were no notes in my clothing this time. My running shoes contained no pink scraps of paper. I turned all the pockets of my clothes inside out when I unpacked, hoping for her notes.

I missed those scraps of paper. Maybe Sophie outgrew love notes. The irony hit me. She'd always been the one to write them.

I didn't remember a single time I sent her flowers or cards for any occasion, even our anniversary. The memory sent a blade of pain between my ribs and twisted it. I heard in my mind, the disappointment in her voice, seven years' worth. "Can't you just pick me up some flowers?" She asked. "The grocery store has them in the produce department, for Pete's sake."

I didn't get it. Flowers died. Like, little boys.

When I turned my pockets inside out and found nothing, I began to understand.

16

"Camp Paradise Cigar Club, come to order." Glenn sauntered to the front of our bench, opened a box of cigars. "It's time you young bucks learned the art of manliness."

Friday nights had evolved into Camp Paradise Cigar Club. Glenn started it, said we needed an activity to make us real men.

Glenn, Travis, Sergeant Thorstad, and I were the usual suspects. Visiting instructors and brass joined us from time to time, but mostly, it was just the four. Glenn received a new shipment of cigars, and he was eager for us to try them.

I inspected the cigars. I'd never been a smoker. If my dad had caught me with a cigar, I'd have learned the art of manliness from his belt. "What kind are these?"

Glenn pulled a cigar out of a tube, extended it in my direction and ignored my question. "Your first love affair with a cigar is like meeting a beautiful woman for the first time. You take your time and enjoy the experience. The wrapper should be well-made, no knots or defects. Feel how smooth that is?" He placed the cigar in my hand. "Use this for cutting, not your knife."

"What's this?"

"It's a guillotine cutter. Place the cigar foot in it. Yeah, like that, and cut."

I fumbled around but managed to get the thing cut

to Glenn's satisfaction.

I automatically placed the cigar in my mouth. I felt as if I was still in high school, and I'd just sneaked out back of the field house to have a smoke.

"No, hold it away from you like this."

Glenn held his cigar away from his body and rotated it, lighting it carefully and evenly. The tip glowed in the dusk. There was a lot more production to this cigar smoking business than I'd thought.

I dropped my hand to my side and curled the unlit cigar in my palm.

A voluminous cloud of smoke billowed from our little group. I was sure our position was clearly visible from the air.

Travis drew on his cigar and smoke trailed beside my right elbow.

The glow of cigars flared around our bench, reflecting back the dying rays of Afghanistan sun. Our names were carved in that bench. We became brothers through that small act, and I was reminded of our friendship each day we were in camp.

Travis turned toward me, and I could see my face reflected red in the evening rays of sun in his sunglass lenses. I thought I looked rather manly with the cigar, though it was unlit.

"Where's Phoenix? They didn't make you get rid of him, did they?" Travis asked.

"No, Reynolds was taking a flight back to Kabul. No Dog Left Behind said if we could get Phoenix to Kabul they had a way to get him shipped back to the States, so Reynolds agreed to take him along."

"What'll happen to him once he's in the States?"

"That's the good part, my Sergeant from HPD is picking him up at the airport and will take him home to Sophie."

"I bet she's excited."

I started to feel nauseous, and it wasn't the cigar smoke. "Um, yeah."

Travis studied me in the setting sun. "You didn't tell her, did you?"

"I will, I just haven't figured out how to break it to her yet.

"That's easy. You call Sophie, and you say, 'I'm sending you a puppy.'"

"It's not that easy. I've wanted a dog for years, but Sophie always said no. They were too much trouble. She's afraid it'll tear up the house."

Travis took another draw on his cigar. "Well, you'd better warn her before Phoenix shows up on her doorstep. By the way, we're having a manliest beard contest. Categories are Manliest Beard of Camp, Best Mustache of Camp, and Most Creative of Camp."

"I think I already have a good start on the manliest," I said, scratching my fingers into the unruly hair that engulfed my face. "What are the prizes?"

Travis blew out a lazy stream of smoke before answering. "Bragging rights, I suppose."

"I'd have liked a plaque."

"Where will we get a plaque out here?"

"I bet Glenn could come up with something. Isn't he supposed to be the King of Procurement? At least that's what you told me."

"You're right."

Glenn caught the last few words. "The King of Procurement needs to get what?"

"A plaque, for the winner of the Manliest Beard of Camp Paradise," Travis said.

"Hm. Yeah, I think I can come up with an award.

Give me a month or so."

"It'll take them that long to reach their full glory anyway," Travis said.

"Speak for yourself. I think I already have a magnificent beard."

Glenn still only had the thinnest of mustaches, and Travis hadn't even begun to grow his beard yet.

I had high hopes to claim the title.

"You still haven't lit your cigar." Glenn inspected the stogie hanging from my fingers.

"I'm saving it for later."

"I have a feeling you're too much of a wuss to smoke it."

I couldn't stand it when Glenn gloated. I made an attempt at lighting the thing. I was rewarded with a glow of light. I inhaled deeply and immediately realized that was the wrong thing to do. I slid to the gravel gasping like a fish out of water. I flashed back to the morning the middle school bully delivered a fist to my stomach on the playground.

"Are you all right?" Glenn feigned concern, but it was hard not to miss the mirth in his face, even as the T-wall spun and I found myself studying the underside of the bench. Someone accumulated a lot of chewing gum under there.

Gravel poked my back in all sorts of uncomfortable places, and my stomach threatened to turn itself inside out. Next thing I knew I was being heaved up from under the bench. I immediately double over and emptied the remnants of my dinner on Glenn's boot. My retching was drowned out by Travis's loud baritone laughter.

"McCann, you destroyed a great cigar and my favorite boots in one night." Glenn grabbed a bottle of water and drenched his boot, scraping the sides on the gravel.

"Let me get you to your cot. You look green." Travis draped my arm over his shoulder, and half dragged, half carried me into the tent. Getting away from the smell of tobacco was good. Even the smell threatened to induce more retching.

Travis, good man that he was, dragged me to my cot and deposited me there. "You want a drink?"

"The thought of it makes me want to puke some more."

"OK, sleep it off. See you in the morning."

I curled into the fetal position and shoved my blanket into a wad against my stomach. All in all, it was quite a successful night. I managed to both placate Glenn and disgust him. I had a good start on the Manliest Beard of Camp Paradise, and Phoenix would soon be home, waiting for me to finish my tour. I drifted off to sleep with the smell of tobacco still clinging to my clothes.

~*~

In my dream, I was home in our king-sized bed. Sophie leaned over me, kissing me. In the background, a phone rang incessantly. "Sophie, I'll get the phone." I rolled over, and the sour stench of vomit and stale cigar smoke filled my nostrils. I opened one eye, and unfortunately, I was back in the tent at Camp Paradise, still wearing yesterday's clothes. I squeezed my eyes shut, tried to recapture that moment with Sophie, but the phone in my dream was still ringing. I dragged myself over to the desk and didn't even bother to read the display. "Hello?"

"Hello? Is that all you can say when you see my name pop up?" Sophie was not too pleased, judging from the sound of her voice.

"Hi, sweetie."

"Don't try to placate me."

The room was spinning, so I sat down on my computer chair. I was still riding out the after-effects of the night before. "I'm not trying to placate you." Even the yellow desk light was too bright that morning. I shut it off and let the room bathe in the glow of my laptop. What day was this? I glanced up at my calendar, each complete day neatly marked through with a black line.

Saturday. I had to be at the academy in two hours. My tongue stuck to the roof of my mouth, sandpapery. I set the phone down on my desk and groped around in the semi-dark for my drink bottle. All the while I could hear Sophie's voice as if it was far away, fussing. I wished my head would stop throbbing.

"Mac, did you hear me?" She was not giving up, whatever it was.

"Yes, I hear you."

"I'm hanging up my cell phone. Call me on live video. Right now," Sophie said.

The phone clicked off.

I ran my hand through my hair, before grabbing the hand sanitizer bottle to quell the stench of cigar smoke. When I clicked on Sophie's photo, there in full-screen hilarity, was Phoenix. I forgot my hesitation at Sophie's bad mood and felt a smile stretch across my face. Man, I missed the little guy. His face peered into the screen, his tongue hung out to one side in a comical way. His eyes were bright, and beyond his head, the tip of his tail wagged like a pendulum. I wanted to believe he was happy because he saw me.

My head was still fuzzy from sleep and cigar smoke. "Hello, boy," I mumbled through clumsy lips.

The next picture was not so pleasant. Sophie's face was right up against the screen, and she clearly was not happy to see me. "Sergeant Henshaw brought him by this evening. He came to the door and said you'd sent me a gift."

"Good old Henshaw. I knew I could count on him. Did you thank him?"

But Sophie had not stopped talking long enough to hear me. "When he said he had a gift for me, I thought, 'Finally, Mac remembered our anniversary.' You do know today is our anniversary, don't you?"

I wondered half-seriously if I could put in paperwork to extend my tour, but Sophie got over things pretty fast. Usually.

"Mac? Do you have anything to say?"

"His name is Phoenix."

17

"Cease fire!" I whipped my pistol from its holster.

Foizi swung his gun erratically around the practice firing range until I was looking at the black hole of the barrel.

Travis ducked, Glenn cursed, and I turned my pistol into position.

Foizi's face was in my pistol sight. *Lower your weapon. Lower it!* My finger tensed ever so slightly on the trigger. With earplugs in, my rapid breaths thundered.

Foizi grimaced and pointed the barrel of the AK47 to the ground just as my finger was applying pressure.

There was a millisecond for me to stop. I lowered my pistol and released the breath that felt as if it would explode my lungs. I strode across the range and jerked the weapon from Foizi's hands. The whole incident took only seconds, but each action seemed an eternity as it played out in my head in slow motion. "Do you know you were almost shot?" My voice shook, and I grappled to control it.

He hung his head.

I took a deep breath and swallowed, but there was a peach-pit-sized lump in my throat. "What you did is called flagging. Wave that barrel like a flag again, and it'll be a quick way to leave this earth."

"I forgot," Foizi said. He looked miserable.

"Keep the barrel downrange," I said between gritted teeth.

The guys were like kids on a playground during training. We had to impress on them how dangerous Range was. Foizi was still a kid himself, a lanky twenty-three-year-old father of two. He was nine years my junior, but to me, he was still a kid. He needed to understand it was no time to goof around. As close as we became with the students, there were still incidents where instructors were attacked. We didn't have the luxury of complete trust.

I handed him the AK47. "Let's try again."

Foizi nodded.

The shame on his face made me address him again. "You can do this, Fozzy," A nickname we hung on him.

Foizi nodded again, this time determination was plastered across his face.

"Unload and show clear," Glenn called over the bullhorn.

I waited until all ten students cleared their weapons before I approached the target stands. I marched down the lane, stapled a new paper target to the wood frame for each student and walked back up the line toward them, hand on my pistol all the way. Beneath my bullet-proof vest sweat ran down my back between my shoulder blades. I'd never taught a class in the States where I had to worry about students shooting me. Green on Blue attacks had been increasing. As much as we joked and cut up with our students, we never really knew who might be the one to shoot us in the back next range time. Taliban had a way of infiltrating police academies. It had happened before. My goal was to train these guys to the best of my ability but also to make it home in one piece.

I reached the lineup and walked the row,

straightening students' stances. Adjusted a barrel here, a hand-hold there. Foizi still looked off balance, so I tapped his foot with my own to get him to distribute his weight evenly. When everyone appeared ready, I nodded to Glenn.

"Load," Glenn shouted.

Ten magazines slammed into rifles, and the metallic sound echoed off the sand-filled Hesco barriers that surrounded our practice range. We counted on the wire-framed, canvas-lined walls to stop any errant rounds. They also protected us from incoming fire.

Glenn placed the bullhorn in front of his mouth and clicked the button.

"Treat every weapon as if it is loaded. Never point your weapon at anything you do not intend to kill. Keep your finger straight and off the trigger, until you're ready to fire."

He paused to wait for Rasool to interpret and then added, "Be aware of your target, background, and surroundings. Make ready," Glenn continued. He glanced at Foizi.

Foizi gripped the barrel of his AK47 until his knuckles showed white. The end of the barrel shook, but this time it remained pointed at the target.

"Standby."

The hair stood up on the back of my neck.

"Fire."

The sound of ten rifles crashed off the walls of the Hescos. Again, we had the students unload. Again we retrieved targets. We kept this up until we had completed several iterations. When the guns had been cleared and the last targets collected, Travis and I approached Glenn.

"Mac and I have a prize for the best shooter today," Travis said, as he produced a watch in a box from his pocket. The watch was just like mine.

"Line up with your targets in hand," Glenn said over the bullhorn.

Students stopped talking and retraced steps to their shooting positions. Each one had a fist full of paper targets. Every student was so different in appearance. I could see the impact of several nationalities having occupied Afghanistan. It seemed every nation left part of its gene pool there.

"Abdul, let me see your targets," I said.

He handed them over. Self-assurance showed in his eyes. Abdul was the father of three and a learned man. He kept meticulous notes and shared with the other students. I could always count on him to keep them on track.

Travis and I studied Abdul's targets. Round holes punched through the paper made a tight pattern on each one. Abdul was a serious contender for the winner.

He grinned when I handed him the papers and patted him on the back. "Good job," I said.

The men were competitive. It worked in our favor to teach them when we did exercises such as this. Next in line was a student nicknamed Boom-Boom. He'd earned that moniker the first day we practiced with RPG's. To prevent the scenario we had with Foizi, we trained with plastic RPG models. Boom-Boom was so named because he beat all the other students to the RPG and refused to relinquish it during any of the tactical exercises. He loved that weapon, and he answered to the nickname with pride.

Boom-Boom's target patterns were not as precise

as Abdul's, an outcome I would have predicted. His preoccupation with big guns did not lend itself to smaller weapons target practice. Still, his effort was applauded.

Foizi stood with his head down, nervously tapping target papers against his thigh.

"Let me have a look." Travis extended his hand, and Foizi reluctantly gave up the papers. It wasn't a great score, but it was an improvement over the last time we'd practiced.

"Fozzy, your patterns are getting better. Next time we go to the range you and I will get some extra practice in, what do you say?"

A nervous smile spread across his face, and he nodded. Despite his clumsiness with weapons, Foizi was a friendly guy, always acted like a clown with his fellow students. He had a lanky frame and short-cropped, wild hair. His uniform was always a mess.

The last student in line was a seventeen-year-old who fudged his age on his application to the Afghan Uniform Police. The minimum age to qualify for application was eighteen, but evidently, someone looked the other way when his request was turned in. To the extent that Foizi's uniform was a mess, Ace's was immaculate. His boots were always clean, laces tied, which was not the case for most of our students.

I found it amusing that most of them, accustomed to wearing sandals, thought laced boots were too confining. We would march out to the range only to have to stop and order someone to tie his boot laces. One student or another always walked, laces dragging the ground behind him, boots dog-eared. But not Ace.

He handed his targets to Travis and leaned across us as we studied them. Travis and I counted the number of holes punched through the inner circles. Flipped the papers back and forth. It was a close match between Abdul and Ace.

"What do you think?" Travis's brows lifted.

I walked back to the front of the line. "Abdul, let me see your targets one more time." He handed them over, and I carried them to the back of the line where Travis and I compared them to Ace's.

The students were unusually quiet. Every ear strained to hear the first words out of our mouths.

I looked at Travis, and he nodded. I walked back to the front of the line and returned the targets to Abdul.

He took them with a questioning look.

"Travis, come on up here and help me announce the winner," I said.

Travis ambled to the front of the line, fished a box from his pocket, and handed it to me. He took the bullhorn and, with a nod from me, announced, "The winner of today's shooting competition is Ace."

"Please come to the front to receive your award," I said.

Ace's face colored, and he walked quickly to the front.

I was the first to reach him. I grabbed his right hand and clapped him on the back.

The other students clapped raucously.

"This is from Travis and I, to show how much we appreciate the hard work you guys put in each day." With that, I handed the box to Ace, who drew his brows up in a question. He fumbled with the top and flipped it open.

A collective "Ah" escaped from the students.

The silver watch face gleamed in the dry Kandahar

air. Ace pulled the watch from the box and excitedly strapped it to his wrist. He admired it for a moment before an exclamation came from his lips. He pressed his wrist next to my strapped-on watch and said something in Dari I could not understand.

"He said 'Thank you, Mac. Every time I look at it, I will remember you. I will never take it off, never,'" Rasool said.

If I had a son like him, I would have been proud. The thought settled into the back of my mind, but I shoved it further down to the 'what could have been' compartment.

"Line up single file, back to the academy," Travis said.

Gravel crunched under the feet of ten students, walking in single file for the instructor's safety. We could keep a better eye on them that way.

The wind, ever-present, blew grit into my eyes. Some of the students burrowed down into their scarves to shield their noses and mouths. They looked impressive in steel blue uniforms, squared off caps, and black boots. I felt a burst of pride.

I glanced down at my boots. O Positive, my blood type, was printed neatly in black marker on the tops. Earlier in the day, I thought I'd come close to needing that information. I hoped to make it off Camp Paradise without doing just that.

18

"Tricia wants a divorce." Travis grabbed a swig from his water bottle and set the treadmill another level higher. The belt flew, and he spoke in short bursts. I struggled along beside him on the next treadmill. Travis was a long-distance runner, one of those guys who went into withdrawal if he couldn't make it to the gym. That day he needed exercise for a different reason.

My knees were taking a beating trying to keep up with his speed. I lowered the number on my treadmill. "What happened?" I asked.

The belt on his treadmill gave a high-pitched whine.

"Our bank balance kept declining. At first, I thought Tricia was taking classes, or hanging out with friends." He shifted the treadmill incline up a notch. "Tricia was never one to stay still for long." Sweat flew off Travis. "Today I got an e-mail from her. She was taking classes all right. Guitar, from some hippie guy. Next thing I knew she told me she was sleeping with him."

"What will you do?"

"I thought I'd take emergency leave to see if I could save us." He grabbed another drink from his water bottle. "She said, 'Don't come.' Said it was too late, wouldn't do any good." He grimaced. "Don't come? Who says that after years of marriage? How did she just shut us down?"

"I'm sorry." It was all I could say, and it felt inadequate.

"I've been there for her through every trial in her life. When she had emergency surgery and when her parents died," Travis said.

We ran along for another thirty minutes.

Travis was sweating out his pain.

I was sweating for a different reason. Travis put in the work, tried to have a good marriage. I left my wife to hide from my own pain.

Travis's treadmill belt was screaming. His footfalls were closer together. He was stomping out his past.

I didn't have another thirty minutes in me. I shut the treadmill down and decided to hit the free weights while I waited on Travis. Bicep curls felt good. The burn made me feel alive. When I completed my reps, Travis was still running. He was in his zone, so I let him be. I arrived at the tent gritty, tired, and badly in need of a shower. I grabbed my towel, trudging down the gravel path, and headed to the Conex boxes.

The sun had slipped down the mountainside, surrendering itself to dusk. The stars were beginning to pop through, and I recalled Travis's words about feeling small. I wished for redemption, only this time for Travis.

Soldiers were milling around the outside of the Conex boxes.

I started to get that skin-crawling feeling I used to get on patrol as a police officer. The feeling something was about to go wrong. An odd thing had taken place that morning. None of the local workers showed up. When that happened, it made me nervous. They knew something we didn't. I grabbed the nearest soldier's attention as he passed. "What's up?"

"Shower's closed."

"Why?"

"Pump truck came to empty the tanks and clear a blockage. We stopped them and searched the truck. It was packed with explosives."

My skin prickled. I was still staring at the "closed" sign, partly in disbelief and partly because I desperately wanted a shower to feel human. I could almost feel the water washing off the day's dust.

Travis came puffing up, towel slung over his shoulder. He turned around when he saw the sign taped across the shower entrance.

We returned to the tent in silence.

When we got back to our tent, I ran inside and grabbed a few bottles of water. Outside beside the trash barrel, I hung my head over the side and doused it with water and shampoo.

"Great minds think alike." Travis grinned at my elbow, shampoo dripping down his face. "I may live in a tent, but I don't have to smell like it."

"Then while you're at it, get your feet. They stink all the way down the hall," I said.

Travis threw water in my face. I grabbed the empty bottle and pitched it at him. It was good to see the old Travis back again.

Later, alone in my room, I went through my evening ritual of answering e-mails.

Sophie,

We had a successful day at the range. The students shot well, and everyone seemed to enjoy it. We had a couple of students that'd never fired a weapon before, so it was fun watching them. This is the first formal class they've ever been to. A lot of these guys are hired and put right to work and have to wait for a slot in an academy, so this is essential for them.

The important thing is no one got hurt. I checked the zero on my rifle, and it was right on. I even shot my pistol.

No shower tonight. Taliban almost blew up our Conex Boxes. Just another night in Camp Paradise.

Love, Mac

The emptiness of the tent got to me. Down the hall, I could hear Travis arguing with his wife on the phone. I needed to see Sophie's face, to see our home in the background. On the computer, I searched for Sophie's name, hoping she was online. "Sophie?"

The picture pulled up, and Sophie had a smile on her face.

"I was just answering your e-mail, but I'd rather see you in real time," I said.

Travis's voice boomed over mine, from down the hall. He and his wife were still arguing.

"Who was that?" Sophie asked.

"Probably Travis. He's having a horrible week."

"What's going on?"

"I think his wife left him."

Sophie's face crinkled. "Oh, Mac. I'm so sorry."

"It happens," I said. "Last leave one of the guys went home, and all the locks were changed on his house."

"Awful."

"Yeah, it is. How are things going with you? You look cute," I said, wanting to change the subject.

Sophie was covered in flour. She was wearing one of my old tee shirts, baggy and tucked under an apron. She had finger stripes of white flour on her cheeks. There was a smudge on one ear. She wiped her hands on a towel and adjusted the laptop screen.

"What are you baking? Whatever it is, I want some." I wished I could smell through the computer. Better yet, I wished I were home.

Sophie pushed a strand of hair behind her ear depositing even more flour on herself. I didn't dare tell her because she'd wipe it off, and it looked too comical right then.

"I was waiting to tell you later, surprise you, but you know how the neighbors are always asking for my homemade bread?"

"Do I know? You've made so many loaves and given them away. I've told you for years you should start your own business, but you don't believe me when I say you're a great baker."

"That's because you're my husband. You have to say that kind of thing." Sophie's mouth turned up in a tease.

I missed that teasing girl. I growled. "No, I don't, Soph. I'm telling the truth. Why are you all covered in flour? Is one of our neighbors sick, and you're making them that cheesy bread I love?"

"No one's sick. I was a vendor at the Baker Street Farmer's Market last week. I rented a table, got a banner made. I kept it a secret from you until I knew how they'd sell."

"What? That's great!"

"It was fun. I wish you could've been here." Her voice caught.

"Did you take pictures?"

"No. It was just me doing the setup and takedown, and I didn't want to bother some stranger to take a picture for me."

"Where did they have it?"

"Downtown, on the square. The church has a

vacant lot, and they put straw down. There are hundreds of vendors. I met many of them, and they're nice. There were organic produce and things from local farmers." She disappeared from the screen, her voice faded in the background. "Hang on a minute. I'll show you." She reappeared with a small glass candle holder. She held it up like a prize, and inside was a golden candle. "It's homemade. There are bee-keepers with local honey and candles made from beeswax."

I wasn't interested in candles, but I'd watch Sophie all day long. She was my home. "You're making cinnamon rolls?" My mouth watered. When we were newlyweds, she'd sneak out of bed early and have a hot tray of them ready when I woke up on my day off, which, being a rookie cop, could have been any day of the week except Saturday and Sunday. A smile crept across my face. "I miss your cinnamon rolls."

She turned the laptop camera down so I could see a silver cookie sheet covered in pinwheel shapes with cinnamon swirls in them. They were puffing up, rising. My stomach gurgled.

"If this picks up like I hope, you can have as many as you like. I'll be baking rolls every day." She turned the camera back on herself. This time she was running the mixer, dumping in more flour until it billowed out of the bowl. It was impossible to talk until she turned the thing off. She held up a hand to mean wait one minute. She ran the mixer for a bit and shut it down. "Sorry, but once I get into production mode, I have to keep going otherwise things get backed up, and I waste electricity heating an empty oven."

"That's OK, I'm having fun watching you mix stuff. How did the rolls sell?"

Sophie spread her arms wide. Flour drifted off her

fingers to the floor, but she was too animated to notice. "I sold out. I only brought 10 loaves with me, and they were gone within twenty minutes. The rolls didn't sell as fast, but they went, too. And the cinnamon rolls went in the first ten minutes." She set the mixed dough on the top of the stove to rise.

I knew the routine. I'd watched her do it a million times. Usually, I was there because I was hoping to eat at the end of her baking. This time I looked on because I wanted to be near her.

She rinsed the bowl, prepping it for another batch.

"I didn't clear anything last time. All my profits went for the table rental and the banner. But I'll double my inventory and see how it goes tomorrow. If it sells as well as last week, I'll turn a small profit."

"That's great Soph. I've wanted you to do this for a long time."

She picked up a recipe card, frowned over it, and pulled a package of dried cranberries from the pantry. "Maybe it took you going away for me to have the time to think about it and put it into motion."

I tried to get the thought of hot cinnamon rolls out of my mind. I glanced at the old roll on my desk. It wouldn't do. "Hm. Maybe. Or maybe it's time you did something for yourself, a business that is all Sophie's. When I come home, I'll build whatever kind of bread display racks you need."

"Oh, babe, that would be awesome. I do think they'll sell better on one of those slanted wooden racks, so people can see them. They look dull sitting flat on a table with just a tablecloth."

I got my pad of paper out and sketched a display rack for Sophie's bread. I drew a little sign at the top. It read, "Sophie's Southern Breads." I held the pad of paper up to the camera, adjusting it so she could see what I'd drawn.

She smiled, put down her oven mitts, and propped up on the kitchen stool with hands on either side of her face. Her nose had a smudge of flour on it.

I didn't always feel like we had to talk. I liked that. Funny it took me going away eight thousand miles to learn how to enjoy our marriage.

A sharp beep cut through the silence. I twitched, turned toward the door, and listened. Sophie jumped at the same time. For a second, I thought it was the early warning system at camp, but I relaxed when Sophie pulled on her oven mitts. It was the oven timer.

She pulled a hot tray of rolls out and set them on top of a cooling rack. She shoved another tray of risen dough into the oven and gently closed the door. Set the timer. "I have to mix another batch Mac, so we won't be able to talk for a minute or two." She smiled a floury smile and flipped her mixer on. There were smudges on her cheeks.

Man, what I'd have given to be there to wipe those smudges off.

My cell phone vibrated. A text came through. My room whirled, and I braced my hand against my desk when I recognized the name.

Sophie turned off her mixer and peered at me as if she were trying to read the name on my phone, too. "What's wrong?"

"Nothing." I stuffed the phone in the pocket of my cargo shorts.

The oven beeped, and Sophie ignored it. Slowly, she took off the mitts, placed her hands on the counter as if to support herself. "Is it someone there, serving in Afghanistan with you?"

"I don't know what you're talking about."

"I'm talking about Travis and the guy who had his locks changed. I'm talking about you and me, Mac. Have you found someone else?"

"It's, no. It's not someone here."

"Then it is someone? Who, Mac?"

I had tangled myself up in words again. I didn't know how to untangle myself, so I just told the truth. "Dispatcher from HPD. You don't know her, Soph. It was before I left, long before I left. I told her I never wanted to talk to her again. This is the first text I've received since I got here. You have to believe me."

"Mac, talk to me."

"I don't know what to say."

"What does that dispatcher have to do with you?"

"We'd been texting each other off and on."

"Texting?"

"Yeah, and—"

"And what?"

"You were busy with Little Mac and so tired when I'd come home from work—"

"I was exhausted from caring for our son. Our son!"

"She was having marital problems. She needed someone to listen to her, but it never went any further than that. It's over now, Soph. Over. I haven't spoken to her since—"

"Since when?"

"Since Little Mac died."

In the background, I heard Phoenix barking. It sounded so homey. My background noises were explosions and heavy machinery grinding down shell-pocked streets. "I needed you, Sophie, and you weren't there."

"I was on-call myself, twenty-four seven, with a colicky toddler."

"I played with him when I got home from work. Don't make it out like you were the only one who loved him. We played cars." My voice cracked. I pictured those cars sitting on a shelf at our house on Wells, collecting dust.

"Sure, you played with him, but when did you help with potty training? Where were you? On the phone with that woman? You took what was mine and gave it to someone else?"

"What about me, Soph? I'd come home from pulling bodies from car wrecks, and you were too busy to listen."

"You didn't talk. You retreated to that stupid combat game. Do you know how I longed for you to get us a sitter so we could go on a date and do nothing but talk? Do you think I only wanted my life to revolve around kiddie shows and nap times? I wanted to have a friend and lover again, and you were never around."

"I was there," I said.

"Emotionally you checked out. You were too busy killing the enemy on that dumb computer screen."

A loud metallic beep of an alarm went off somewhere. It sounded like it came from camp. Was it the early warning system?

Sophie gripped the counter. The color drained from her face. I threw my door open and surveyed the hallway, heart pounding. All was quiet.

Sophie ran to her oven and yanked the door open. Thick black smoke from burned bread rolled out in a wave. She gagged and choked, pulled on oven mitts and removed the smoking pan of blackened bread. The shrill beep of her smoke alarm raked the air.

"Sophie, you have to believe me. It's over," I said.

She moved to the counter with the hot pan. "I have to turn off this smoke alarm. I can't hear you—"

An explosion violently shook my tent. The impact rattled my shelves, rumbled through my computer chair and threw me to the floor. Books and DVDs fell. The towel on the makeshift clothesline beside me fluttered as if in a breeze, but there was no wind.

Sophie dropped the pan of burnt bread to the floor. "Mac!"

19

I scrambled to my feet and rushed into the hallway, only to come face to face with Travis, colliding with him.

Travis jammed his helmet on his head. He was dressed in black-and-green checkered pajama pants, a T-shirt, and boots. He already had his vest on over his shirt. The pajama pants would've been comical any other time. "They're firing mortars. Get your kit on," Travis said.

I dashed into my room, threw my vest on over my polo shirt, and grabbed my helmet and weapon. Sophie's face appeared on the laptop across the room. Her eyes were wide with fear. Why hadn't I shut that laptop down? "They're firing at us," I yelled above the chaos.

"E-mail me so I know you're safe," Sophie said.

"I will." I slammed the laptop closed and joined the rest of the guys outside. Travis, Glenn, Thorstad, and I ran to the T-wall outside our tent.

Mortars shook the ground. Overhead, screams of jets ripped the air, and the deep vibrations of helicopter blades rattled through my head as choppers passed near.

I checked my gear, cinched my helmet down tighter, and felt over my pouches, checking for extra magazines. I was as prepared as I could be. I took stock of the guys around me.

Glenn leaned back against the T-wall, smoking

another of his cigars. The end glowed blood red in the dusk. "If I'm going out, I'm going out savoring the flavor of my best cigar." He looked as if he was having just another night out with the guys. I guess he'd done this so often it had become routine. His deliberate calm was infuriating.

I breathed deep to try and control my pounding heart. I walked a few feet farther down the T-wall, closer to Travis to cool down. My finger rested on the trigger guard. I automatically fell back into officer mode. All my senses were heightened, and the slightest twitch of my guys got my attention.

Travis wiped off his sunglasses with his shirttail and jammed them back on top of his head. Even at night, he kept them perched on his skull. Must have been a security blanket for him.

"We're not in Brentwood, Tennessee, anymore," I said.

Travis nodded, not amused. Dark splotches circled below his eyes. He'd slept better in a war zone before his wife announced she was leaving him.

I wondered if I'd soon join his ranks. *Focus on the situation at hand.* My safety and the safety of the guys around me depended on my concentration. There'd be time later to try and heal my marriage. I hoped.

"The last thing we want is for them to blow a hole in our perimeter," Travis said. He checked his gear as he spoke.

I could see him silently taking inventory, making sure he had extra magazines.

Thorstad chewed a wad of gum frantically. His hair tufted up in the front like a little boy awakened from a nap. He swigged from a power drink bottle, noticed me watching. "Want some?"

"No, thanks," I said at first but thought better of it. I needed to stay hydrated to keep alert, and no telling how long we'd be along this wall. I made a mental note to make sure I carried water with me the next time this happened. "Hey, I changed my mind. I'll have a drink if you don't mind sharing."

Thorstad handed the bottle over, and I took a long draught of lemon lime, cooling my throat. "Thanks." IEDs went off frequently outside the walls, but mortars were being fired directly into the compound. They shook the ground and rattled everything. Luckily for me, so far their aim had not been great.

Travis leaned toward me so I could hear him better over the screech of jets. "Once they start the rocket attack, they'll try and make a ground attack also. If they breach our fence line, the perimeter could be compromised, so keep an eye out."

I nodded.

My head pounded with the sound of each mortar. It seemed we stood there for hours. Finally, the attack ceased.

"Stand down," Thorstad called from ahead of me.

Things quieted fast. Quick Response Vehicles made their way around camp to make sure things were secure. It didn't appear we had taken on much damage, only shook up the camp and stirred up a lot of dust and smoke. The enemy's aim wasn't precise with mortars.

"This is what they do: drop three or four mortars on us, and that's it," Travis said. "Just enough to make everybody crazy. I'm going back to bed." I could tell Travis was nearing the end of his tether. He dragged himself across the gravel to the wooden door of our tent and slammed it as he entered.

I jumped when the door bounced against the doorframe. I still felt as though I was wired to an electrical outlet.

Glenn's chuckle sounded from behind me. "I've got your back, Little Mac, don't worry."

I whirled around and faced him. "Don't ever call me that again." My scalp tingled. As amped as I was from the attack, I had no patience. And I was still stinging from Sophie's accusation. "I don't need any games tonight," I said.

"First time under fire, Little Mac? How's it feel to be a real soldier?"

"Don't."

"What's the matter? Nickname sting?" That was all he got out of his mouth.

The pain of the last few months coiled itself into my fist, and I slammed it into the side of his face. My knuckles raked his jaw, and the cigar went pinwheeling into the dark, showering sparks behind. Satisfaction filled my gut. Glenn rolled to the side and dropped slowly to the gravel with a grunt.

Regret hit, not because I had any great compassion for Glenn at the moment, but because fighting in camp was a one-way ticket home. Stupid. Stupid. I'd traveled all the way to Afghanistan and could ruin it by losing my temper. I heard nothing but my own sharp breaths. In my peripheral was gray fog. I looked around to determine if anyone had seen us but since the Quick Reactionary Force cleared the area, everyone else was back at the tents.

Glenn sat, rubbed his jaw, and started to make another comment until he saw the steel in my eyes. "Whoa, friend. Settle down. No harm meant." He scrambled up off the ground, brushed his pants off, and felt around in the loose gravel for his cigar. He finally located the dying ember and picked it up to inspect it. "Still in one piece," he said under his breath with relief. He brushed the dirt off the end of the cigar, moved around the wall to our bench, and slid onto the seat. He turned on his cigar lighter and soon the cigar was glowing again. "McCann, get over here."

I walked over and leaned stiffly against the wall next to our bench. My temples throbbed with anger.

"That was a pretty good punch. I bet you were a force to be reckoned with on the streets back home," Glenn said.

"I've had my share of fights." I rubbed my knuckles, which tightened with pain. Moonlight glinted off Glenn's face, and to my satisfaction, revealed a swollen bottom lip. He balanced the cigar gingerly in his mouth.

I took a deep breath. Slowly the burn left my face. Exhaustion replaced anger.

Every minute or so a long trail of smoke curled lazily skyward from Glenn's cigar.

I finally took a seat next to him. I wound down from adrenaline.

Glenn studied the ash growing along the end of his cigar. "What was that all about?"

"You have another one of those cigars?" I ignored his question.

Glenn fished around in his pocket and pulled out a cigar tube and unscrewed the top.

"Where's your cutter?" I asked.

He dropped the cutter in my hand and watched me as if I were his apprentice. I cut the cigar and returned the blade to Glenn.

"Now, let me see you toast it properly," Glenn

said.

His attitude frustrated me, but I grabbed the butane lighter from his outstretched palm. I clicked it on and started to apply the flame, but Glenn moved my hand.

"The flame should never touch the cigar."

"Sorry, King of Procurement."

"Rotate the cigar and lightly toast it. That's right."

I was rewarded with a glow, like a pile of fall leaves when they burn until all that's left are twinkling embers.

"Draw the smoke into your mouth and hold it there. Don't inhale it the way you did last time. It's not a cigarette," Glenn said. "The whole point of a good cigar is to enjoy it slowly so you get the full flavor." His voice had lost the edge it usually carried. When he spoke to me, it was more as if he was talking to a little brother than a subordinate.

I drew the smoke carefully into my mouth, and when I released it, a smooth stream of smoke curled into Kandahar. It rose above Camp Paradise. I followed the trail with my eyes. I felt myself rise with it, above all the turmoil, pain, and loss.

Glenn studied me. "Will you answer my question?"

"My son's nickname."

Glenn drew on his cigar with a long, slow breath. When he breathed out, the smoke spiraled deep into the night.

"He died a year before I arrived in country," I added. I hadn't meant to spill my guts, and to Glenn, of all people, but speaking the words relieved the pressure deep inside me.

"It seems we have more in common than I first

thought." Glenn leaned back and rested against the bench.

A red glow twinkled on the end of my cigar. I turned it toward Glenn so he could see. "Looks like a thousand fireflies. Like we used to help my boy catch in a mason jar on humid nights. Sophie would pull an old jar she'd cleaned out, and I'd get a hammer and nail. I'd punch holes in the lid so they could breathe. Then we'd sit on the front porch and watch the sun go down. Cicadas would start up, sounded like a bunch of raspy-voiced drunks. Little Mac loved it all. I'd help him chase fireflies. We'd get as many as we could in the jar and set it down on the porch steps. He kept his face pressed against the glass so long, watching the yellow lights inside."

Glenn took another draw on his cigar. "I always thought Lauren and I'd have a son." His voice was muffled, but it wasn't from the smoke.

"Why didn't you?"

"Lauren was unable to get pregnant." He mouthed the word "pregnant" as if it left a bad aftertaste. "We tried. Then they found cancer. I knew I wouldn't make a good single father." He twisted around on the bench and extended his hand to me. "Truce?"

I shook Glenn's hand and noticed the gorilla grip from our very first meeting was gone. He'd given me a regular handshake. "I'll tell you, McCann, real love is sacrificial. It's not flowers and candy and trips to Paris.

"It started out that way with Lauren and me. I sent her flowers all the time. I gave her gifts. In the end, it was only me, holding her hand and keeping her company while she slowly left. I couldn't make her stay. I couldn't keep her on this earth. It was beyond my capability. All the flowers in the world couldn't keep her here. Don't you see? Don't waste your time on chasing something meaningless."

"It was working for Travis," I said.

"You think so?" Glenn asked. "His room's right next to mine. I couldn't help but overhear his conversations with his wife. She wasn't happy. What you interpreted as romance was really Travis vainly trying to heap wood on a dying fire. He was desperate, so he pulled out all the stops, sending flowers every week, making calls home all the time, and sending extravagant gifts," Glenn said.

"But that's what Sophie wants."

"She doesn't want gifts, man. Wake up. She wants you."

I could feel the blood drain out of my face. I'd taken the one thing Sophie wanted and moved it miles away? But how could she want me? Where did she get that kind of love? "It isn't humanly possible to love someone that way. At least, I've never seen it. She doesn't know who I really am."

Glenn's cigar burned to a nub. He methodically pulled a new one out of his shirt pocket and deliberately took his time lighting it. I knew he was giving me mental space to approach the subject, but I felt the crushing weight of Little Mac's death again. It sucked the air out of my lungs in just the same way the brittle, dry heat of Afghanistan did.

"Who are you, then?" he asked.

"A murderer."

I expected Glenn to be shocked, but he just toasted the end of the cigar in the flame, rolling it back and forth until I wanted to curse.

"I killed my son by my negligence," I said.

"OK."

"What?"

I jumped from the bench and paced back and forth in front of him.

"Tell me what happened." Glenn sucked in a long draught of smoke and let it slowly escape his mouth.

I launched into the scene. My mind rebelled at going over the details. Is forgetting possible?

When I reached the part about the ambulance, Glenn sighed. He didn't move. The only tell he had, like in a poker game, was the tip of his cigar bobbed ever so slightly.

"Then you are no worse than I."

"How can you say that?"

"Because I was the one who had her ventilator shut off."

"That's not the same at all."

He glared at me.

"I was my wife's executioner. I was the one who had the power to decide when it was time to pull the plug. She trusted me, and I betrayed that trust."

"Not the same. You stood by your wife while she fought cancer."

"But in the end, what did it matter? I told her we would beat cancer together. I told her she would make it. When the doctor said she wouldn't, I refused to discuss death with her."

"Maybe she didn't want to discuss it?" I said.

"No, she tried many times. She'd say, 'Glenn, let's talk about my funeral.' I'd glare at her and leave the room. In my mind, I could keep her alive. Somehow, I'd find a way, and I failed her."

I dragged the toe of my boot through the gravel.

"Is that all she said?"

"No, she said it was OK to talk about death.

Lauren said she knew she belonged to Christ and that she would be with Him soon."

There was that name again. The name Sophie clung to. I didn't know Him.

"I guess that gives you some comfort," I said, "But I don't believe in that stuff. It's too far out there for me. I need to experience something before I believe it. I mean, if I can touch it, put my hand on it, then it's real to me. It's like this cursed dust that's everywhere. I'm covered in it. It seeps into my clothes and my shoes. Dust is real. It grinds in my shoes as a constant reminder that I chose to come here and that by causing Little Mac's death, I will never be clean again."

Glenn ground the stub of his cigar into the gravel with a twisting motion of his boot. "Christ never did anything for me. If He exists, if He is who Lauren said He is, then why did He take her from me? Wouldn't He know I needed her?"

"I got nothing for you on that one," I said.

As I said it, a light blew across the sky. Out here, shooting stars were so familiar, you could become jaded by their frequency. But this one lit up the sky in a way I have not seen before or since. "Did you see that?" I pointed over Glenn's shoulder.

"What?"

"A shooting star, man. It was the brightest I've seen since I've been here."

"Maybe God's trying to tell you something, eh?" Glenn laughed bitterly.

"You don't know, but the night we buried Little Mac, I asked—"

"What?"

"I asked for a sign that God was there."

"What did you ask for?"

"A star."

"I guess you just got your star. Let me know how that works for you." Glenn stood and ambled toward our tent.

I slid back on the bench and drew smoke slowly into my mouth. I was surprised at the subtle earthiness. My body relaxed, and for the first time since I was in Afghanistan, I allowed my mind to rest. I felt hazy, slightly euphoric, and numb. Afghanistan noise faded into the background, and I leaned back and pondered the God Sophie talked to.

"Was that you, God?" I exhaled, and the words seeped out of my mouth and ascended with the rising smoke trail.

20

The morning beeps of MRAPs screeched through my tent walls. The sounds were my daily alarm clock. I cleared my throat, sandpapery from Kandahar dirt and cigars. I grabbed a fresh bottle of power drink and washed the remnants of last night's cigar smoke away.

I e-mailed Sophie first thing when I got back in my tent, yesterday, letting her know we were all right. *Let there be an e-mail from her.* When I pulled up my e-mail, there was only a short reply.

I prayed for you. Please be safe.
Sophie.

Not *I love you,* not *please come home to me.* I started to reply three times, but the words were stilted. I erased them. I had no idea what to say to Sophie or how to heal us. Instead, I went to the hospital website, punched in my login, and clicked the "Pay Now" icon. And with that Little Mac's last medical bill was paid.

Between me being in Afghanistan and Sophie managing the bills at home, we finally did it. I pulled up my computer game and tried starting a few missions, but it didn't have the same draw as before. I kept hearing Sophie in my head. Did I hide by playing combat games? I shut the computer down, feeling dissatisfied and lost. I wandered down the dark hallway of our tent.

Glenn's door was propped wide, and he was

cutting open a brown shipping box on his desk.

Travis barreled past me. "Did it get here?"

Glenn stepped back like a proud daddy. On his desk was a wooden box.

Travis pulled up with a start at the sight of Glenn's face. Glenn's lip was still swollen from our altercation the night before. It was shaded with spectacular circular colors ranging from black to purple. Glenn grinned. He actually looked proud of it.

"Whoa! Who gave you the fat lip?" Travis asked.

"Mac." Glenn smirked wickedly.

"Ha! That's a good one. Now tell me how you really got it."

"Blackburn, you are aware of the prohibition against fighting in camp?" I asked.

Travis nodded, still mesmerized by the awesomeness of Glenn's wound.

"Therefore, Glenn was not involved in any altercation, understand?"

"Got it. I still want to know who didn't hit you." Travis smiled.

I moved around the desk and ran my hand across the polished wooden box. "What's in there?" I asked.

Glenn shot me another of his looks as if to say, "Haven't I taught you anything?" but thankfully, he didn't say it. "Behold, a one hundred capacity humidor." Without waiting for me to ask, Glenn started demonstrating the features like a salesman at a car dealership. "Mahogany finish, Spanish cedar tray, humidifier, and a hygrometer." Glenn waited for my admiration. I could see it in his eyes.

"Nice, very nice." I didn't know what else to say. He looked disappointed at my lack of appreciation.

"I have news, too. I just paid the last medical bill

Sophie and I owed."

Glenn's face smoothed out into a lopsided smile. After last night, he understood how important this was to me.

"I didn't know you had medical bills," Travis said.

Glenn glanced my way. "There's a lot of things you don't know, Blackburn. For instance, did you know you have to keep the humidity between sixty-eight and seventy-two percent for optimum cigar storage?"

Over Travis's head, I nodded my thanks to Glenn, and he smiled his acknowledgment. Then he returned to loading the humidor with his outlandish collection.

"I never knew you had so many cigars," I said.

"I've been collecting for quite some time."

"What's this one?" I said, picking up a dark cigar, holding it to my nose and sniffing.

Glenn took it gingerly from my hands as if it was a treasure dug from the pyramids. It smelled like it should have stayed in the pyramids.

"Set me back ten dollars for that one alone."

My pop addiction was looking downright frugal. I made a note to relate this to Sophie the next time she made fun of me. Would she be sending me any more packages? I didn't even know if she'd want me back when my tour was up.

Glenn selected a cigar for himself, and before he closed the lid offered Travis and me one.

" No, thanks. I know how much this cost. Give me one of your cheaper smokes."

"Pick one for yourself with my best wishes then," he said.

I studied the different shapes, lengths, shades of wrappers. "I still like those."

"A distinguished gentleman's choice." Glenn handed me one and carefully closed the humidor. He grabbed his butane lighter, and we strolled out to the bench.

We were treated to a spectacular sunset. The sky was bright orange, the color of ice cream on a stick I bought as a kid. The rumbling of vehicles and helicopters played out like a soundtrack. The sounds no longer merited my attention. When I'd first arrived in country, every noise jarred me. After a while, I slept through the night with no problem.

Travis drew on his cigar and blew out a long stream of smoke. "I signed divorce papers today."

He tried to say it nonchalantly, but I could tell it was eating a hole in his gut. I felt bad for him, but the last thing I wanted to discuss just then was divorce.

Glenn toasted his cigar.

In the background, faint explosions echoed in the starry Afghanistan night.

"Why do you hide the fact that you're a Southerner?" I asked Glenn, hoping to change the subject.

"Give me a minute to get this baby going." Glenn sparked his lighter and twirled the cigar in the flame, back and forth, until it glowed. Satisfied, he clicked the cigar lighter off and took a long draw. His cheeks rounded out, full of the sweet smoke.

"I mean, Savannah is a great place," I said.

Glenn held up a hand. He opened his mouth, and a smooth stream of smoke drifted above. He inspected the cigar, seemed satisfied with it. "Northerners are enamored with the South, are they not? They love our music laced with hometown values. When they listen to it, they pretend they live in Mayberry. They love our fried food, chicken crispy and still spitting grease as it's pulled from an iron skillet. Peach ice cream that rivals any gourmet menu. Yes, they love our food and music."

"I'd agree with that but how does it figure in with your denial?" I asked.

Glenn ignored my question and continued. "Northerners wither when the humidity hovers at ninety percent. They mop their heads and retreat to their air-conditioned hotels. As hot as it is in Kandahar, it can't compare to the sweltering humidity of Savannah in July. Northerners can pretend they understand Southerners, but they don't. There's as big a difference in our cultures as if we were from separate countries, which, when you think about it, came horrifyingly close to happening.

"You said 'our.'"

Glenn grinned sheepishly. "I did, didn't I? For all the admiration of our quaint ways, lies an unspoken arrogance toward their neighbors to the south. It's there, smoldering below the surface. You can't tell me you haven't come up against it?" Glenn asked.

"I'd hoped we were viewed as the South of today, certainly not for our past problems. That's why I talk about the space program and how high-tech my city is. We're anything but a cotton town."

"The reality is, Mac, that we're still viewed as hillbillies. Stereotypes are difficult to put to rest. Hollywood's South is not my South. It's annoying when I hear some actor butchering a southern accent. It doesn't bother me if it's done innocently. It's outright bigotry that bothers me." He contemplated the bench and flicked an ash away from his coffee cup. "I won't tolerate bigotry of any kind, not for skin color, or geography." Glenn's mouth tightened.

"Are you hiding from your ancestry to avoid conflict?" I asked.

"You paint me as a coward. I haven't been forced to put it into words until now. I wanted to be successful and I felt being labeled might hold me back in people's eyes."

"So you cut the accent and any references to Savannah," I said.

Glenn nodded, though reluctantly, I thought.

I clipped the end of my cigar and flicked the lighter. "When I was eleven years old, my father's job was transferred from Maryland to Huntsville. My first thought was, is there anything good in Alabama? I drove my dad nuts in the following weeks, quizzing him about the state. 'Do they have an airport? Do they only listen to country music? Will we have to eat grits?'" The cigar glowed as I rolled it back and forth beneath the blue flame. "My older brother, who was nineteen at the time, moved out of state. Dad used to joke that I threw the biggest fit relocating, and I was the one who stayed. Unlike you, born in a Southern state, I was transplanted, and I fell in love with the place and the people. And as for bigotry in my city, I don't see it to the extent it's portrayed."

"Do you mean to say it doesn't exist?" Glenn asked.

It was my turn to hold up a hand while I drew in spicy smoke. It warmed my mouth, and once again, numbness filled my head with a mild euphoria. I blew the smoke out and watched it rise above our bench and mingle with the smoke from Glenn's cigar. "That's not what I'm saying at all. Evil exists everywhere." In my mind, I saw the shadow men, the ones who would surely approach Bashir at some point and try and recruit him into a life of sexual slavery. "I love the South because I see potential. We've overcome so much already, and I believe we'll continue to move toward being a place where people truly are treated with equality. Surely, I'm not the only one in Alabama who feels this way."

Glenn looked doubtful.

"Maybe what you said about me when we first met is true," I said.

"And that was?"

"I'm an idealist. I like that about myself." If only I could give myself the same hope I so readily gave others.

21

"Sophie?" I could wait no longer. If she wanted to end us, I needed to know. I wasn't the kind of guy who could live in uncertainty. I needed concrete facts. I tapped my foot as my computer made its slow-as-molasses attempt at signing on to the Internet. Eventually, it did connect. I repeated her name, hoped she could hear me.

"Hi." She was withdrawn.

I couldn't pinpoint her feelings. I studied the curve of Sophie's lips and wondered if I would ever kiss them again. Then the picture froze, and in the background, I heard her asking, "Mac, can you hear me?"

The connection was lost.

I fumbled with my phone and dialed quickly. Sophie worried if I didn't call when the Internet shut down. The phone connected and her voice swelled with relief. "Oh, hi."

I ran my finger down the side of my cell phone, suddenly shy, like a teenager in love for the first time. "You all right?" I asked.

"Yes, I'm fine. It's a little scary when that happens. I used to be able to handle it...until the mortar attack." Her voice was strained, but she kept her tone calm.

"I used to be good with a lot of things before the mortar attack." I tried to reassure her. "I used to be good with going to the gym to work out and leaving my rifle in my room. I used to be content with walking down the gravel drive to the showers early each morning, feeling exposed even though I was dressed. It'll be OK, though. You know what I always say, 'Welcome to Camp Paradise.'"

We both let out a short laugh.

"I'm calling you back on my laptop. Maybe it'll behave this time."

"OK. I'll be looking for you."

I clicked off my phone and hurried to pull up a live video. It worked, thankfully.

"Sophie, I love you. Please forgive me."

Sophie looked as if she was struggling with an answer. She shook her head. "Just like that? I'm not some video game that you can just turn on and off when you feel like it, Mac."

"I know what I told you came as a shock, but it's the past, Soph. I don't know how to say it any other way. I don't know what you want. Please, tell me how to make things right."

Blush spread up her neck and across her cheeks. "I can tell you about a dinner I went to this week. I saw some things I wanted to talk to you about."

"Sure, anything, Soph. I just want us to be OK again." Whatever that was. I wasn't even sure I'd recognize it in our relationship anymore.

"It was nothing big, just a gathering of a few couples for potluck. I was by myself, of course, and I guess because of that I noticed things. One couple barely looked at each other the whole night. They each told stories about their week, but they weren't even in each other's narratives."

Phoenix jumped up on the bed beside Sophie. She absent-mindedly scratched him behind his ears as she spoke. "They looked so weary and sad. Like field hands who had been at the plow so long they never even glanced up at the beautiful sky anymore. Just kept looking down at the dirt, unfurling from the plow."

Phoenix relaxed down into the bed and rolled over on his back. Sophie rubbed his belly.

"On they plodded, and the scenery never changed." Sophie paused, took a sip of water from a glass she kept beside the bed.

Funny how I noticed the details of our life together so clearly once I was away. She always kept that glass by our bed.

"I remember you and me being like that," she said softly. She stopped rubbing Phoenix's belly, and we were both silent. The sound of his relaxed breaths filled my tent. Soon, he was snoring. "I remember you working three jobs just to get us through. I was home with Little Mac," Sophie said.

His name seared me.

"We just hoped to get through one day, and the next and the next, didn't we?"

I nodded. I remembered those dark days. I'd rather have forgotten. "I'd come home tired from work and dealing with people's problems. I just wanted to be left alone. It seemed all day that everywhere I turned people had their hands held out, needing help. The calls I went on were traffic accidents, murders, and horrific things no man wanted to discuss with his wife. I'm sorry, Soph. You got the leftovers." A deep sigh worked its way up from my core. It seemed I had been holding that particular breath for years. It was release. Not defeat, not surrender. It was a different kind of sigh. It was a coming home sigh, and Sophie was my home. "Computer games were my escape. You were right, Sophie, only I didn't want to see it. I couldn't see it. It was too easy to come home, sit in that chair, and block everything out. Besides, you were so self-sufficient. You made it easy for me. I'd come home to a hot meal and a clean house. And you did extra things for me, too, little things, like that bread you knew I loved, with the cheese stuffed in the middle. I never thanked you out loud for that. I just thought you knew how much I appreciated you." My voice cracked.

Sophie rubbed Phoenix's belly. He stretched and snored.

Could we return to the time in our marriage where we were as content?

"There was another couple, Mac. They chilled me even more. They used sniping, cruel remarks toward one another. Sharp weapons forged in bitterness." Sophie stopped and adjusted the laptop. "I remember a movie you and I watched. It was the couple's second marriage for each one. The wife asked the husband to promise she would never be back in the dating world again."

I shifted in my computer chair. I could feel it coming. I knew Sophie well enough. She wanted something from me, but the old fear returned. I didn't know if I could give it. Practical things like bill paying, fixing things around the house, those made me comfortable. When we hit emotions, they tangled me up. "Yeah, I remember that scene."

"Promise me." Her eyes were soft, her voice warm, like maple syrup.

"OK. Promise what?" I'd give her anything.

"Promise me when you come home, we will never take each other for granted again. Promise we won't become those couples."

I sighed deeply, and it came out like a rumble, a low primitive growl. I'd do anything for Sophie. "I promise."

I signed off and carefully placed my vest, helmet, and M-4 within reach of my bed. I started to change into my shorts and T-shirt but thought better of it. I left my cargo pants and polo shirt on. Shorts wouldn't provide much protection from flying debris. I took one last swig of my power drink and turned off the light. The hum of the generator down the hall lulled me to sleep. The last thing I pictured was Sophie.

The next morning, I pulled up my e-mail before I even rolled out of bed. I lay on my cot, laptop balanced on my chest.

Mac,

I forgive you. I truly do. It doesn't mean that I'm not hurt, which I am. Deeply. I've been thinking about our conversation, and I see where we have wounded each other time and again. I don't want to hurt each other anymore. I want to heal and go on.

When we last talked, you seemed so much like the old Mac, the guy I fell in love with.

I remembered our first kiss. Your breath reeked of onions, and you were so clumsy but so sweet. I remember the stubble on your cheeks and the way you cupped my face in your hands. I had a crush on you for so long.

The day you took me riding in your new truck was like a fairy tale, but when you told me you were leaving to join the Army, I almost called the whole thing off.

I was afraid I wouldn't be strong enough to live with the constant good-byes that go with being an Army wife.

Because I knew I was already falling in love with you.

I remember snuggling down into your old worn leather

jacket. You pulled me up against you like you never wanted to let me go. I still remember the smell of your cologne. I could feel your whiskers, all scratchy on my cheek.

You traced on my back.

I asked you, "What did you write?" and you said, "It's a secret."

I just now realized what it was you were writing.

I—love—you.

Is that it? You were the first one to send a secret love note, not me!

I'm tracing with my finger right now on the screen. Can you see it? Can you feel it?

I love you.

I guess this is my way of saying I want to try again.

Sophie

P.S. I'm starting a game called Tag. This is how it goes. I tell you a memory, and then you are "it," and you have to send me one.

Tag, you're it!

I closed her e-mail. She'd figured it out, after all those years. A smile filtered across my face. Her description of that day took me back to that red truck, the day I fell in love with my girl. I never knew that was the day she fell for me. It was my turn to tag her back. I pulled up a new e-mail but it was hard to concentrate with all the constant noise.

On the other side of the thin plywood partition, Glenn was talking loudly on the phone to someone from the States. He was placing an order for who knew what. That guy shipped more packages than a delivery service.

Farther down the hallway Travis's snores shook

the tent. He'd been sleeping in a lot, avoiding us. His phone rarely rang anymore.

In between, was Stockton's room. He wasn't there, which was a relief. When he was there, it was mainly late at night, and he stayed up until all hours making a racket with his music. I had to knock on his door on more than one occasion to tell him to turn it down.

The cursor blinked at me from a blank page. What should I write? I wasn't used to sharing feelings with Sophie, and I knew that's what she wanted. It threw me off balance.

I'd rather talk about my day, training the guys. How the food was good, and I was thankful for that. How I respected the soldiers, who came in from the field. I always nodded a hello when I passed them on the gravel road on the way to the DFAC. Some answered me, and some didn't. There was a long history of strained relations between contractors and the military. I would have been lying to pretend it didn't exist. Some of the military resented us. They felt we got in the way of them doing their job. Others saw what we did and appreciated it. It all depended on the man.

Separating myself from the soldiers was impossible. I felt a kinship with guys like Sergeant Thorstad that was difficult to explain to Sophie. My goal had been to be one of them, and for a while, I had been. But ties stronger than the brotherhood of soldiers pulled at me. Sophie captured my heart.

Sophie,
I guess one of my strongest memories of you was the day I left for Basic Training. You stood there with me at the bus terminal until it was time to board.

I'd told you to stay home, let me say good-bye the night before, but you wouldn't listen. You were always stubborn like that. The truth is, I was glad you came to see me off.

We didn't talk very much. There wasn't much to say, and I was afraid I'd make you cry because you looked so sad already. They announced we could board the bus, and I remember you grabbed me like you wouldn't let go. I was going to ask you to marry me before I left.

Did you know that?

But I didn't because I wanted to save up my first few paychecks and get you a ring.

I remember when the bus pulled away I looked down at you and tears were running down your face. It was the hardest thing I've ever done, leaving you like that. But I did it for you and me. I wanted to start a life for us.

Soph, I came to Afghanistan for the same reason. When I get home, we will start fresh, and things will be better. I promise.

I'm going to close this now. Writing this has made me feel things I haven't felt in a long while.

I love you, Soph. I always have, even when I messed things up. I never stopped loving you.

(I'm tracing the screen back to you)
Mac

P.S. Tag, you're it.

22

"Hi, Mac? Can you get on live video? I hate to stay on here because they charge just to connect to you on the phone."

"Are you all right?" I asked.

"Yes, fine. Turn on your laptop, OK?"

I hung up my phone and hurriedly clicked on the icon on my desktop. It seemed to be running slow. When we were off work, everyone tried to get online to talk to family, and my guess was it overloaded the system. Finally, it pinged, and her live video showed up.

She held a piece of paper in her hands. She could barely stand still, she was so excited.

"What's that?" I said.

"A contract to supply one of the local restaurants downtown with my bread and rolls." She danced around the kitchen.

"I'm so happy for you, Soph!"

She positioned the paper on the kitchen table and smoothed it out.

"I can't believe it. So far, I have six varieties of bread, and they're all selling well. I just signed a rental agreement to use an industrial kitchen near the restaurant. That way I can bake it and transport it quickly. Besides, I've outgrown our kitchen."

"I miss your baking. Camp feeds us well, but I miss coming home from work and getting a whiff of homemade bread," I said.

"You'll smell it a lot more. I'll probably never get the aroma off me. I can't wait for you to come home. You'll get to see my table at the market. I have a banner and everything. You know my vintage bicycle? I have baskets on the front and back, and I deliver bread that way."

"Really?"

"When the weather's nice, I use my bike. You know I practically live on that thing. Otherwise, I take the car."

All that talk of bread and Sophie on a bicycle was carving a knot of yearning inside me.

Sophie studied my face. I must have been frowning.

"What are you thinking? Aren't you happy for me?"

"I'm happy, Soph. All this talk is making me a little homesick."

"Well, maybe it's time," Sophie said.

Not the reaction I anticipated. "What does that mean?" I asked.

Sophie pulled a kitchen chair from under the table and slid onto the seat. She rested her elbows on the table and cupped her chin in her hands. "I'm glad for once you're missing me. Just think, in a few weeks you come home on leave."

"Where do you want to go for vacation when I'm home?"

She tipped her head sideways and looked at me quizzically. "There's only one place."

"The beach," I said.

"How'd you ever guess?"

"What about somewhere different for a change? Maybe the mountains?"

"The beach is us. I'll never forget our honeymoon there, and every time we go back, I get the same feelings. I fall in love with you all over again."

"I'd be a crazy man to turn that down," I said.

"Yes, yes you would."

"All right, then. The beach it is. I'll leave the planning to you. Did you get the e-mail with my travel dates?"

"Yes. I keep counting and recounting the days, and I'm finding it hard to believe you'll be here. I know time goes fast for you, but it seems like we've been apart a lifetime," Sophie said.

"Teaching pretty much fills my days. And I think being in a different place makes the time go quickly. You're still in familiar surroundings," I said.

"I know, and I look for you every morning out of habit when I wake up. But I feel like a different person, and I like that," Sophie said. "This contract with the restaurant has shown me I'm capable of running my own business. Even our relationship is getting stronger."

I spun the wedding band on my finger. "I'm trying."

"I know you are and really, Mac, that is worth more to me than any present you could give me, or any trip you could take me on. It's what I've wanted for so long."

I didn't know what to say. Glenn was right? Sophie only wanted me, not extravagant gifts.

Sophie moved closer to the screen and gave me an air kiss. "I feel as if I'm about to go on a date with a most handsome man from overseas." I was about to send her a kiss back when Travis rapped on my door.

"Everything all right in there? We're going out to

the bench to smoke."

"Yeah. I'll be there in a minute," I said.

"What was that all about?" Sophie asked.

"That was Travis. They have a cigar club on Thursdays."

"Cigars?" Sophie's nose crinkled.

"Yeah. It's kind of cool," I said.

"I suppose you'll want to cancel your order for suckers and have me send you cigars instead."

"Don't worry. That's not about to happen. Speaking of pops, I'm in desperate need of three bags of them."

"Oh?"

"Two to give away and one for me."

"All right, they'll be in the mail tomorrow."

"Super." I stayed online. Just stared at her. I ached for her.

She sent me another air kiss, said good night, and signed off.

I closed my laptop.

The sounds of war crowded in, as if to suffocate me. But in my mind, I was back home in a kitchen that smelled of hot bread fresh out of the oven, and I had my arms around my lover.

23

Flight 1811 was headed for Atlanta, Georgia. I followed the plane avatar on the screen in front of me. Not much longer, and we'd be landing. After fifteen hours in the air, I'd be happy to land in a cornfield. A roar from under the right wing, immediately followed by a violent vibration stopped my thoughts. The plane shuddered.

"What do you think that was?" I asked the man to my right.

He was seated next to the window. He leaned as far forward as he could and studied the wing. "I don't know. Feel that vibration? Something's not right," he said.

The Fasten Seat Belt sign flashed on.

"Please secure your trays in the upright position. Stow any bags or purses beneath the seat in front of you," the flight attendant announced, her voice tense.

I scrambled to dig my seat belt out from beside me, clicked the buckle shut and tightened the belt across my lap. I survived a mortar attack in Afghanistan. Would I die in a plane crash before I saw Sophie?

There were no more announcements. The flight attendants rolled their cart down the aisle and offered sodas, water, and alcoholic beverages. I nudged the guy to my right.

"Still nothing?" I asked.

"Can't see any damage," he shook his head.

A bell tone rang, and the passengers were silent.

"The captain wants you to know that we've apparently blown a tire. We will be arriving in Atlanta on time but will wait on the air strip until maintenance crews can change the tire and make sure there are no other issues. We apologize for any inconvenience. Please remain seated with your seatbelt fastened."

"A blown tire didn't sound nearly as bad as what I had pictured in my head," the guy next to me said.

"I hear that," I said.

My ears felt like they were popping as the cabin pressure adjusted. We were headed for the landing. I closed my eyes and pictured those in my life who were so important to me. Sophie and Little Mac. What was it King David said? 'I can go to him, but he can't come to me.' If I didn't make it, would I be with Little Mac?

My thoughts were interrupted by a terrifying blast, and the plane shuddered. Metal groaned. A young girl a row ahead of me cried. We were on the ground, moving along like a crippled bird, but we were on the air strip. We were alive.

With one last screech, the plane limped to a halt.

"The captain has decided to allow you to disembark. Please be careful when opening overhead bins as contents may have shifted during flight," the attendant announced.

I still had a four-hour layover in Atlanta, but it was on American soil.

I was off the plane, working my way through the crowd to the nearest men's room. My shirt was soaked through with sweat. I would have preferred a locker room with showers, but they charged for those. On the way, I called Sophie. The call went through. Her voice was giddy.

"Mac, I can't wait to see you. I was almost tempted to drive over there to pick you up just so I could see you four hours earlier, but I didn't think you'd want to spend four hours in a car after fifteen in the air," Sophie said.

"It's OK. I'll be there soon. I'm going to go clean up now. I'll get a shower when I get to the house, but right now I want to wash up a little. I'm pretty nasty."

"See you soon," she said.

"See you soon," I echoed. I'd wash up in the sink as best as I could. I would have shaved, but I glanced in a mirror and congratulated myself on the decision to keep the beard. I studied it in the mirror, took out my comb and tried to tame it.

I had Gul trim it before I left camp, and he shaped it nicely. I brushed my teeth and swished some mouthwash around in my mouth. It was odd to be able to use tap water to brush my teeth. At camp, we used bottled water or mouthwash. The local water was full of parasites.

I exited the restroom and looked for a fast food restaurant. Sophie tried to get me to eat healthily, but I hadn't tasted fast food in months. When it was my turn in line, I bought everything: a burger, fries, shake, soft drink, apple pie. By the time I was through eating, I had regretted the extras.

Boarding the flight home, I could barely make myself stand still in line to get on the plane. Time was ticking down, and it seemed harder to wait to see Sophie the closer it got. I watched the countryside go by through the window of the plane. Green. Everything was so green, a nice change compared to miles of desert.

Soon after landing, I walked down the concourse,

backpack slung over my shoulder. I didn't check a bag. Didn't want to keep up with it. All my civilian clothes waited at home for me in the closet. I enjoyed the sounds and smells of home. People hurried everywhere. Did they even appreciate the freedom they had? I hopped on the escalator and quickly started ducking and scanning for a glimpse of Sophie. I pegged her right off the bat. She was standing in the front of the line with a little American flag in her hand. She was wearing some kind of silky dress, the color of the Afghanistan sky at sunset. I stopped moving when I saw her. Just stood there for a moment. She was stunning.

People were grumbling behind me, bumping into my back, walking around me like I was some kind of moron. But it took a moment for my legs to start moving again. All I could think was, *I'm in trouble*. I dropped my bag and gathered her into my arms. The smell of her blackberry-woodsy perfume curled around me. Her arms went around my neck, and she kissed me. People were watching, but we didn't care. After a moment I made myself pull back, held her at arm's length. Drank her in.

"Let's go home," Sophie said. Her words tasted like honey.

Sophie led me to our red vintage auto in the terminal. Even the old car felt like home.

We popped the trunk, and I threw my bag in. Before I could close the lid, Sophie's arms were around me again. We stood like that for a moment. I was breathing in her fragrance, feeling her hair against my face.

"Come on. I want to get you home. You have to be exhausted."

Sophie slipped into the driver's seat. I was grateful she wanted to drive. I was feeling the effects of all the travel. It was impossible to keep my eyes open.

"How was your flight?" Sophie asked question after question.

I jerked awake.

"I can't believe you're here for real and not just a picture on my laptop." She took my hand and twined her fingers in mine. Every mile or so she glanced over at me. "I'm afraid if I take my eyes off you, you'll disappear."

I felt the same way. I looked back and forth out the window, taking in the scenery. I couldn't get over the trees, flowers, and grass, acres and acres of green grass. We had trees in camp, but due to all the traffic, the leaves stayed pretty much covered in dirt. It was a shame because sometimes I could see the beauty that used to be there, back when it was a fruit cannery.

We had a twenty-minute drive, but I didn't care. I wasn't in a hurry to go anywhere. I just wanted to enjoy being home. I was surprised at my attitude. I was a driven man before I left. I'd told Travis before I departed Afghanistan that I didn't even like disputes anymore. I stay out of them. I just nod my head and go on.

We pulled into the driveway of our little Craftsman-style house and parked. Sophie had draped the front of the porch in red, white, and blue bunting. There was an American flag hanging from a bracket on the side of the front porch.

"Did you put that flag bracket up yourself?" I was impressed. To say Sophie wasn't handy with tools was an understatement.

Her face grew flushed. "No, the neighbor next

door hung it for me. She saw me struggling with the screwdriver and rescued me."

We jumped out of the car, and before I was even in the front door, I heard Phoenix's excited barking.

Sophie unlocked the door, and he immediately jumped, bouncing his front feet on my chest. Phoenix tried to lick my face, and all the while made a whining, crying noise that I'd never heard him make before. I set my bag down and sat on the floor with him. I wrapped my arms around his stout body. "I missed you, boy," I said. I burrowed my face in the fur at his neck. Emotion welled up in me, and my eyes filled with tears. They moistened his fur.

I pictured him once again as a pup, discarded like trash. How I wished for someone to pluck me out of my sin in the same way I'd rescued him. I cleared my throat. "He looks good, Soph. You're a good dog mommy."

"When I took Phoenix to the vet for his shots, they said he's up to fifty pounds now," Sophie said.

"Do they think he'll get bigger?"

"No, they said he's pretty much topped out. When he first showed up on our doorstep, I didn't want to have anything to do with him. I fed him and brushed him, cleaned up after him, but that was it. I didn't want to become attached to him." Sophie's hand slipped down, and she rubbed Phoenix behind his ears. A favorite spot for him. He looked up at her with adoration in his eyes.

"I knew you never wanted an indoor dog, and I dumped him on you. I'm sorry," I said.

"Every evening he slept closer and closer to our bed. I stepped around him and tried to make it clear the bed was off limits," Sophie continued. "One night, I climbed into bed, and there was this scrambling noise and the next thing I knew, I was looking Phoenix eye to eye. I didn't say anything. He turned around in a circle and lay at the foot of the bed, on your side. I didn't have the heart to make him leave. I think he knew it's where you sleep," Sophie said. "He's been there every night since."

Phoenix rolled over on his back, so I could rub his belly.

"He made me feel safe all the nights I was alone," Sophie said.

"You should have seen him when I found him. He was a little guy. Come to think of it, I have pictures on my hard drive. I'll show you later." I gave Phoenix a quick belly rub, but I was ready for a shower. I couldn't stand the two days of grunge much longer. "I'm going to hit the shower."

She came up to me and kissed me again. "Are you hungry?"

The greasy hamburger sat like lead in my stomach. "Uh, no. I ate at the airport."

"OK." She smiled and grabbed me for one more hug.

I stood in our old tiled shower. Same one I'd used for years, but everything seemed new. The water was as hot as I wanted. I turned the handles up full force. I stood under the stream of water as long as I wanted. I felt like a teenager again, staying in the shower until my mom yelled that I'd used all the hot water.

In the middle of my reverie, I was acutely aware of my friend Gul and his son. I couldn't get their faces out of my head. Each joy I found was tempered by the fact that they didn't have a chance to experience it. Not that I'm one who felt I should punish myself for our abundance. No. What I felt was an overwhelming desire to help them as I was able.

I toweled off and dug around in our dresser for clean clothes. I was a new person.

Sophie was waiting for me in the kitchen. She'd made me a loaf of cheesy bread. But before I took a bite, I found a tray of cinnamon rolls cooling on the counter.

I laid the cheese bread down and took a bite from a warm cinnamon roll, glaze dripping down my fingers. I ate the roll in two bites and licked the glaze from my fingers with a smacking sound.

"Nice to see you didn't lose your manners in Afghanistan. Look at your clothes." She stood back and gazed at me. "You've lost weight, and they're hanging off of you."

I caught my reflection in the microwave door. Months of working out and long hikes had paid off. My old clothes swallowed my frame. I cinched my belt in several notches and reached for another cinnamon roll.

"Go easy on those, babe, or I have a feeling you'll fill those clothes back out," Sophie said and winked. The corners of her mouth turned up in a grin.

I took her in my arms, pulled her against me. She tasted like cinnamon, smelled like warm rolls fresh from the oven. My hands were in her hair, her breath against my cheek.

Phoenix whined.

Sophie pulled back and laughed. "He doesn't like us kissing."

I led her to the bedroom. Leaning out the door, I told Phoenix, "Stay there, boy. Mommy and Daddy will be out later." I closed the door firmly behind me.

The last thing I saw was Phoenix near the door, keeping guard.

Too many miles had separated us. But soon that would all be behind us. We were starting a new chapter in our lives. I could feel it. Would Sophie continue to believe in me?

24

I rolled over, disoriented. For a minute I wondered where I was. I should have been in my cot. But soft sheets wrapped around me. A digital alarm clock cast a green glow. Ten o'clock at night?

Light streamed under the bedroom door, and the sound of dishes clanked in the kitchen. I stumbled to the bathroom and turned on the light. I didn't recognize myself. I wasn't accustomed to seeing a beard in that mirror. I liked it. I jumped in the shower and took a hot, lathery shower, reveling in the extravagance of unlimited clean water. By the time I dressed and walked into the kitchen, the clock on the wall read eleven.

"Is it really eleven at night?" I came up behind Sophie, who was washing dishes at our sink. I put my arms around her. Hugged her from behind.

"Yes, you slept quite a while. You're obviously still on Afghanistan time."

She was correct, and my stomach demanded breakfast. "Do you have any eggs and bacon?"

"Now that's a silly question." She pulled out a tray of bacon, already cooked. "I fried it while you were asleep, I knew you'd wake up and want breakfast."

"You're spoiling me, but don't stop." I leaned into the fridge, took out the egg carton, removed three eggs, and placed the container back. What a huge fridge. "Has the refrigerator always been this big?"

Sophie looked at me as if I were odd. "Yes, of

course."

"The whole house seems larger." I walked out space on the kitchen floor and showed her. "This is the size area I'm living in. This is how big my room is in the tent."

Her face showed a mixture of curiosity and disbelief. "Wow."

"Yeah, I know. It's funny how fast I got used to it, too. Now, this house feels like a mansion." I snapped a piece of bacon off with my fingers and chewed it while I cooked my eggs. "Over easy. They never let me eat them over easy in-country."

"Oh, why?"

"Salmonella." I flipped the eggs onto my plate, added bacon strips, and pushed the toast lever down.

Phoenix sat at attention by my feet.

I slipped him a piece of bacon when Sophie wasn't looking.

"Don't give him any bacon, by the way. I have him on a strict diet, and I don't want him to learn to beg at the table," Sophie said.

"Oh, absolutely." I sat at our table and cut into my eggs.

Phoenix slipped in under my chair.

I sneaked him another piece of bacon.

Sophie turned around as Phoenix swallowed. "Did you just give him bacon?"

"What are we doing today?" I tried to redirect Sophie's attention. I could swear Phoenix smiled at me.

"Well, tonight I'm getting some sleep. I figured you'd be on your old schedule. Tomorrow I have to man the table at the Baker Street Market. I have thirty loaves of bread baked and five trays of yeast rolls. Four trays of cinnamon rolls, minus what we ate tonight."

She gave me a wink.

"I'd love to help you with your table."

"Great. Then after you eat, I'm going to bed. The tablecloth and banner are rolled up in the foyer. I'll show those to you tomorrow." Her gaze fastened on me. They glistened. "I love you, Mac McCann. Did I ever tell you that?"

"I love you more, and my heart is bigger," I said.

Sophie trudged off to bed. She was as exhausted as I was. She leaned out the bedroom door and threw me an air kiss, just as we did each night online. "Good night, babe."

"Good night, Soph." I relaxed in the recliner. Phoenix started out sitting at my feet then propped his front feet on my legs and slowly worked his way into my lap. He was big for a lap dog. I leaned around his fifty-pound frame and clicked the remote on our TV. Pretty soon I heard soft breathing coming from the bedroom. I turned down the volume on the television and listened. I could listen to that sound forever and not tire of it.

Phoenix licked the side of my face, and I laughed then shushed myself.

The sports channel was showing highlights of my favorite baseball team.

It didn't get any better than that.

~*~

"Morning, Soph. What time is it?" I must have dozed off in the recliner because the next thing I knew Sophie was trying to tiptoe past me. Phoenix woke me, jumping off my lap.

"I let you sleep as long as I could. "It's 10:00 AM."

I pushed myself out of the chair, stiff. "Tonight, I'm sleeping in our bed."

"I have to eat and then I need to pack for the market," Sophie said.

"What time do we have to be there?"

"Twelve, to get our table location and set up."

"OK. I'll shower and change clothes." When I came out, Sophie was nowhere to be seen. I walked through the house calling for her. Finally, I looked out the front window and spied her.

She sat in the wicker swing I hung on the porch for her years ago. I winced when I saw that swing. She and Little Mac used to read there every morning. She had a cup of coffee, and she was sitting in the early morning sunshine. Sunlight filtered through the purple climbing flowers she'd planted on the trellis I'd built.

She gazed across the street, over the stone wall of Dogwood Hill Cemetery. Her head turned east, gaze searching past the old section. I was likely the only person who knew what she probably saw in her mind.

I pushed the front door open and took a seat next to her. I joggled the swing and some coffee spilled on her jeans. "I'm sorry." I jumped up to get her a kitchen towel.

"It's OK, babe."

"What are you doing?"

"I sit out here in the morning. Sometimes I bring the laptop. The first thing I do every day is check for your e-mail." Sophie glided the swing back and forth with a push of her foot.

I joined her on the swing, and we sat quietly. This was the first time in months my muscles weren't knotted with tension.

"I miss him," Sophie said.

My breath caught. I got up and quietly moved back into the house. I could see Sophie through the window. She was staring out across the lawn.

Phoenix wagged his tail and wanted to play. He brought me his stuffed toy. I threw it again and again, and he brought it back each time. Phoenix was so faithful. Conviction hit me. Sophie was the epitome of faithfulness. Could I become that for her again?

After a while, Sophie came inside, and we didn't mention the conversation. I had a bad habit of avoiding uncomfortable discussions. It began as a rookie cop. I knew that about myself, but I always seemed to find excuses not to change.

I grabbed her banner and unrolled it on the floor. It was professionally done, silk screened and read *Sophie's Southern Breads*. "This is nice," I said.

Sophie knelt on the floor to admire it with me.

"You named the business. I went down to the sign shop in town and had them make a banner. I think it turned out pretty well."

"It's great, and I can't wait to see it with your bread on a table underneath."

Sophie glanced at the clock. "We need to pack up."

"OK, you just tell me what to do, and I'll help."

"I need this banner and tablecloth in the trunk of the car. Then we'll wrap the cinnamon roll trays with plastic wrap, load them and the bread in the back seat, so they don't get crushed. I had business cards made up in case people want to place an order. I need to bring those and that business card holder, and some water bottles for you and me. It gets hot sitting in the sun."

"I had no idea there was this much work involved."

"Oh, it's not that much. Not when you're doing what you love."

Had I ever done what I love? Then I remembered. That was one of the reasons I went to Afghanistan. The military. Sad that what I loved, Sophie hated.

Together we packed the bread, rolls, and everything else into the sedan. One thing was evident to me. If Sophie was to continue in this business, we had to get her a bigger vehicle. Cars weren't made to be delivery vehicles. But it was only a ten-minute drive. We lived so close to downtown. We pulled up and unloaded.

Sophie was already talking to the coordinator.

"Can you tell me where our table is located?"

The woman, small and stout in a flowered straw hat, pointed down the end of the lane. We would be on the front row, near the end. A pretty good spot according to my calculations, as people who walked the first aisle would have to circle back past us when they reached the end.

We carried the tablecloth and banner and set them up first.

Sophie set her business cards out on the holder. They matched the graphics on the banner.

I made a couple of trips back and forth with stacks of bread and cinnamon rolls. At last, we were set. I stood back and admired our work.

Sophie stood behind the table.

"Hey, let me get a picture of you to show the guys back at camp."

"I'm a mess from carrying all this in the heat."

"Come on, Soph, please?"

She nodded reluctantly and smiled when I took a camera shot on my phone. I pulled the photo up and showed her. Her hair shone in the afternoon light. One day she'd be glad I took this photo. She could look back and remember how it all started.

I pulled up a chair behind the table next to Sophie and sat with my hands in my lap. "Now what do we do?" I asked.

"Now we wait for customers to show up."

"Is that all?"

Sophie laughed. "Yes, that's all. However, if you get antsy you can take that old milk glass plate I brought with me and cut up some of those cinnamon rolls into small pieces, about the size of a piece of fudge. Put them on that plate, and we'll give out samples. That always gets us a lot of sales."

I pulled out my knife.

Sophie jumped. "Wait, what is that?"

"It's a knife."

"It's a dastardly looking knife."

I grinned wickedly. "I know."

"Well, keep that thing out of sight. I don't want to be thrown out of Baker Street Market for brandishing a weapon." She smiled, and her eyes had a dancing sparkle in them that I loved.

"This knife is one of the tools of my trade."

"Keep that particular tool of your trade hidden."

I started to carve up the rolls when Sophie grabbed my wrist. "Wait." She produced a squeeze bottle from her purse. "Hold out your hands."

"What is that?'

"Hand sanitizer. I can't have you getting germs on my rolls."

I held out my hands, rubbed the gel into my palms and quickly waved them in the air to dissipate the smell before it threatened to saturate more than the surrounding air.

Behind us, someone dropped an aluminum pan on the gravel, and the metallic bang made me jump. The lines between Huntsville and Kandahar blurred. My knife reflected light off the keen blade. The crowd noise could have been Taliban, could have been an attack. I jumped up, knocked my folding chair away from the table.

"Where are you going?"

"I just need to clear my head," I said.

Sophie's brow wrinkled. Her eyes darkened with concern. "Are you OK?"

"Yeah, it's that hand sanitizer, the smell of it. I practically have to bathe in that stuff in Kandahar. The smell's just a reminder. That's all."

"Oh, babe, why didn't you say so?" She capped the bottle and put it in her purse then taking it out, she chucked it in the metal trash barrel across the table. "I'm sorry, I didn't know that bothered you."

I didn't need a fuss made over me. I returned to my seat and picked up the knife. "It's OK. Let's get these rolls sold." I made quick work of the cinnamon rolls with my knife and laid them out on the plate like Sophie wanted. I sheathed the knife and stuck it in the cooler under our table.

It looked like sale day at Abdul's. Customers were converging from two different parking lots.

"How many people come to these things?"

"Enough that I sold forty loaves of bread last week, and I forget how many trays of cinnamon rolls."

They surrounded our table and gathered samples from the roll platter. In minutes it was empty.

"You could go broke handing out samples like that."

"I know, that's why I limit myself to one platter per week. It's just enough to get good word of mouth going, but I don't lose that much inventory."

I popped a piece of a cinnamon roll in my mouth.

"Hey, are you eating our profits?"

"No," I mumbled through the crumbs.

"Do you want to walk around the market? I have to stay with the table, and I've seen almost all the vendors before," Sophie said.

"I'll stay here with you," I said.

"No, Mac. Go take a look. I want you to see what they have available. These are the people I work with every week, and I'd like you to meet them."

I reluctantly got up and pushed my chair back under the table. "I'll just make a quick run through and be right back."

I wondered if she was getting tired of me being home already. I wandered down the straw covered lanes lined on either side with tables. Just about any organic fruit or vegetable in season was available.

After a while, I relaxed and enjoyed watching people shop. Time slipped by me. I appreciated the luxury of not knowing what time it was, not having to be in any place at a particular time. I walked lazily past an ice cream vendor and watched as people juggled ice cream cones in the scorching heat, ice cream dripping down their hands. Again, I thought of Bashir. He would have loved cold ice cream.

I turned to the back corner and discovered jewelry vendors. One booth had delicate necklaces that reminded me of Sophie. Handmade pottery pieces were strung on a thin black strip of leather. They were individually numbered, and the artist was right there, ringing people up.

I wandered down the side of the table just looking. I turned to go when something glittered in the sunlight. It was an intricate carving of a small butterfly, strung between two beads on a delicate silver necklace. It was simple, but it made me smile and think of Sophie. "How much is this one?" I asked the artist.

The price she quoted made me step back for a moment, but I couldn't get away from that necklace. It reminded me of Sophie, tiny and fragile, but so fearless she could fly. I reached into my pocket for my wallet. The woman wrapped my purchase and handed it to me in a bag. I carefully hid it in the pocket of my cargo pants.

"Is this for someone special?" the artist asked.

"Yes, I'm home on leave from Afghanistan. It's for my wife. She runs the bread business on the next aisle."

"I think I've met her. Is her name Sophie? She helped me set up my display one morning when a worker failed to show. She's a kind person. You're very fortunate to have her for a wife."

My mouth turned up in a smile. "I'm the lucky one," I said.

The artist nodded. "Let me get you a gift box. I'll be just a minute."

She dug around in a packing box under her display table, and as she did, I had a clear view to the next aisle over.

Out of the corner of my eye, I saw the dispatcher. She was in the next aisle buying flowers. I placed my hand on the display table to steady myself. Then I took off around the corner headed to Sophie's table.

The artist straightened and called out to me. "Did you change your mind about the box?"

I didn't answer her. I was already moving as quickly as I could to our table. I glanced at my watch. It was almost time to shut down. I arrived in front of Sophie's table, panting and sweating.

"Mac, are you all right?"

She always could read me.

"I'm all right."

"Is it the heat?" And then, almost to herself, she added, "How could it be the heat? You're used to working in hundred-degree temperatures in Afghanistan."

"Do you have a bottle of water?"

She dug around in the cooler and pulled out a dripping bottle. I took it from her and held the cold plastic to my forehead. The chill felt good, took some of the pain away, almost as good as chugging an iced coffee. I twisted the top off and took a long drink. "Thanks."

As I was handing the bottle back to Sophie, the woman worked her way down our aisle. I saw her at the far end. Six tables between her and me. She hadn't spotted me. Yet.

"Let's pack up. Are you done for the day?" I asked, keeping my back to the woman.

"Yes, let me find my keys, and we can take all this down and pack the car."

Sophie dug around in her purse for her keys. "I can never find my keys."

"Why do you need keys?"

Five tables down.

"To unlock the trunk, to put this stuff in."

Four tables down.

"OK, give me the keys, and I'll unlock the car, I'll pull it around the side street, and we can load it there.

It'll be less walking." I grabbed the purse and started digging past the makeup, lipstick, and coins. "Where are your keys?"

Three tables down.

"Mac, what is wrong with you?"

"I need to get home."

"Now?"

"Right now."

Two tables away.

I dug some more in Sophie's purse, finally found the keys, and dropped her bag back in her lap.

"Why are you in such a hurry?"

"Going to get the car. I'll pull in that alley right behind you, and we can load up." I didn't even wait for an answer. I took off at a run behind our table, doubled back up the other aisle and across the road to the parking lot. I breathed like Travis on the treadmill the day he found out his wife was divorcing him.

I reached the car, opened the door, and threw myself into the seat. For a minute I sat, hands on the steering wheel. Sitting behind a steering wheel was the last place I wanted to be. I had driven as little as possible since the accident. At least I was away from that woman.

After a minute, my breathing slowed, and I turned on the ignition, rolled up the windows, and blasted the air conditioning. There was one good thing. We had a new air conditioning unit put in the old car. It worked like a dream. I turned the vents toward my face and held it there like Phoenix might when he rode in a car. I closed my eyes.

After a few minutes, I drove out of the parking lot. I drove slowly beside the market. I could see in between the tables, and the woman was gone. I pulled slowly into the alley behind Sophie's table and hopped out of the car, leaving the air conditioning running so it would be comfortable for Sophie. I popped open the trunk. "Are you ready to go?"

Sophie rolled up her banner and stacked empty bread boxes.

I picked up the cooler and placed it in the trunk.

Sophie came up beside me with the empty boxes and put them in the trunk. "Mac, are you OK?"

I put my hand on her arm and gave it a gentle squeeze. "I'm fine, Soph. Really."

She looked at me oddly. "I'll believe you this once. But don't do that to me again. You scared me to death. And I'm driving."

That was OK with me. I didn't want to be behind a steering wheel right then.

We drove in silence to the house, but it wasn't the comfortable silence that signals togetherness. It was a silence that felt like separation.

When we got home, I jumped out and unloaded the car. I was beat. I slumped down in my recliner. Sophie went into the kitchen, and I heard her banging pots and pans around.

"Mac, I'm tired. Do you mind if we eat out?" she asked, reappearing from the kitchen.

"Do I mind? I'd love to eat out."

"Are you sure you feel up to it?" There was hesitation in her voice.

"Yes, Soph, I feel up to it. I'm sorry about back there. I just had a headache."

"A headache?"

"Yeah, but I'm better now."

"Do you want some aspirin?"

"No. I'm better now, really."

"Maybe if you get some sleep tonight, you'll feel better in the morning."

"Yeah, that's all it is. I just need sleep." Sleep and then the truth. Sophie deserved the truth.

25

Sophie jumped out of the car. "Let me check the mail." She came back down the sidewalk, shuffling envelopes in her hands.

I unlocked the front door, and a fresh, sweet breeze of lavender enveloped me.

Phoenix rose from his dog bed and stretched. He must have been napping, but his guilty posture gave him away.

I ran my hands across the couch cushions, still warm. Phoenix had been sleeping on the sofa. The mischievous guy must have jumped down when we pulled into the driveway. A smile tugged at my mouth.

"Mac, another bill from Body Rip?" Sophie called from the kitchen. She leaned around the doorway.

"Remember what you said, that I work hard, and I deserve to do something for myself." I made a muscle. "Do you really want to give this up?"

Sophie shook her head in exasperation.

"What's the plan for tomorrow?" I asked.

Sophie checked off items on a notepad. "We need to finish packing for the beach. We leave at seven tomorrow morning." She tapped the pen she was holding on the side of the counter.

"What else?" I said.

Her lips formed a tight line.

"I want to visit Little Mac's grave."

"Tonight?"

"It's just a short walk."

"I can't."

"You can't?" Sophie exhaled and seemed exasperated.

"Don't ask me to do it, Sophie."

Sophie moved from the kitchen and tried to squeeze past me to the bedroom.

"I've been waiting for you to suggest going to the cemetery, and you haven't. I'm visiting our son's grave tonight. Whatever you do is your choice. Now please let me by, so I can get my jacket." Sophie walked stiffly from the room and didn't say another word.

It wasn't like Sophie to give up trying to persuade me so easily. I followed her to the bedroom. "If it means that much to you, let's go." What a horrible choice of words. I wished I could call them back.

"I don't know who you are. What do you mean, 'If it means that much to me'? What does it mean to you, Mac?" She wasn't mad, just hurting. Pain made her voice ragged.

She needed me to be there for her. But I couldn't. "It means everything to me. It means everything I've lost, all that I'll never have again," I said, stumbling over the words. I grabbed my jacket and shoved my arms into the sleeves. "Come on, Sophie. Don't be angry. I didn't mean it the way it sounded."

She gathered her jacket and a small bouquet of flowers.

We left the house in strained silence.

Little Mac's gravesite was across the street, through the walkway, past the weathered stone wall that surrounded Dogwood Hill. That cemetery was just a big extension of Sophie's childhood yard. Watching her march across the yard reminded me of the first time I'd been to Sophie Mullin's house...

I had knocked on the wooden screen door. It bounced in the wood frame, creating a hollow sound.

"Just a minute," Sophie had called from inside. When she opened the front door, Sophie smelled like spring rain and fresh-mowed grass. Her cotton sundress hung loosely from thin hips. Hips that made me want to dance with her in the fading sunlight on the lawn. She gave me that quirky smile and shut the door behind her. She sat down on her mama's old wooden porch swing. I settled in beside her, breathing in her freshness, gazing at her like she was a goddess.

"You live across the street from a cemetery?" I asked.

"It's not that weird," she'd said.

"I've lived here my whole life. I learned to ride my bike down those asphalt lanes. When I was a little girl, it was my playground. My best friend and I used to play hide and seek among the tombstones. When I had spend-the-nights, we'd sneak across the street with flashlights at midnight and tell ghost stories…"

Later, we inherited the house when Sophie's mom passed.

This night, cicadas sang in a crescendo from hundred-year-old oaks.

It was an ancient cemetery and served as a history book of sorts. Each year storytellers dressed in costume and regaled visitors with adventures of cemetery residents. Because there were many notable people buried there, the stories were exciting.

We passed the headstone of a man who was famous for being the owner of a top producing milk cow. The story had fired up Little Mac's imagination. We spent many hours walking the cemetery together. Sometimes I'd bring his tricycle, and Little Mac would pedal furiously down the asphalt lanes...

I paused to read the man's tombstone. In 1892 his heifer won a world award for top butter producer. He threw one of the liveliest celebrations the city ever witnessed, just for his cow.

"Little Mac made me tell him that story every night at bedtime," I said.

"Which one?" Sophie asked.

"The one about the cow who had her own party."

Sophie circled back and gazed at the man's headstone.

"He loved the voices you did to go along with it. I always heard Little Mac giggling from his bedroom. You were in there tucking him in. I'd listen to the two of you over the running water as I loaded the dinner dishes in the washer." She brushed dead leaves away from the gentleman's grave.

"Little Mac made me tell it every night, but I changed up the story and added voices and sound effects," I said. And now Little Mac was buried in Dogwood Hill, not too far from his hero. "Sophie, there's something I have to tell you..."

Sophie had her back to me. She started off toward the east. "Hurry, Mac, the sun's going down. It'll be dark before we make it home."

I ran to catch up with her. The smell of new earth traveled to me on a breeze that made me shiver. A crimson tent awning was set up. Underneath were folding chairs on a hunter green funeral carpet. Someone would be put in the ground the next day. I felt compassion for the family, whoever they were.

We picked our way across the grounds. Sophie knew all the shortcuts. She marched ahead of me, stepping wherever. It never bothered her to step on a grave.

Me, I picked my way around the head and foot stones, trying not to step on someone's family member. My grandmother said it was bad luck to step on a grave. I never really believed her, but still, it didn't hurt to be careful, just in case.

Sophie stopped. In the fading light, she knelt at our son's grave and placed the flowers in a little urn we had added to the headstone.

I couldn't go any closer. It was the worst kind of fix, trying to be there for Sophie, and yet I couldn't stand beside Little Mac's headstone.

Sophie straightened and waved me over.

I shook my head. *Can't do it, Soph. Please understand.* I pleaded with my eyes. I looked for a place to sit down while I waited for her, but there were no benches in that section, and I was not about to lean on someone's headstone. My grandmother would probably return from the grave to scold me.

The light faded quickly. Sophie was an ashen figure in a sea of dusty light and shadows.

I heard her more than I saw her approach. She sighed.

She took my hand, and we walked out of that shadowed place, into the glow of a streetlight that wrapped our home in gold.

We moved in silence, down the stone steps that made their way down the embankment to where the yard leveled off, and up the stairs to our house.

I turned back and looked across the street one last time before we went in.

I love you, son.

~*~

Phoenix bounced around us. We were his god and goddess, and he never let us forget it. I was thankful for his antics.

Sophie trudged across the foyer and hung her jacket on a hook. I could see what a toll all this was taking on her. She understood me, and I didn't have to explain. She moved to the kitchen wordlessly and started a pot of hot water for tea.

I sat at the kitchen table and absentmindedly flipped through packets of tea she kept in a small basket. "I've become friends with a barber who works at camp," I said. "We sit at Green Beans Coffee, at a little table and drink chai together sometimes. Seeing this tea reminded me."

The pot whistled, and steam condensed, running down the side of the spout, hissing when it hit the hot burner on the stove.

Sophie opened a packet of green tea, dropped it inside her mug, and poured steaming water over it.

"Do you want some tea?"

Surprising myself, I said, "Yeah. That would be great. I never drank hot tea until I went to Kandahar. I used to make fun of it, you know?"

Sophie handed me a mug.

"Glenn, back at camp, taunted me about my iced coffees in the same way. I used to say hot tea was a sissy drink." I picked through the tea packets and found one I liked. "You have chai," I said.

Sophie studied me over the edge of her mug, gently blowing across it to cool her tea. "I never thought I'd hear that come out of your mouth," she said. A grin pulled at the corners of her lips.

I opened the packet, let it fall to the bottom of my

mug, and poured steaming water over it from Sophie's teakettle. I watched the hot water swirl over the tea bag.

"You were telling me about a barber," she said.

"I walk him to work almost every day. We have to escort the civilian workers to their shops from the front gate."

"Why?"

"Security reasons. One of them could be, uh."

"Oh." She looked back down into her mug. Her mouth tightened. "One of them could have a bomb planted on him?"

"Yeah, something like that." I took a drink of chai. The spicy tea warmed my throat. "Anyway, I get to walk with him frequently, nearly every day. He's teaching me Dari."

Sophie put her mug down and smiled. "Say something in Dari for me?"

"Promise you won't laugh?"

"Promise." Sophie leaned forward.

I was afraid she would be disappointed. "Yak roz dee-dee doost, degar roz dee-dee baraadar. This means, the first day we are friends; the next day we are brothers."

"What a beautiful saying."

"My pronunciation's a little rusty, but you get the idea."

"Did the barber teach you that one?"

"Gul Hadi, he's become my window to the outside world there, Soph. He's not like the radicals. He only wants to be left alone to raise his son and live his life. He's got a great sense of humor."

"I've never known anyone who spoke Dari," Sophie said.

"I can't really speak it. I understand a lot more of it now, and I know basic one-word commands that we use for our students in training, that kind of stuff. But this is the only sentence I've memorized."

"Still, that's something." She nodded her head and then took a sip of tea.

"Actually, how I met him is a funny story. There's this sergeant I work with, a really great guy. His name is Thorstad."

"Thorstad," Sophie repeated after me. I could tell she was trying to keep everyone straight in her mind.

"Yeah, he's another one in our tent who's military. We're a mixed bunch in tent 29. Travis, Glenn, and I are contractors, and Stockton and Thorstad are career military."

"Anyway, I call Thorstad the Pied Piper of Kandahar because he keeps candy in the pockets of his BDUs and hands it out to all the local kids."

"He sounds like a kind person."

"One day, Travis and I were getting a haircut, and this little kid comes up to me, actually comes up to Thorstad, and holds his hand out."

"A little boy?"

"Yeah, cute as can be. Thorstad gives him sticks of red licorice whips, and the boy runs off, sits in an empty barber's chair and thoroughly enjoys the candy. So I asked where he was from, and Travis points to Gul, and says, 'Well, that's Gul Hadi's son.'"

"How old is he?"

"Oh, I don't know. It's hard to tell. I guess our age maybe."

"No, I mean the little boy."

"Bashir? He's four."

"His name's Bashir?"

"Yep."

"What does he look like?"

"He has nut brown skin and hair the color of black licorice, that bluish-black color. His eyes are the color of Little Mac's."

"His eyes are green?"

"Green as yours."

"Oh, Mac, I'd love to see him. Do you have any pictures?"

"No, afraid not."

Sophie twirled her mug, spinning the tea bag around inside.

"Some of those pops you send me go to him. He loves them."

"That makes me happy knowing we've done something for him. Tell me, is there anything his family needs that we can help with?"

"I've been turning that same question over in my mind, Soph, and the things they need are out of our jurisdiction right now."

"Like what?"

"Like a decent education. Gul is limited by what he can provide. A barber doesn't make much of a salary. Don't get me wrong. Compared to what a lot of people are living on there, Gul's doing pretty well."

"Well, I can keep sending pops though, right?"

"Right."

"And if there is anything else you stumble on that we can do for them, you already have my agreement, even if you can't get hold of me first," she said.

"Agreed."

I took a sip of my chai. Drinking chai and talking about Gul Hadi and Bashir. I glanced up at the kitchen clock. "It's getting late. I'd better finish packing for the beach and set the alarm. We need to leave by seven." I groaned as I said it. I was so tired, and we had little time to sleep. Maybe I could catch a nap in the car if we took turns driving. I moved to the bedroom and started packing clothes for the trip. I had a flashback to when I laid out clothes for Afghanistan. It wasn't that long ago. I glanced up, and Sophie was carefully folding her clothes, placing them in her bag. I smiled to myself. At least this trip Sophie is coming along.

26

"Let's unpack later. I want to walk on the beach." Sophie had dropped her bag beside the bed and was already changing into sandals.

The delight in her eyes was like medicine to my soul. The beach had become an annual pilgrimage for us. We spent our honeymoon there, and the memories drew us closer every time we came back. After a six-hour drive, the beach called to us.

I threw the sliding glass door open and let the ocean breeze into our condo. I stepped out onto the balcony of our seventh-floor room and filled my lungs with salty air. A group of pelicans flew at eye-level. They studied me with beaded black eyes as they passed.

A strip of white beach stretched across the horizon. From my vantage point, I could see a pod of dolphins rising and dipping in the waves. Already, stress was leaving my body; my shoulders felt loose. "Come on. I'll race you to the beach," I said and slid the patio door shut.

Sophie ran ahead and tried to block me from the doorway. We pushed and pried at each other's hands on the door, but she managed to slip beneath my arm, turn the handle, and fly out the door like a bird freed from a cage. She sprinted to the elevator and mashed the button several times. She looked back at me, teasing, laughing.

I caught her just before the doors opened,

wrapped my arms around her, pulled her to me for a kiss. I heard the elevator doors open and a gasp. We must have been a spectacle, there in the hallway. Let them look. Hadn't they ever been in love?

Downstairs the sun beat heavily in a three o'clock scorcher. I took my shoes off, and Sophie threw her sandals beside the pool. We ran down the wooden boardwalk to the white sandy beach. My feet sank into hot sand. It was soft and gave way with each step, making it hard to keep up with Sophie. She splashed into the surf ahead of me, turning back to wave me on.

"Come on, Mac! The water feels good!" She wrapped her skirt around her legs to keep it from the waves. The waves splashed against her and threw droplets of salt spray across her top. She looked giddy, drunk on salt water and sun.

I waded into the water beside her, knee-deep. The currents pulled at the sand around my feet then pushed me back again toward shore. It was everything I had dreamed about for months, and I meant to enjoy every minute.

Sophie's eyes gleamed green as the tide. Her cheeks were flushed from the run and her hair curled in ringlets from the humidity. She kicked her foot through a wave and sent a spray of water in my face. Sophie giggled.

It was healing to be back at the beach. I breathed in the ocean air. If I closed my eyes the warmth of the sun and the fresh breeze took me back seven years to our honeymoon. Another spray of water hit my face, and when I opened my eyes, Sophie was running up the beach, laughing.

"Catch me," Sophie said.

I took off through the waves, jumped to the hard-packed sand and pursued her. I finally trapped her at the pier. This time she threw her arms around me. She brushed the hair from my face, hair that I'd let grow wild in Afghanistan. She traced my beard with her fingers. "What made you grow a beard? When we were dating, I begged you to grow one, but you always refused. Now that you went off without me, you come home with one."

"I wanted to try something new. I was tired of rules, you know? At HPD, I wasn't allowed a beard."

She tickled my face and brushed her fingers across my beard.

"Do you like it?" I asked. "I mean, you begged me for a beard for all those years."

She smiled up at me and tickled my chin. "As a matter of fact, I do like it. It makes you look like a surfer."

"I always wanted to surf. There aren't many waves to catch when you spend your summers lifeguarding in a pool."

~*~

We drove down the beach to our favorite restaurant. The host at the front door handed us a pager. "Wait time is approximately an hour," he said.

We spent the time looking through gift shops across the street, waiting for the pager to buzz when our table was ready.

"Look, Mac. That gelato shop wasn't here our last visit," Sophie said, dragging me by the arm to a pastel colored store. "Let's see what flavors they have."

"OK, if we have any room left, we'll stop in here after dinner."

As we entered the door to the shop, our pager buzzed.

"Come on, Mac. Save room for dessert."

We crossed the street and entered the restaurant. The server led us through a shoulder-to-shoulder crowd to our table, dodging trays balanced on the arms of other servers, squeezing our way between tables placed so tightly there was little room to pull a chair out.

Live music blared from a small stage. Alongside was a faded couch. Patrons sat on the couch, drinks in hand, enjoying the music. A local band was in full song.

The fish was served up quickly. I plunged my fork in and enjoyed the best fresh seafood I'd had in months.

Sophie twined her fingers in mine as we ate. "Time for dessert."

"I'm ready. Just let me move around a little bit first, make some more room for it." I leaned back and patted my bloated stomach.

"I don't know if you need any gelato." Sophie laughed. "I don't even know how you finished that platter. It was huge."

I paid our check, and we hiked across the street once again to the gelato shop. The crowd stretched from inside the shop out into the street. We joined the end of a long line of dessert seekers.

"Are you sure you want to stand in this long line? We can come back tomorrow," I said.

"I'm really craving gelato."

"OK, I guess I can walk it off on the beach later tonight. There'll be fireworks at midnight." I stretched my neck to see how much longer we would be in line.

That was when I saw him, a ghost of a boy. His curly, strawberry-blonde hair grew almost to his collar. Faded blue shirt. He was dressed in the khaki cargo shorts I'd picked out for him and red sneakers. His socks were mismatched. I never could find the right socks, and the day we went for a haircut I'd dressed him.

He grasped the hand of a man about my age. I couldn't see the boy's face. "I need to find a restroom. I'll be back in a minute."

"All right, but don't be too long. The line's moving quickly."

I worked my way alongside our line and inched closer to the boy. As I caught up to them, he turned. My heart was pounding and my throat constricted. For a second, I wished.

But his features were not my son's.

He looked at me curiously, and the man with him studied me as if I were some kind of stalker.

I ducked quickly into the restroom. The walls echoed with stall doors slamming. The hand dryer whirred, and toilets flushed alternately. I ran to a sink, splashed cold water on my face, scrubbed my hands, and dried them off. In the mirror, I saw them. Fathers and sons, a parade of what might have been. I had to get out of there. I was feverish and frantic, like an animal caught in a trap. Why did I agree to the beach? We should have gone to a solitary place, a cabin in the mountains. Not the beach, where every other person had a small child in tow. I made my way back to Sophie just as she was about to order.

"What took you so long?"

"Long line." My voice wavered when I said it. I glanced around to see if the boy was still there, but he'd disappeared.

We carried our gelato to a picnic table outside the shop and sat down.

I was grateful for the distraction because the specter of that little boy still haunted me. I scooped the cold dessert into my mouth and swallowed. "I don't understand the pointlessness of Little Mac's death," I blurted out before I could stop myself. I was still reeling from the encounter in line.

Sophie put her spoon down, mid-bite. "What do you mean pointless? His death was not pointless."

"But it seems meaningless. Isn't death supposed to have some kind of meaning? Your father died serving his country in the military. My dad died from burns he had rescuing those teenagers from that wreck."

Silence.

"You haven't talked about that wreck in years," Sophie said.

"Yeah. I never told you how my dad described it to me. The screams he heard coming from the car. But he sacrificed himself. He said he never felt the flames when he cut them loose from their seat belts. It didn't register until he saw the charred flesh on his arms. When he went back in for the third one that was when the car exploded. He passed the day after he told me that story."

"That's when you decided to be a cop, wasn't it?" Sophie gazed into my eyes.

"Yeah, I wanted to be like him. I wanted to save people. I wanted to make things right."

I'm sure she saw in my eyes that I hadn't made things right, that I had only made things terribly wrong. I looked away.

"You couldn't save little Mac. You tried, babe. You

tried."

"What good was the end of his life? He was too little to affect the world around him. His death had no meaning."

"Maybe he had more influence than you know. It's my prayer that God will use his death to help some other little boy."

"Why didn't He help Little Mac?"

"I don't have an answer for that, and you know it. That's an unfair question. I just know God was there, and He will use it for good. He promised me."

27

That night, back at the condo, we fell into bed exhausted. Moonlight from the window made a muted glow across Sophie's face. I watched her sleeping so peacefully next to me. Smoothed her face with my fingers, felt the softness of her cheeks. Her mouth puckered in a pout. I traced the outline of her lips with my finger.

Little Mac looked so much like her. He had my hair but her features. What kind of man would my boy have been? Would he have made a difference in this world? *Forgive me, son.*

I tried to watch Sophie, steal one more look at her, but it was impossible to keep my eyelids open.

I awakened to the sound of my own voice as it echoed off the plaster condominium walls. My arms thrashed through the depths of sleep. Flailing, desperate to get help. Cold sweat covered my face and ran down my neck, soaking my T-shirt. Even in my dreams, I failed to rescue him.

Sophie sprang up in bed and flipped on the bedside lamp.

"Mac?"

I sat stiffly in bed beside her, not focused on anything in particular.

Sophie touched my shoulder. "You were having a nightmare." She drew her hand back and wiped her palms together. "You're soaking wet."

"I'm all right," I said. But my dreams conspired to

punch a hole in the facade I'd so carefully constructed.

We'd been married seven years that June, long enough for Sophie to read every worry crease in my forehead, like someone reading tea leaves.

I stripped off my sodden clothes and jumped in the shower. I held my face in the stream of warm water and closed my eyes. I stood there until steam enveloped my body, muffling the noise in my brain. I wanted to numb the painful memories, but they didn't make painkillers strong enough to heal what ailed me. I was not sure how long I stood there, but eventually, I turned off the hot water and went back to bed.

Sophie wasn't asleep as I'd hoped. She waited up for me. Why was I surprised?

"Did the shower help?"

"Yeah." I pulled a clean T-shirt over my head, shoved my arms in the sleeves, and climbed into bed.

Just leave it alone. I'll talk with Sophie tomorrow. Who was I kidding? I'd used that excuse for months, and I couldn't remember one single day that I'd followed through. It was time to tell Sophie the truth. "I have something to say to you."

Sophie rubbed my arm. "What is it?"

"It was my fault."

Sophie frowned and pushed her hair out of her eyes.

"What was?"

"The accident," I said.

"No, it wasn't. The other driver was listed as at fault."

A strangled wheezing sound clawed its way up my throat. "The other driver *was* at fault, but..." I breathed out, still wheezing. "My phone beeped. It was sitting on the seat. I glanced over to see who was texting, and when I looked up, the other car plowed into me." *Oh, God.* The words were finally out of my mouth.

Sophie crawled around in bed to face me. "What?" Her voice squeaked, pitched like a guitar strung too tight and about to break.

"Who was texting you? It wasn't me. You'd just left our house." A glimmer of suspicion grew in Sophie's eyes. "Mac! Answer me." Sophie seemed small and brittle, more even than the day we'd buried him.

"The dispatcher." I waited, but instead of the outburst I'd expected, she was silent. Her silence was more excruciating than any words. Only Sophie had the power to release me. She had to say it. It would be a mercy killing. This time I was the moth at the light.

"Say it. You can't forgive me." I begged her, yet inside I had one strand of hope. Like a three-stranded rope that's been sawed through until there's only one strand left. I hung by that strand, and Sophie wielded the knife. A knife I'd given her.

But she wouldn't say it. Sophie had too much self-control. The color drained from her face, left the freckles on her nose in stark relief. Her eyes shimmered with unshed tears and muffled choking sobs came from her throat.

She jumped from our bed and quickly slipped into her skirt that was thrown carelessly on the floor just a few hours before. A few hours before, I had been her lover, her provider. The one she depended on to make everything right.

She pulled her thin blouse over her head and jammed her feet into her sandals.

I stood there frozen. Just watched. Watched my

world come crashing down.

She grabbed her purse.

"Where are you going?" Please, Soph, not like this.

"Away." She moaned from between white lips. "Away from you. I can't do this anymore." And then the dam burst with a torrent of her words. "When Little Mac died, I tried to carry on. When you decided to go halfway across the world, I hung in there. I'm a law enforcement officer's wife. I know how to deal with loneliness. At first, I begged you to come home, but then I realized you probably needed time to heal, so I gave you what you asked. Now I need time alone."

"When will you be back?"

She stopped midway through putting her sweater on. "I don't know." She shoved her arms the rest of the way in.

I made a halfhearted attempt to touch her, but she twisted past. My hand was left hanging in the air. Her perfume drifted away from me. The door closed, and silence wove a smothering blanket. She was never coming back. I'd always remember that moment, for I knew I would not have another with her.

Glenn was right. My Achilles heel was that I hoped for second chances. I was a wandering star in a field of blackness. I had become Glenn. Back at camp, a re-enlistment packet was on my desk. I could continue as a police trainer, and Sophie would have her freedom.

All it needed was my signature.

~*~

"Sophie!"

The crowd flowed around me like a living stream.

I tried to cut across the flow, but I dodged parents with cotton candy and children. The night air was damp, and the full moon crashed off the waves. I hadn't stayed in our room long. I had to find her.

It seemed the entire city was out for a stroll, headed to the beach, for the midnight fireworks display.

I caught sight of the back of her head as she moved ahead of me through the crowd. I walked faster to catch up, called her name again, but the noise of the crowd drowned me out. "Sophie I'm here," I called out to her. I willed her to hear me, repeated it in my head. But she couldn't read my mind. Or could she?

Sophie turned, and a smile full of yearning filled her face.

But her smile wasn't for me. I drew my gaze down the street, targeted the line of her vision, and my glance landed on the ghost boy once again, illuminated by a street light. Small tow-headed boy, same shirt.

I was bumped from behind, but my eyes remained fixed on Sophie, afraid panic would seize her the way it had me. But she amazed me. Instead of running away as I'd done, Sophie walked directly to the boy and started up a conversation with the father.

I couldn't hear what they were saying, but her hand caressed the boy's head and lingered for a moment, just a moment, across his blond curls. Then she drew back, tucked her hands behind her back, locked her thumbs as if to prevent herself from hugging him.

I made my way beside her as the man and his son walked off. When I caught up to Sophie a mixture of longing and regret clouded her face.

She jumped, startled when I came into view. A

small breeze rose and turned up the ends of her hair. Her cheeks and lips were pink from the day's sun. She glanced my way hesitantly, and I didn't know if she would leave.

"Sophie—"

"Did you see him?" Her voice wavered, and she clasped her hands together tightly.

"I saw him."

"He looked just like Little Mac from behind. He even had the same shirt I bought," Sophie said.

"I know, Soph. He was in line earlier at the gelato shop with his dad."

"Let's go back to our room," Sophie said.

As soon as the door to our condo was shut, she walked across the room and braced her arms against the desk. Her back was to me, and she looked spent.

"You've known about this for over a year, but for me, it's as if it just happened," Sophie said. "I was getting to the place where I could enter his room without breaking down, and now this…"

"I was wrong to withhold the truth. When I saw Travis's marriage crumble, I was afraid ours would be next."

"I don't know if you've considered how hard this has been for me. When I heard those explosions outside your tent, I was horrified. All I could think was that our son was gone, and I was about to lose you, too. I'm too young to be a widow."

"Please forgive me."

"Remember what you told me when you first arrived in Afghanistan and I was begging you to come home?" she whispered. "You said, 'We can do this. I know we can.'"

I nodded, mechanically at first. Then the

realization hit me. She was repeating my own words, as her way of saying she wanted to give us another chance.

A flood of forgiveness washed over me, deeper and wider than I'd ever felt before. I couldn't comprehend that kind of mercy. It didn't seem humanly possible.

Sophie placed her hands in mine. I rubbed her hands as if to warm her, as if to fight off the chill of death that hung over our marriage.

"Now it all makes sense. It didn't before. Why you left the way you did, so soon after we lost him. I was hurt, angry, and alone."

"I never wanted to hurt you. I was running from the accident and from myself. I know it sounds stupid, but the more miles I put between me and Little Mac's grave...I thought I could outrun my guilt."

She leaned back and made me look into her eyes. "I don't hate you. I can't hate you. Ever. I knew you were evading me. I wish you had trusted me enough to tell me. Promise me something. Promise you will tell the truth. Lies put distance between us, more separation than if you were still in Afghanistan."

"I promise." I kissed her forehead.

Sophie pulled me closer, and we melded into one person.

For the first time in a year, we were a couple again, embracing each other as if one would let go of the other, we'd lose the tiny island of peace we'd just found.

28

"I have a mission to finish if we can hang on." I released Sophie's hand and ran my fingers through her hair. A forced grin spread across my face. We would make it. Only this time, I was the one who needed reassuring. Returning to Afghanistan was harder than I'd expected, and it took all my will to drive toward the airport.

Our car was the only speck of color on the highway. The road was gray, the sky was gray. During the two weeks, I was home on leave, the seasons shifted into full-blown fall. Patches of rain-soaked grass in the median encircled brown puddles from last night's thunderstorms. High winds stripped trees of any remnant of fall. The grayness matched my mood.

"Time will go slowly while you're gone. But I've got to build the business, so I'll be putting in a lot of hours. This will work, Mac." Sophie tried to make her enthusiasm rub off on me. "When you get home for good, I should have my hours established. The time apart will give me room to get the business grounded."

It all sounded so logical, so orderly. My mind shouted. I want to be here to watch you build your business. I want to see your dreams come true, not spend the next months imprisoned behind cement walls.

Sophie curled the tips of her fingers back into the palm of my hand and closed her eyes.

I shifted in the car seat and pulled her against me.

She rested her head against my chest, and I focused on the rhythmic beating of her pulse, her steady breaths. I memorized them so I could play them back in the emptiness of my tent at night. "I'll miss you, Soph."

She turned her head up and studied me. "I'll miss you, too." She gave my hand a squeeze. "You love teaching, don't you?"

I tapped the steering wheel with the wedding band on my finger. Could I find the words? "I wish you could meet the students. Most of them have an insatiable desire to learn. This academy is their only opportunity. I tell them to enjoy the time in school, treat it like a small vacation. That's something they'll never have. We feed them well and provide beds and uniforms. Some go home at the end of the day. Some have the option to stay. The ones within traveling distance go back. But the locals usually stay anyway because we feed them. There's also TV and showers.

"It's normally one of the few times they don't have to worry about being shot at, about IEDs. Yeah, I hope to see a difference in them by the time they graduate. It'll feel good. A lot of them have never been through a police academy, never even fired a weapon. For the first time in my life, I feel like I'm making a difference."

I pulled up to the passenger drop-off zone. I put the car in park and turned off the ignition. I started to get out of the car, and the feeling hit me. My heart was being shredded. Despite all my bravado, I might not make it back. I might not be able to hold Sophie again.

"Let me move the car to the parking deck and you can come inside to say good-bye," I said.

Her eyes softened. "Please don't make this harder on us. I'm not going in. I can't get beyond the passenger check-in anyway. Let's say good-bye here." Her voice pitched higher. She was as awful at good-byes as I was.

"Before I go, I have something for you." I dug in the pocket of my cargo pants and pulled out a gift bag. I handed it to Sophie.

"You bought me a gift?" She shook her head in wonder.

"I know it won't make up for the birthdays and anniversaries I've missed, but I saw this at Baker Street Market, and it reminded me of you."

Sophie pulled the square of folded tissue paper from the bag. Her hands shook. She carefully opened the wrapping. The silver butterfly necklace dropped into the palm of her hand, and she breathed in sharply.

"Do you like it?"

"It's beautiful."

I traced the wing of the butterfly with my finger. "It reminds me of you, Soph. You're so beautiful, and to the world, you appear fragile. But I know you have the strength to fly."

Sophie looped the chain around her neck. "Can you hook this, babe?"

I closed the hook on the chain and leaned back to admire the necklace on Sophie.

"I won't take it off until you come home."

We'd been parked in a passenger drop-off zone long enough. The terminal security officer gave us the "move along" eye. I ought to have recognized that look. I'd given it to many while on patrol myself.

"I need to get going. We've been parked here too long." I opened the car door, walked around to the trunk, and pulled out my bag. I had to stay in motion just to keep it together.

Sophie got out of her side of the car.

I stepped up on the curb beside her. She wrapped her arms around my waist. Seven years of motion ingrained in us. We fit together the way I was sure no other two people ever would. She laid her head against me, face curled against my neck. I felt a sigh course through her body. I pulled Sophie tighter against me. If I stayed longer, I'd lose my composure. Reluctantly, I released her and stepped away. With one swift motion, I slung my bag over my shoulder. "Bye, Soph."

Her head turned down. Her hair fell across her face. She tried to hide her tears, but they fell to the pavement, dark circles on the cement.

I willed my feet to move quickly. I opened the door and swung my bag inside. With a sideways turn, I waved, but Sophie was gone, hidden behind the reflection in the glass door. Instead, I saw myself, mirrored. Alone.

I swallowed hard. Forced the peach pit in my throat to go down. This was for Sophie. This was for us. The first time I was running. Now I headed forward. I'd finish what I started and come home to be the man she needed. I hoped.

~*~

I picked up the pinwheel from my desk, carefully wiped the dust off the plastic blades, and tipped it with my finger. It spun, but with no breeze to sustain it, soon stopped. It was the only link left between Little Mac and me.

Classes at the academy were over for the day. The students were on their way to a well-earned rest. I picked up the picture of Sophie and I that I'd packed. I didn't even tell her I'd taken it to Afghanistan with me. It was an old photo, taken when we first found out she was pregnant with Little Mac. She was sitting in my lap, and behind us, a fireworks display lit up the sky. In her hand was the blue pinwheel.

Travis knocked on the door. I stuffed the pinwheel in the pocket of my backpack.

"It's time to award Camp Paradise's Manliest Beard." Travis had been waiting for this day for weeks, carefully cultivating his beard.

I looked in my scratched mirror. Travis had me beat. I followed him down the hallway and stepped into the blinding daylight. I quickly shoved my sunglasses down over my eyes.

Glenn and Thorstad were already assembled at our bench.

Travis stepped in front of the three of us. He yelled above the noise of camp. "First, I would like to welcome you all to the First Annual Camp Paradise Manliest Beard contest. As you know, the categories are Manliest Beard of Camp Paradise, Best Moustache, and Most Creative."

I held up my hand. "If we could take a minute before you announce, let's line up for a picture. I want a record of this."

Thorstad took my phone and positioned us along the T-wall. Travis and Glenn still wore their work clothes, polo shirts, cargo pants, and boots. I'd already changed into my tennis shoes, shorts, and a T-shirt. I was more than ready to relax after a long day in class. We posed, proud of our facial hair.

Glenn decided to keep his to a neatly trimmed short beard. A brown line of moustache covered his upper lip.

Travis sported a scraggly blond beard.

Mine was red, full on the sides and shorter at the bottom. I thought of shaving it before I went home but decided to keep it. It kept my face warm at night when it was cool and protected me from the desert sun.

Thorstad was participating but dropped out at the last minute. He only had a scraggly, wispy beard, and he finally gave up and shaved it off.

I was disappointed. I thought if Thorstad had stuck it out a few more weeks, he'd have had something.

Travis stepped up. "All-right, we took a poll in the academy. I had the students vote."

He held a piece of paper with the vote tally written in scribbly handwriting. He looked toward Thorstad.

"The winner of Manliest Beard of Camp Paradise is—"

A blast shook the ground. Rockets roared, then another loud detonation. Dust and smoke filled the air. The camp warning system shrieked, "Incoming. Incoming."

We looked at each other, stunned. Simultaneously we took off for the tent and our kits. I sprinted into my room and grabbed my vest and helmet. Another explosion rattled everything around me, then another closer in sequence. The concussion from an RPG shook my tent, and I staggered, falling to the floor.

29

Two-by-four shelves I'd so carefully built along the wall collapsed, and bodybuilding supplements, books, first aid supplies, and movies crashed on top of me in a heap. Dust and smoke filled the tent, burning my eyes and lungs. I crawled out from under the debris, did a quick check to make sure I wasn't wounded, and slung my vest and helmet on.

Explosions came one after another. I checked my magazines. The guys in our tent yelled to one another, checking for casualties, reassuring each other we were OK.

Where was Travis?

I jumped across the mess on my floor and barreled down the hallway. Travis wasn't in his room.

I reached the outside T-wall and Travis was there, his M-9 drawn. His back was against the wall, but he didn't have his helmet or vest. He hadn't run to the tent with the rest of us.

Guys yelled for everyone to head to the bunker. Travis's gaze met mine, and we knew. No bunker for us.

Glenn planted himself against the wall. He wouldn't be hanging out in that fortification either.

"Secure the front gate!" Travis yelled. "Taliban will attack the guard towers. They'll try to blow the gate and swarm in."

I was determined no enemy would make it through the gate. I gripped my M-9. Time compressed.

Jets screeched overhead. Dust and shrapnel blew through the compound with each explosion. I glanced at Travis ahead of me on the wall. He should be in his vest and helmet. Glenn and I'd cover him so he could make it back to the tent.

"Kit up," I yelled above the constant explosions, motioning Travis toward the tent.

Travis took off at a run and made it into the tent. The door slammed behind him. I moved forward to cover Travis's position, waving behind me for Glenn to follow.

Glenn ambled casually along the wall as if it were a drill. He took up my former position. I would have been amused if I hadn't been riveted on the front gate. At first, I thought Glenn was checking for magazines until I saw him retrieve a cigar tube from a pocket. He unscrewed it and produced a fat cigar. Glenn fumbled in another pocket and grabbed a lighter. I marveled he could light the cigar without shaking. Every fiber in my body vibrated from adrenaline.

I drew a sharp breath to calm my nerves, but before I could exhale, a sixty-two-millimeter recoilless rifle round slammed into the T-wall. A wave of energy clouded with dust and shards of concrete from the blast slammed me to the cement.

My shin seared with pain. I ran my hand across it and pulled back with my own blood. I stared at it, watched it run across my palm. Not a large wound. I wiped my hand across my shorts.

I turned to check on Glenn and froze. He writhed on the gravel. His face was white, and he clutched what was left of his calf. Blood spurted through his pants leg and between his fingers. His pants were scorched and torn where his leg should have been. The iron-like smell of blood mixed with the pungent odor of cordite suffocated me.

"Oh, God!" Words clawed their way up from deep in my chest from a place I had not known before. It wasn't a prayer, but a shout of anguish. I threw myself to my knees and immediately put pressure on the wound. Warm blood squeezed between my fingers, no matter how much pressure I applied. I stared in horror at Glenn's life spilling between my fingers, over the ragged strips of pants leg, over the gray gravel. I placed Glenn's hands over his leg and yelled next to his ear, "Keep pressure on it."

Glenn's eyes were fixed off in the distance. His mind seemed to hover somewhere between earth and sky.

I wasn't sure he could hear me above the explosions, and even if he could, he looked as if he was in shock.

I moved mechanically. The black tunnel of fear threatened to close in on me. The same tunnel from the day Little Mac died. The roar of jets and small arms fire dampened out until all I could hear was the bass drum pounding of blood in my ears. I stared at the blood on my hands and Glenn, but instead of Glenn, I saw Little Mac clinging to me.

Cold tingling crept down my arms to my fingers. The ground and sky swirled into one dizzy picture.

Glenn groaned again, and I jerked back to the present. My friend was dying. But he couldn't die. Not Glenn. Glenn always seemed above the fray to me. He'd been so withdrawn from life it seemed he was out of reach of ordinary pain.

I willed myself to take a deep breath and shook the mind-numbing fear out of my head. The tunnel would not win this time.

Days of practicing first aid kicked in, and I went on autopilot. I broke out my IFAK and applied a tourniquet. Pulled out a field dressing and tore the plastic covering off with my teeth. I pulled the cloth pad out, pressed the pad to the stump of his calf. "Hold this," I yelled once again above the roar of battle. I sounded more in control than I felt. I was amazed he was conscious with the extent of his wounds. If I could keep him awake, he stood a better chance.

I yelled over the constant blasts to him as I worked to stop the bleeding. I wound an 'H' bandage around Glenn's stump.

Glenn winced, but he ran his hand alongside mine and held the pad in place.

A figure sprinted past me. Stockton. I jerked my head at him and yelled above another rocket blast.

"Here. Take care of Glenn." I needed someone to keep the pressure on Glenn's wound so I could cover us in the event the enemy made it through the front gate, and Stockton carried no weapon. His help would free me up to keep watch.

Stockton glanced nervously side-to-side as if he hoped I was addressing someone else. He didn't attempt to slow down. If anything, he sped up. "Headed to the bunker to get a medic!" he yelled at me.

My voice cut like shrapnel. "Now!"

Stockton returned reluctantly to my side, and he placed his hands where I positioned them.

"Keep pressure on the wound." My eyes burned into his. "You let Glenn bleed out, it won't go well for you," I yelled above the blast of another explosion.

I scanned the building to the southeast and traced the roofline with the barrel of my weapon.

From the roof, they could look directly across the street into our camp. I suspected there were spotters.

A head popped up, just along the roofline. I raised my M4 and tracked him through my sight. I was willing to bet he was visually ground-guiding rounds. *Come on buddy, give me a reason to pull the trigger. Let me see a weapon.* Someone would pay for this, but the head disappeared out of sight before I could get a shot off.

Another explosion shook the ground, and I was hit with a dense concussion wave, unlike anything I'd experienced before. The invisible force shoved me into the T-wall. I dropped my weapon and scrambled to retrieve it from the gravel. From the trajectory of the rounds, I was pretty sure they were trying to hit the academy. It was almost impossible to hear the shots before they went ripping past me, and the roar of generators close by hampered my ability to determine the direction of the shooters.

Seventy Afghan students were housed within the green sniper-fabric-covered fences of the academy. Seventy students put their lives on the line for peace. They deserved our protection.

I heard a familiar shout, and as I turned, Travis ran at a full charge toward me from the tent. His helmet and vest were in place, his M-4 held at an angle to his chest. In my peripheral vision, Stockton jumped to his feet, abandoned Glenn and ran like a wild man toward the bunker.

I cursed the coward.

I motioned toward Travis, but he'd already assessed the situation and knelt, pressed on Glenn's wounds. Good ole' Travis. What I could have done with a hundred men like him at that moment.

Soldiers barreled around the corner driving a Gator and hopped down. They swarmed like a nest of fire ants. Two of them sprinted alongside me and hauled Glenn on board the Gator.

I followed alongside, providing cover in case we were fired upon.

Detonations were closer to the academy.

Glenn's white face searched mine. He mouthed words. I leaned closer as they secured him in the Gator.

I barely heard the words coming from his lips. I leaned a little closer. It must have been important the way he struggled to be heard above the constant barrage of fire. Maybe he wanted me to get word back to a relative in the States. Maybe he wanted me to take care of his belongings. I leaned in, my ear almost touching his mouth.

"Who won Manliest Beard?" A spark of mischief gleamed in his eyes. I knew then he'd make it.

"You did," I yelled into his ear, above the roar of incoming.

He smiled and lay back in the Gator, satisfaction on his dust and sweat-smeared face.

The Gator spun down the gravel path to a waiting helicopter. A silver glint of light flashed up at me from the bloody gravel. I bent closer. It was Glenn's butane lighter. I rescued it from the dirt, wiped it on my shorts and dropped it in the pocket of my cargo shorts.

The other pocket of my shorts vibrated. It was my cell phone.

Without thinking, I automatically pulled the phone out and touched the screen under Sophie's name.

"Mac, I couldn't get the Internet to pull up. Is

everything OK?"

My breath caught.

"Soph!" My voice fought to be heard over the whump, whump of the helicopter that was evacuating Glenn. The mechanical bird lifted slowly, churned dust and debris in a whirlwind around me. I pressed the phone to my mouth as I watched the helicopter take wing, turn sharply and power away. I supposed they were taking him to Kandahar Air Field, though I wasn't sure. From KAF Glenn would be airlifted to Germany, usually the first destination for wounded soldiers. I'd have to track Glenn down later. Emptiness settled into my gut when the metal bird pulled away. Glenn had begun as an enigma and turned out to be one of the closest friends I had in camp.

"Are you all right?" Sophie's voice went into that squeak it got when she was stressed. Her words broke into my thoughts.

Take a deep breath, steady.

"We're under attack."

"Where are you?" The phone must have been pressed against her mouth because I could hear her breaths coming in short spurts.

"I'm at the wall. Travis and I are watching the front gate. The guy behind me got hit. Pray for him. We had to medevac him."

"I'll pray," Sophie said.

I could tell she was limiting her words. She knew I had to get off the phone. Sophie knew what it was like for me to be in danger, though this was the first time I'd ever asked her to pray. It surprised me when the words burst from my mouth. That word was foreign and comforting at the same time, but prayer was the one thing I knew Sophie could do for us. How had she put up with this stress for all these years? It came clear to me, like walking out of a fog bank into blinding sunshine. She made herself do it, for me.

Sophie was my hidden police partner, the strength behind my badge. She was the one who kept our family together while I worked long hours.

The phone connection was getting worse. Besides that, the distraction would put Travis and me in jeopardy. I had to hang up, though every fiber in my body rebelled against it. Her voice was my lifeline.

Static took over and decided for me. The last words I heard from Sophie were "love you."

The line went dead.

I didn't get to say it back. I turned the phone off and stuffed it in my pocket.

Travis and I had our backs to the wall, our weapons ready. We were able to talk between blasts from the mortars aimed at our camp.

We stood guard for hours. The sun arched across the sky and threw shadows across the tents as it retreated. I was bone-weary of watching the gate, waiting for a suicide bomber we hoped would never materialize. I unscrewed the top of a bottle of water, took a long drink, and offered the bottle to Travis.

"Drink?"

"Thanks." Travis turned up the bottle and almost drained it. He wiped his mouth on his sleeve and handed the bottle back to me.

"That Sophie on the phone?"

"Yeah, I brought the stupid phone out with me, forgot it was in my pocket."

"She OK?"

"Sophie has seen me in tight situations before, on the force."

"But this is different."

"You're not kidding. I've never had RPGs shot at me before."

"Tricia heard me come under attack lots of times."

It was the first time he'd mentioned her in a while.

"How are things?"

"The divorce finalized. It's weird. Things don't seem any different to me because I'm still in Afghanistan. I mean, other than not hearing from her. I guess the next leave I take, it will hit me."

"That's tough."

"Yeah. Tricia pretty much cleaned me out. Had a good lawyer. I'm extending my tour. If I can't stay here, I'll get them to give me orders for some other place." He removed his helmet and wiped the sweat from his forehead before putting the headgear back on.

"I just don't know what went wrong. I keep going over it in my head. Did I neglect to do something she needed? What would make her leave me?"

"You've been more of an involved husband to Tricia than I've ever been to Sophie."

"Then what was it? I had a new book in my hands every other week. I thought I could fix me."

"Maybe you weren't the one who needed fixing," I said.

Travis went silent on me, which was good. I knew he was considering what I'd just said.

I tried to change the subject, but unfortunately, the only thing I could think about was Sophie. "I go home in a few weeks," I said.

"I know. It'll be weird without you and Glenn." Travis held out his hand, took my water bottle, and drained the last of it.

"You can meet Sophie and me for dinner the next

time you're home on leave. We'll pick a place somewhere between Brentwood and Huntsville."

"That'd be great."

There was a blast about a quarter of a mile from us, in the third-story building that overlooked the camp. Dust and smoke poured from the building, fragments showered the air. The ground shook under our feet, and we stopped talking. *Come on in, boys, come get what I have waiting for you.* But there was no movement.

"Are they at it again?" Travis finally asked.

"I think that was us," I said. "That was the building all the firing has been coming from. Evidently, we pinpointed the source and took it out."

A few bursts of firing echoed inside the city. Shooting quieted down. Sirens took the place of gunfire.

Quick Reactionary Force Vehicles patrolled our path. That was our cue we could return to our tent. We went out four, came back three.

When we pushed open the tent door, dust and smoke swirled in.

In Travis's room movies, books, and trash were on the floor in a heap. Part of his shelves had pulled away from the wall and hung lopsidedly across the corner of the room.

His eyes glazed over when he saw it.

"I know what I'll be doing for the next few hours."

I winced when I passed Glenn's room. I'd get in there later and pack his stuff for him, find out where to ship it. The silence coming from his room only underscored our loss.

I surveyed my room then called down the hallway, "Same mess here." I slung my vest off and hung it on the hook I'd made on the wall. Placed my helmet nearby and anything else I might need quickly. There was no assurance the enemy wouldn't hit us again tonight.

I bent over and picked up movies, books, and papers and put them back on my shelves. I didn't want to trip over stuff if I had to jump up in the middle of the night. I turned on my laptop and found the Internet was running, so I wrote Sophie a quick e-mail. I promised if we ever had an attack I'd write SAFE in the subject line. I kept my word.

The Internet had been shut down until now. They always closed access to it when there was a casualty. Families were finding out on the internet about the death of their loved one before officials could contact them. The thought made me tense, to think of Sophie finding out about my death from social media. That's why I tried not to complain when I couldn't get online.

I hit "send" and closed my laptop. I found a water bottle, dampened a paper towe,l and pressed it to my shrapnel wound. I changed into long pants. I'd sleep in them, just in case…

30

Mac,

I didn't sleep until I saw your name in my inbox.

I pulled up the account of the attack online and read it. I want you to know, we prayed for you here and the guy who got hit. I thank God you're safe.

How are you?

I felt so helpless, holding onto the phone and hearing explosions going off all around you, and me not being able to do anything. I could only listen and pray, but I did pray.

We are one, Mac. When you walk the dusty roads of Afghanistan, so do I. You were not meant for that place. You were meant for green lawns and thunderstorms that spring up without warning on hot summer days. You were meant for backyard grills and Fourth of July fireworks. Not mortar attacks. Not IEDs.

Come home to me soon,
Your Sophie

~*~

After breakfast, Travis and I toured the camp to see what kind of destruction we'd taken. Our concern was the academy. As we approached the building, the first thing I noticed was the green sniper fabric torn in strips. Right near the door. Fabric flapped eerily in the wind. Any other time of day, this area would have been filled with soldiers. We were fortunate. A tree at the front of the building was shredded like a giant weed eater had gotten hold of it. It reminded me of destruction from tornadoes back home.

We entered the building to find Thorstad doing the same thing, checking on damage.

"What did you see?" I asked.

"Pretty weird, an RPG went through the exterior door and all the way down the hallway. If a class had been in session, someone would have been killed. Other than the damage outside you've probably already seen, I didn't find anything new."

"Did you see the pickup?" Travis asked.

"The roof caved in. Another instance of, 'thank goodness no one was in there,'" Thorstad said." We were pretty lucky all in all. Except for that interpreter in his cot."

Travis and I looked at each other.

"We hadn't heard about him," I said slowly. Faces flashed through my mind. Someone's husband would never come home. I sucked in my breath. *Not Rasool.* "Was he one of ours from the academy?"

"No, he worked with the Afghan Army. He was asleep when the attack began. RPG went right through the roof of the tent. Poor guy probably never heard it coming."

"Is that the tent we had all those injuries in?" I asked.

"The same one." Thorstad shook his head. "I'm glad I'm going home. I'm done with this."

Thorstad. My comic-book-reading, candy-delivering friend. Home seemed pretty far away to me right then. Our yellow Craftsman on Wells that needed so much work felt like heaven.

We continued to walk the rest of camp. Classes were shut down, and there was not much else we could do except prepare for the upcoming week. We made the full circle and ended up back in our tent. Travis and I had a little more housekeeping to do. I sorted through papers in my room, placed more books and movies back on my shelves. I checked the news online before I dropped off to sleep.

Camp Paradise was mentioned, just not the kind of story we wanted to make:

Dispatch from a major news carrier:
October 27, 2011
Kandahar, Afghanistan

The attack began around 2:45 PM. Kandahar Training Center was fired upon by an unknown number of gunmen from positions in an empty three-story building a quarter of a mile from the camp. A spokesman said Taliban took responsibility for the attack. The base houses the Kandahar Provincial Reconstruction Team that leads efforts to aid the local government. Eight Americans were injured during the attack, seven of them soldiers and one civilian. An Afghan interpreter was reported killed.

I wrote an email to Sophie before falling asleep. It was late. I spent the last few hours straightening my room, but the truth was I was so amped up on adrenaline, I couldn't have slept if I had wanted to.

Sophie,
The academy was hit by four RPGs. I'm back in my tent. It's 4:00 AM. Trying to get some sleep. I'm exhausted.

Thank everyone for all the prayers. The academy

is pretty torn up.
Love you,
Mac

~*~

The academy was back in business. We finished our classes for the day and broke for lunch. Lack of sleep was starting to take a toll on me, so I decided to try and take an after-lunch nap. I pushed the tent door open.

Stockton was on the phone. There was so little privacy around here, I tried to pass his room quickly, so I didn't disturb his conversation. That was when I heard it–

"Yes, that's what I'm saying. They submitted paperwork the other day. I'm getting a Bronze Star."

Bronze Star and Stockton didn't belong in the same sentence. I wasn't an eavesdropper, but I stopped and listened to that conversation.

"I rescued a guy that was bleeding all over the place after the attack. Yeah, I bandaged him up. Saved his life, medics said. Now Colonel Smith is giving me an award. I had to turn in a narrative about what happened. When they read it, they were impressed. The colonel called me into his office and said they would present me with the Bronze Star at the next awards ceremony. Well, yes, it's a very prestigious award."

I forced myself to move on. My stomach lurched. I thought I would lose my lunch.

I turned back and headed to Travis's room. He wouldn't believe it.

And Glenn wasn't even here to refute Stockton's

story; he was back in the States recuperating.

I pounded on Travis's door until it vibrated like a drum.

"What?" Travis threw the door open, annoyed until he saw it was me.

"Let me in. You won't like this."

He ushered me into his room and shut the door. "What's up?"

"I just passed Stockton's room. He was on his phone. He's turned in a narrative on the attack."

"So?"

"So, he's a hero. We've been living with a hero and never knew it."

"Now you've got me confused."

"Stockton told his girlfriend he's to be awarded the Bronze Star." I sank down on the bed. "Stockton, a hero. Heaven help us."

Travis rubbed his hand across his forehead. "But you had to order him to help Glenn. Then he ran off when he saw he could push it off on me."

"I know."

"That's messed up."

"Yeah, it is."

A sharp crack reverberated through the tent. Travis and I jumped to our feet.

Travis grabbed his vest and jammed his helmet on his head. He would not be caught again on the wall with just his M-9.

I ran out Travis's door to grab my vest and helmet. As I passed Stockton's room, his door burst open, and he fell heavily against me and rolled onto the floor, blood spurted through his boot. *They fired into the tent and hit Stockton?* I ripped my T-shirt off, removed Stockton's boot and sock, and wrapped his foot to stop the bleeding.

Travis jumped across Stockton and checked the room. I was busy applying pressure to stop the flow of blood. Stockton moaned like a dying animal.

"Clear," Travis called out then leaned back into the hall. "There's no entry from the exterior. His M-9's laying on the floor." Travis turned to Stockton. "Did you shoot yourself, idiot?"

"Stockton?"

His face was white. His lips parted, and he mumbled. "I was just cleaning my M-9. I didn't think it was loaded."

The 'didn't think' part was too tempting to comment on, so I let it slide.

Travis ripped open a field dressing from his IFAK. He mashed it onto Stockton's foot as I removed the T-shirt. Stockton screamed.

The tent door opened and medics pushed their way in. Someone must have called them. Everyone in camp was on hyper alert since the attack.

"What happened?"

"Accidental discharge."

The first medic shook his head.

"Window or aisle?"

Stockton clutched his foot and was distracted enough by the question to stop his hysterical moaning. "What?"

"Congratulations. With an accidental discharge, you just won a ticket home. It's a joke. I was asking if you wanted a window or aisle seat. It would have looked better on your record if you'd transferred."

Travis and I backed off into my room and let the medics do their thing. They loaded Stockton up on a stretcher and took him off.

Word spread and MPs canvassed Stockton's room. They took our narratives and confiscated his weapon.

The next day when classes were over, Travis and I passed Stockton's room. His door was propped open. His room was vacant except for a few candy wrappers and some empty water bottles.

Travis poked his head in the door. "Looks like he's been sent home."

"Yeah." I stood in the doorway and surveyed the empty room.

Travis pushed past me. "Let's see if there's anything we can use before the new guy arrives, whoever he is."

It was customary to raid rooms as soon as someone went home. With a shortage of building materials and computer chairs, there was always something getting swapped around or re-purposed. The camp was a huge barter system. If one couldn't find what one needed, chances were, someone else had it and was willing to make a trade.

"I always liked this computer chair." Travis sat in the black, high-backed chair. He spun around.

"It's fancier than mine," I said. "And the back doesn't fall off."

Travis stopped spinning long enough to grab something off the floor. When he turned the chair around a single sock dangled from his hand. "Looks like he'll be one sock short when he gets home."

I took a sharp intake of breath when I saw it.

"Caribe" was stitched in tan letters on the toe. It was the mate to the sock someone had left for Phoenix to play with in my room. *Stockton had been my puppy savior.*

31

"I just got your e-mail with the picture of you."

"Which picture?"

"One of you and two other guys standing by a cement wall. The first guy has chestnut brown hair and a beard. He's a big guy, like a football player."

"That's Glenn. Remember me telling you about him when I was home on leave? I worked pretty closely with him. He's the one who was injured in the attack. That photo was taken seconds before we got hit."

"Is he all right?"

"I got an e-mail from him today. He's in rehab. He lost a leg in the blast." The words tasted bitter in my mouth. I was still trying to come to grips with Glenn's injuries. He'd taken a hit that had been rightfully mine. Seconds before the blast, I'd moved ahead along the wall, and Glenn moved into my former position. The thought made the hair on my arms stand up.

"Please tell him the next time you e-mail him that I'm praying for him."

"Yeah, I never thought he'd be injured the way he was. Glenn's been doing this for years, and he seemed untouchable."

"Who's the guy to your left in the picture, the one with the blond hair?"

"That's Travis. He's one of my friends here. He's even-keeled. As a matter of fact," I contemplated Sophie's face. "Sometimes I think his personality is a lot like yours."

"Is that good or bad?"

"It just hit me right now why I get along so well with Travis. He doesn't get upset easily about things, and he's a philosopher, thinks things through. Besides that, he always encourages me."

"That's sweet, babe."

"I'll miss all of them. You work, eat together, sleep in the same tent. It makes it hard to get along sometimes, too, but it forces you to work out your differences and function as a team."

"Mac." Sophie had stopped listening. She stared at something else in the picture. Her mouth opened in a pucker and her brow drew up. "This was taken before the attack?"

"Seconds before."

"The guys standing next to you are wearing polos, long pants, and boots. Why are you in shorts and a T-shirt?"

I sighed. What difference did it make what clothes I was wearing? Sophie was a detail person. "I'd already changed into my shorts and T-shirt because our work day was over."

"And running shoes," Sophie said.

"And running shoes."

"Mac." Sophie couldn't contain her excitement. Her face burst into a smile, the broadest I'd seen since I'd been in Afghanistan. "Mac, do you have your tennis shoes near you?"

I laughed out loud. The question was absurd. Everything in the room was within arms-length for me, even if I was sitting down. "Yes. They're on my feet, as a matter of fact." Her excitement made me smile and something about the way she looked caught me up in her wonder.

"Mac!" The urgency in her voice brought me back. "Mac, take your shoes off!"

I slipped my feet out of my tennis shoes. A tan dust line encircled my socks where they met the shoes, a reminder that a trip to the Happy Sock Laundry needed to happen soon. I was running out of clean underwear. "OK." I held up the empty shoes to the screen so she could see.

Sophie leaned forward in her seat. "Pull the insert out of your shoe!"

"What?"

"Pull that black thing out of the bottom of the inside of your shoe."

"Which one?"

"It doesn't matter. Just do it!"

A shiver crept up my spine. I didn't know what Sophie was playing at, but I had the distinct feeling Someone else was in the room with me, a warm, comforting Presence. That was crazy. It was late, and all the other guys had gone to bed. I shook the feeling off and pulled the foam liner out of the shoe. In the empty bed of the sole of my shoe, were words written in faded blue marker. In Sophie's handwriting, it read, "Psalm 91, The Lord is my refuge."

So that was why she wanted my shoes the day I was packing. I got my secret love note from her after all–

"I was so mad at God," Sophie said.

"What?"

"I prayed for you before you left, and I couldn't get this scripture out of my head. Remember, your boots weren't issued yet?"

"I remember."

"The night I hid that verse in your shoes, I complained to God with every word I scribbled. I wanted to write that verse in your boots because if you were ever under attack, I wanted you to have that verse with you. I knew there was nothing magical about it, but it was an agreement between God and me. It was my way of letting Him know I trusted Him to take care of you."

"That's one of the sweetest things you've ever done for me, Soph."

"Don't you get it?"

"What?"

"God knew which shoes you'd be wearing the hour of the attack."

32

"This six-man class is the best we've taught yet," I whispered to Travis who was standing beside me.

The APTS, or Advanced Police Tactics and Skills, students' graduation was underway. An attack couldn't stop our mission. The guys were all current police officers, three of the six from different cities. They had a drive to learn, which made it a thrill to teach them. They looked sharp in their steel blue uniforms. Hats straight, they approached the visiting Afghan general one at a time, saluted, and took their diploma.

They called Ace's name, and he approached the general. He marched proudly to the front in an exaggerated goose-step march that the Afghans employed. His salute was crisp. He moved down the line, and it was my turn to shake his hand.

"Congratulations," I said. "Good job." My chest swelled with pride. I remembered a story about a little boy struggling to throw a starfish back into the swelling waves. An old man came along beside the boy, watched him pitch the starfish back into the deep. There were hundreds of starfish washing up, stranded and dying on the hot sand. After a few moments, the old man addressed the boy. "Look at all these starfish, and you, only one little boy. What you are doing will not make a difference." The little boy looked up into the hardened face of the old man. "It makes a difference to this one," he said, as he pitched a solitary starfish back into the waves.

That was how I felt the day I handed Ace his diploma. As I shook his hand, sunlight flashed off his wrist. He was wearing the watch he'd won at Range. He was never without it. Normally, he would have had his sleeve rolled up so the other students could admire his trophy. He grinned at me, gave his memorized speech just as we had practiced. He turned sharply, held his diploma high above his head and shouted "Life!" in Pashto.

I didn't know who was prouder, Travis and me, or the students. We spent all week working with the students, perfecting marching and salutes.

After the ceremony, the students dispersed. They would be returning to their home cities, to their families. The academy had been a mini-vacation of sorts for them. No one shooting at them, they were able to eat and sleep and have camaraderie with guys who faced the same threats each day. I'd miss them.

~*~

The next day, a call came through on computer. It wasn't Sophie. I clicked on the button, and there he was...

"Hey, old man. How's it going?" I said, trying to sound upbeat, or however one was supposed to address someone who'd lost a leg.

"Hanging out here in rehab, back in the States," Glenn said. "How's life at Camp Paradise?"

"Things are winding down. The cigar club disbanded after you left."

"No?"

"You were the driving force behind it, you know that. Thorstad got orders to return to the States. He was up most of the last night packing. Bashir will miss him, I'm sure."

"It's for the best my friend, for the best. I told you he let his guard down with the locals. Sooner or later it would have come back to bite him in the—"

I heard a woman's voice off-screen. "It's time for your pain pills, Mr. Thurman."

"Just a minute, buddy," Glenn said. He lifted a small paper cup and threw what were probably pills into his mouth, grabbed a cup of water, and washed them down. He wiped his mouth with the back of his hand and tossed the paper cup into a bedside trashcan. "I can't complain too much. Food's decent. Physical therapy is torture, but hey, what do you expect?"

I found myself absentmindedly rubbing my calf and stopped.

"You want to know the worst part?" Glenn leaned toward the screen.

"What?"

"I wouldn't give the coffee here to that mutt of yours. It's unrecognizable as fit for consumption by humans. You have to really make an effort to turn coffee into burnt sludge. The other thing is, I have to wait until someone can take me outside to have a cigar."

"I pity the one who gets in the way of you and your cigar. Did they patch you up?"

"I've decided to become a pirate." He waved the stump of his leg in the air. Bruised, bandaged and swollen, it was anything but humorous. The pain pills must have kicked in. "I did come away from this with something valuable." He held what appeared to be a certificate. It had an official-looking stamp.

"WinCorp gave me a commendation."

"You deserve it," I said.

Glenn stopped grinning. "I'd trade it this minute to get my leg back."

"You took that hit for me."

"How do you figure?"

"When we moved down the wall, Travis ran to the tent to kit up. You ended up standing exactly where I had been. I should be the one in rehab. You should still be here, annoying people and smoking your ridiculous cigars."

"All that time spent mentoring you wasted." Glenn glanced away. He repositioned himself, dragging his stump onto a pillow. He grunted with effort.

"What do you mean?"

"I mean, McCann, you spend too much time blaming yourself. You've got to let things go, man. So what if I was standing in your spot? Would you have rather it been you? Would you rather go home to Sophie minus a leg?"

I shook my head. "No, truthfully, but I didn't want it to be you, either."

Glenn closed his eyes and exhaled. "That's just it. We don't get to choose."

~*~

All the glory was gone out of it, all the bright hope. Half the men in the tent had cleared out. What was once a hive of activity echoed like an empty tomb. Rumor was they were bringing in two new instructors that week. Rumors abounded.

As I'd told Stockton, wait a week and there'll be a new one. Stockton. One lonely sock with "Caribe" stitched into the toe, hung from my shelf. It served as a reminder that people aren't always as good or bad as they seem. If it weren't for Stockton, I'd never have gotten Phoenix home. He was the one who shoved the No Dog Gets Left Behind flyer under my door. He never got the chance to tell me, but the lone sock spoke for him. That was the brand of sock that someone tied into a dog toy and left for Phoenix to play with in my room, the same day the flier showed up.

There was a lot of gray in the world, certainly a lot of gray in Afghanistan.

Outside our tent, in the distance, more explosions added background noise. Somewhere in Kandahar, there were more injuries, more deaths.

I sighed and pulled up a video game on my computer, but the game didn't seem so important anymore.

Travis hammered on my door. "Mac, did you hear?"

"What?"

"During our graduation ceremony, the chief of police in downtown Kandahar was killed by a suicide bomb."

"That's the precinct where three of our students who just graduated work," I said.

"I know. Right after graduation, the students hit their posts to cover the station after the bombing. They never even got to make it home to celebrate with their families, just went straight to work."

Travis looked worn. I hadn't hung out with him for a few days. He pretty much kept to himself.

"You want to watch a movie?" I thought Travis was probably feeling the emptiness of the tent, too.

"Sure."

"Sophie just sent me a whole box of cinnamon rolls," I said.

Travis threw himself on my cot. I started up the external hard drive and popped the movie in. I searched around in my gorilla box and pulled out the cinnamon rolls, throwing two of them to Travis and keeping two for me.

"I've wanted to see this anyway," Travis said.

As the movie started up, I turned to Travis. "Makes me think of when I got my Ranger tab."

"Did you ever see any action?"

"No. I ended up getting out of the military shortly after I married Sophie."

Travis took a bite of the cinnamon roll and chewed. We would both be on sugar highs by the time the movie ended. "You regret getting out?"

"No, that's what I keep trying to tell Sophie. I don't regret it. I'd do it all over again for her. But I do miss the military."

"I'd never been anywhere but Brentwood, Tennessee, before I came here." Travis unwrapped two more rolls.

"Sometimes I don't know if coming here was the right thing to do or not," I said.

He looked at me and chewed thoughtfully. "Don't you think everything in your life prepared you for this point?"

"Such as?"

Travis held up his hand and ticked a point on each finger. "Such as being in the Army. You were already prepared to live overseas. You were used to adapting to different conditions. Then you served in the police department. That qualified you to train law enforcement officers here."

I held up a hand and stopped him at that point. "I have to tell you. I've been holding out on you."

Travis was silent. His eyebrows shot up.

"This will be hard to say because I've always considered you as one of my best friends at camp. But Glenn had me pegged early on. I was running."

"I thought so, too. Only I wanted to let you have your privacy," Travis said.

"Travis, I had a son, the best thing that ever entered my life, other than Sophie."

Travis's eyebrows bunched up, and his lips drew a tight line. "Where is he now? I never heard you mention him."

"He died. It was an accident. I had a wreck with him in my pickup truck."

"Man. That's hard." Travis's face was contemplative. Understanding passed across his expression. "Sophie blamed you for his death?"

"No, never. That's what made it so torturous. Every time Sophie tried to comfort me, it was like shoving a knife in my gut. It got to the point where I couldn't stand to be around her any longer. The guilt was killing me, killing our relationship. That's why I signed up for Afghanistan. I figured it was my only chance to heal myself, to save our marriage." I twisted open a bottle of power drink and took a swig. I thought of long nights in the most magical place, how I hated to leave her at the airport. I thought of the power of forgiveness and a good woman's love, and another thing I just couldn't put my finger on. "Yeah, it was hard. But it was strange. The thing I feared most never happened."

"You were afraid she'd leave you?"

"Yeah."

Travis stared hard at a camel spider stalking across the tent floor. Without hesitation, he squashed it with his boot. Never missing a beat, he spoke what was in the back of my mind. "That's ironic, isn't it? You were afraid Sophie would leave you, and she stayed. I knew Tricia would stay forever, and she left."

The sadness that settled over the room was so disheartening I had to break it. I grabbed a box of cinnamon rolls to see if there were any left, but it felt light. I held the box up and shook it. Somehow, we'd managed to empty an entire box. An envelope fell out. Another one of Sophie's cards.

Travis's hand closed over the envelope. He waved it in front of me. "What price will you pay to get this back?"

"I think I've already fed you half a box of cinnamon rolls."

"Good point," he said.

The card slid out of the envelope and fell open to the floor. There was a drawing inside.

"Sophie usually writes stuff," I said, picking up the card. "I've never had her draw me a picture before."

"What's it a picture of?" Travis asked.

I studied the scratchy drawing. "Looks like a patrol car. Aw, I don't know. Sophie's a better writer than an artist. Here." I pushed the card at him. "You tell me what it is."

Travis studied it, and the corners of his mouth stretched wide across his face.

33

"It's a baby carriage," Travis said.

"A what?" My hand shook as I grabbed the card from Travis and studied it. It still looked like a patrol car to me. I stopped the movie and pulled the Internet up. I didn't see Sophie's green symbol. She wasn't online.

Travis jumped off the cot. "You're going to be a daddy." He clapped me hard on the back between my shoulder blades.

I was still standing there staring at the crudely drawn box with wheels and a handle.

A baby.

I put the card down and fished my phone out of my pocket. It rang and then went to voice mail. "Come on, Sophie. Pick up." I punched her number again with the same result. I didn't know what to do with myself. I couldn't contain the happiness that swept over me rushing like a flood. I felt giddier than if I'd just smoked three cigars. I paced the floor, set the phone down, then picked it up again. I stared at the display and willed her number to show up. I wanted to hear it from her lips. I wanted to hear her say she was to be a mommy.

"I have to get home," I told Travis, still staring at my phone.

"You don't have too much longer. Oh, man, I'm so happy for you." He beamed. "This calls for a celebration." He ran down the hall shouting Thorstad's name.

In a minute, they were both back in my room.

Thorstad, the gentle giant, grabbed my hand and pumped it. "Congratulations, man. You will never know how that will change your life until you experience it."

He didn't know I'd already experienced it, and yes, I knew how it would change my life. I felt as if this child was a sign that we could go on. A sign that Sophie and I would make it after all.

"Cigar Club," Travis shouted. "I have the perfect way to celebrate. I just got a brand new box of cigars in honor of Glenn's award. Let's go have a smoke."

"I'm in." Thorstad moved toward my door.

Travis stopped and looked back. "You coming, McCann? You have to. You're the man of the hour."

I stuck my phone in my cargo shorts in case Sophie tried to call me back, and we all marched out the door.

The night was blue-black once again. Stars were everywhere. I'd miss that sky. Everything looked brighter that night. Everything looked good.

A baby.

We gathered around the bench, the last of the Camp Paradise Cigar Club. Travis broke out his cigars and felt around in his pockets. That was when it hit me. I ran my hand around the inside of my pocket until my fingers closed on a metallic object. I pulled it from my pocket. Glenn's lighter glinted in the moonlight. I'd kept it for good luck. "Hey." I caught Travis's attention.

He stared at my palm. "Where did you get that?"

"It's Glenn's. I found it on the ground the day he was hit."

Travis held his hand out, and I placed the lighter in his palm. It was symbolic, like the passing of a baton. Travis's grin spread across his face.

"I can't think of a better person to receive this," I said.

"Thanks, man. I wish Glenn were here to celebrate with us, but I'm glad he's back in the States. He did more than enough time here."

I nodded agreement.

Three cigars glowed in the Afghanistan night.

Travis tipped his cigar toward Thorstad and me. "To Glenn. May he recover quickly."

"Hear, hear," Thorstad said then nodded toward me. "To Mac and Sophie and the new little McCann."

We stood out there an hour or so until the cigars were stubs. My head was numb. Life was good. "I'm going back inside to check my e-mail," I said.

"We're coming, too." Travis put out the last of his cigar.

Thorstad did likewise.

We barreled into the room and pulled up my e-mail, but there was no letter from Sophie. Not yet anyway. "I'll send her some flowers." An electric current ran up my back. This was right. I rolled my old chair up to the desk and pulled up the number on the Internet for Antonella's Florist.

"Antonella's Florist, this is Anthony. How may I help you?"

I leaned forward in my computer chair while I pulled my credit card out of my wallet.

"Anthony! This is Mac McCann."

I ran my fingers over the raised numbers on the plastic card. "I have an order to place with you."

There were sounds of paperwork being shuffled.

"Look, Anthony, can you set me up with some flowers?"

"We have some gorgeous bouquets, just in. If you'd like to come by the shop, I can show them to you." Sounds of an ink pen scratching on paper came through the line.

"That'd be great, but I'm in Afghanistan," I said.

"Oh, I am sorry. We are always proud to help those who are serving overseas."

"Thanks, Anthony. Can you suggest what to order?"

"Of course. We are running a special on our 'Love in Bloom.'"

I glanced around the room. The photo of Sophie and me at the Fourth of July fireworks was on my shelf.

"Mr. McCann, are you still there?"

"Yes. Just thinking. This has to be the best bouquet ever."

"I have our Hugs and Kisses Bouquet with red roses."

"Great. Can you do that and make sure it has a special touch?"

"And that would be?"

I cupped my hand around the phone and asked Anthony to add something. I hoped it would make Sophie smile. I leaned back in my chair and caught myself just before it tipped over. I quickly lunged forward. I couldn't hold it in any longer. I hadn't been this happy in a long time. "Anthony, I haven't told too many people yet, but I just found out. I'm going to be a daddy."

"But Mr. McCann, are you not in Afghanistan?" and then, "I am sorry, I do not know what came over me. That is none of my business. Please forgive."

I laughed with a burst of joy from deep in my chest. Like a flood when a dam has broken, flowing everywhere, bringing new life to a dry land. "Yes, I'm in Afghanistan. Let's just say our baby's due to a little something called beach magic."

"The order has been placed. It will be delivered this afternoon."

"I have your word on that, Anthony?"

"You have my word, Mr. McCann. If I must, I will deliver them myself to make sure she gets them. Take good care of yourself. You must make it home in one piece for your new little one."

"Good man. You have a great day, and call me Mac."

Travis stood to leave. "I'm going on to bed. Let me know when she gets the flowers. Congratulations, again."

I grabbed his hand then threw him a bear hug. We would be brothers for the rest of our lives from this experience. "Thanks, man."

Thorstad came around and grabbed me. "If I don't see you tomorrow, best of luck. It was a real honor serving with you."

"E-mail me when you get your new assignment," I said.

"Will do." He clapped my back one more time then followed Travis down the hall.

Silence settled on my room. I was tired but so amped about the baby I couldn't sleep. I lay on my back on my cot, stared at the tan stitching on the roof seams. Each stitch led to the next and the next. Maybe Travis was right. Maybe my life was like those stitches. Maybe it was ordered, and everything in my life prepared me for that point.

I thought about what Sophie must be doing. I wished she'd call me back. I must have dozed off because a few hours later my phone rang. I knew who it was. It had to be her. I fumbled around in the semi-dark, grabbed the phone, and punched the answer button.

"Mac?"

"Soph!"

"You've been eating cinnamon rolls. I can tell," she said.

"I love you, you crazy woman."

"Did you like my drawing?"

"I couldn't figure out what it was. Travis had to tell me."

"Travis saw it?"

"He was in the room with me when the envelope fell out of the box."

It was enough to hear her breathe on the phone. Enough to know she was carrying our child.

"I love you," I said.

"I love you, too."

"There's someone at the door. Do you want to wait while I get it?" Sophie asked.

"Of course."

"I'm putting you on speaker," Sophie said.

I heard her footsteps as she carried the phone with her. I listened to the door being unlatched. Then a familiar voice.

"Good afternoon. Are you Sophie McCann?"

Sophie made a sharp intake of breath. "Yes, I am."

I heard the man shuffle his feet. "I am so glad to meet you."

"You are?" Sophie asked.

And then, he must have given her the flowers because I heard a little squeak of joy.

"They are so beautiful. I can't believe you sent me flowers," Sophie sounded giddy.

Then, "I'm Anthony Portulaca from Antonella's Florist." Anthony, the sly old dog. He actually did deliver the flowers himself.

I chuckled under my breath.

"Nice to meet you, I have my husband on speaker phone," Sophie said.

He yelled into the phone. I could picture him bent over the speaker. "Hello, Mr. Mac."

"Hello to you, too, Anthony."

"Ah, Mr. Mac, she is as beautiful as you said."

"Thank you, Anthony. I wish I were there to see her with you."

"And hello, little beach baby. I am so happy to meet you."

Sophie giggled, and it sounded like her hand was cupped over the phone. "He was speaking to my belly. How did he know I'm pregnant?"

"I told him when I ordered the flowers. Sorry, Soph. I was so happy I just couldn't hold it in."

"May I carry the flowers in for you?"

"Yes, thank you. Come this way."

I heard the door again and their footsteps on the wood flooring.

"A quaint Craftsman, circa nineteen-fifty, I believe? And look at the floors! You must have refinished them yourselves."

Hours and hours of me running that darn floor buffer we'd rented. It took a while to figure the thing out, but not before I'd put a dent in the drywall and bashed the edge of a doorframe.

"The kitchen is this way. Please watch the step down into the kitchen. The floors are a little uneven. We haven't done the floors in the kitchen yet."

"Ah, but it is glorious, glorious. The woodwork, the crown molding."

"It's all Mac's doing. I don't think there's a spot in this house he hasn't worked on."

I heard what sounded like a glass vase being set down.

"For you. You want me to read the card for you?" Anthony asked.

"Well, that's OK," Sophie said.

But then I heard paper rustling and Anthony's voice again. "It says, 'Sophie, I can't wait to get home to see you and our baby. Thank you for hanging in there, and for loving me even when things were tough. All my love, Mac.'"

I squeezed my eyes shut in embarrassment. Did you really have to read that out loud, Anthony?

There was an awkward silence, and then Sophie, gracious as always said, "Thank you. That was very sweet of you to read that to me." She sniffled.

Listening to all this and not being there was killing me. I tried to picture Sophie's face, wished I had her on live video instead of the phone.

"There, there. I did not mean to make you cry. It is a happy time. You should be happy," Anthony said.

"It's not your fault. Pregnancy makes women emotional. But you're right. It's a happy time. The happiest of all times, and soon, Mac will be home to share it with me."

"I must be getting back to the shop. I am so honored to finally meet the beautiful Sophie."

"Thank you again, Anthony," I yelled over the

speaker, but I didn't think he heard me.

"Yes, thank you again," Sophie said.

Then I heard a vehicle pull away and the front door close.

"Mac?"

"I'm here."

"The flowers are beautiful. There are roses and tulips and my favorite. How did you know to send Gerber daisies?" I reveled in the excitement in her voice. She sounded like the Sophie I used to know. I was also a little proud of myself over the Gerbers. I'd described them to Anthony, and between the two of us, we'd figured out that was what she had planted in the yard last year.

"I saw you grow them in the backyard last summer. I remembered."

And then I heard a sharp intake of breath. Sophie found it.

"A blue pinwheel, just like Little Mac's," she said.

I tried to speak, but my throat closed up. I tried to breathe, loosen up. Swallowed.

"I asked for that for you," I whispered. "I wanted to honor our son. With a new baby coming, I wanted him to know we will never, ever forget him."

"That is the most romantic thing you've ever done for me."

"I love you, Soph. I always have."

The time couldn't pass fast enough. I was ready to get on a plane right then. I'd have stolen Thorstad's ticket if I thought I could get away with it.

34

"Students have been dismissed due to a VBIED detonated downtown, near police headquarters," the sergeant said as he stopped me at the gate.

I turned to go back to my tent. There would be no students for me to escort, no classes.

"Our guys are tied up because of this. Since you're walking back, can you escort Gul Hadi to the barbershop?"

I looked past him and saw Gul waiting patiently at the gate with Bashir. My heart went out to them. This was the only world they knew, a world where they had to dodge explosions just to get to work. I glanced back at the sergeant. To him, Gul was just another worker he was letting in the gate. He didn't know he was more to me than that. The man was my friend. "Sure, I'll escort them."

The sergeant waved Gul and Bashir over and returned to his workstation.

A smile engulfed Gul's face when he saw it was me. He rushed up and grabbed my hand in a warm handshake.

Bashir jumped up and down at my side and tugged at my sleeve. I fished in the pocket of my cargo pants and handed Bashir a pop. He hastily unwrapped it and stuck it in his mouth. A white sucker stick protruded from his apple-shaped cheeks.

Gul took my arm and walked beside me. "How are you?"

"I am excellent, my friend. I leave for the States in

eleven days," I said.

"You are leaving for good?"

I nodded.

Gul spoke slowly so I could understand, trying to make himself heard over the grinding noise of Mine Resistant Ambush Protected vehicles rushing past us, responding to the explosion downtown.

"*Yaar zenda sohbat baqee*. It means as long as the friendship lives, there will be more conversations," Gul said. His generally jovial attitude was dampened.

I wondered if he would miss our friendship as much as I would. It was an odd thing to make friends with someone as far away geographically and culturally as Gul. I couldn't just schedule a vacation to come visit when the whim hit me. It sobered me to think this would likely be one of the last times I ever held a conversation with the man.

"I'll keep in touch with you. I want news about Bashir's first days in school. He's a smart boy. He'll do well."

"He is a bright boy," Gul said. "And my greatest desire is an education for him." Sadness crept from his voice.

I started to ask him what prospects Bashir had for higher education, but what was the point? If he said none, what could I do about it? The question sat in the back of my mind as we walked.

Out of the corner of my eye, Bashir kicked his soccer ball then ran ahead and trapped it with his foot. The thought of having another child filled my chest until I thought I would burst from happiness. Through Bashir, I had experienced the joy of being a father again, though secondhand from observing Gul. Still, the relationship between the two was what I had dreamed I'd always have with my own child. I couldn't wait to get home and be on hand for the birth of our little McCann. I nodded toward Bashir's lanky form. Even for a four-year-old, he was tall. "He's growing."

Gul's expression swelled with pride. "Yes, and he is strong."

Bashir darted ahead of us, kicking his black and white soccer ball to the left, to the right. His thin legs were a blur. Showing off. The ball was so lopsided I didn't see how he could even control it. Stitches on one seam had stretched and left an egg-shaped bump that sent the ball into an erratic zigzag each time his foot made contact.

We walked a few more feet as trucks blasted past us making conversation difficult.

Finally, there was a lull in the line of vehicles, and I turned toward Gul. "My wife is having a baby." I was still in awe of it. It probably wouldn't feel real until I got home. I kept repeating it to myself as if I'd dreamed it and was afraid the dream would vanish.

Gul stopped on the side of the road, grasped my hand, and shook it firmly. "That is excellent news, Mac."

I felt my face draw up in a smile. "Yes, I am very, very happy."

Shouts from across the road turned my head. A soldier gestured wildly toward Bashir. An MRAP sped toward the boy. Dust swirled from beneath the tires of the beast, and exhaust fumes choked us.

My heart felt like it would leave my chest as Gul and I took off at a sprint.

The vehicle could not possibly stop quickly enough.

Someone on the other side of the road saw what was happening and shouted at the driver.

But there was no way the driver would hear them encased as he was behind the impenetrable windshield and armor plated cab. He probably couldn't see Bashir.

Gul called out frantically in Dari to his son, waved his arms at him, but Bashir's focus was solely on the ball. He never saw his dad's desperate motions.

My breath caught in my chest. I willed Bashir to hear his father's warning, but there was no way he could hear Gul's shouts above the grinding, diesel-fueled noise. Bashir gave the ball a powerful kick, straight into the path of the MRAP. His eyes were still on the ball. He never saw the heavy vehicle bearing down on him. Instead, he took off right into the path of the monster to retrieve his only prized possession.

I ran as I had never run in my life. I pushed my legs and lungs past their limits of endurance. Closer. The fabric of his shirt was between my fingers, then the flesh of his arm. I dug in with my nails. I heaved his spindly body tucked against my chest and rolled toward the chain-link fence. Then blackness.

Gul pleaded in Dari, and I slowly opened my eyes to the unforgiving Kandahar sun. A shadow fell across me, and I looked up into Gul's face, which was riddled with concern.

Chunks of gravel bit into my back. A warm sticky liquid ran down my forehead. I reached across and drew back with blood on my hand.

Gul's strong hand wrapped around mine and gently pulled me to my feet. I wavered for a minute and tried to get my balance.

Sitting on the ground next to me was the best trophy I'd ever won for a base slide. Bashir was crying but not from pain. He wailed to his father, "I lost my pop." He was dirty, but he was whole. Bashir's eyelashes curled thick with powder. The whites of his eyes stood stark against the monotone background of his dust-encased face. My arms and hands were covered in the same powder. We were indistinguishable. It was a baptism of dust.

"Thank you. Thank you!" Gul wouldn't stop saying it. I stared into his grateful eyes, and at that moment a knowing passed between us. A bond that crossed borders and governments, something only fathers of sons understood.

"*Awlaad-hoy-e watan, omeed-e watan.* A nation's children, a nation's hope," Gul said.

I nodded. I understood. Better than Gul knew.

We resumed our walk to the barbershop in silence. I dropped Gul and Bashir off and walked thoughtfully back to my tent. My head was still back there on the road to Camp Paradise's front gate. Slowly my emotions were playing catch up to the events. My insides quaked. I moved quickly to my tent and gathered my shower stuff.

Inside the Conex, I was thankful I was the only one. Even greater luck, pump trucks had been there recently, and the drains were working. I threw a blast of hot water on in the shower stall and stripped dusty clothes from my shaking body. They fell in a muddy heap on the damp floor.

I turned my face up to the stream of water. Hot water stung until my eyes threatened to tear up. Abrasions on my elbows and hands throbbed with each pulse of water. Gravel had chewed my skin like a cheese grater. I scrubbed the cuts as best I could with soap and washed the blood and mud away.

What would have happened if I had been a second too late? But I hadn't been. I managed to save another man's son. The look on Gul's face was more payment than I needed or deserved. It helped fill in part of the hole left by Little Mac's death. In Gul's face, I saw what great love he had for his son. In that instant, I saw the hopes and dreams he held for him.

God, forgive me for Little Mac's death.

I held my arm out, shaking from adrenaline. A ribbon of water snaked its way from my shoulder and down my outstretched arm. I was mesmerized by it. The ribbon pushed silt ahead of itself until the dirty band reached my fingertips and then spiraled down the drain. It was as if the last of my guilt and shame swirled down the drain with it.

I was crushed, poured out.

And then I didn't feel alone. The God Sophie loved was there. The one she'd talked about incessantly over the years. I'd been jealous of Him at times. I didn't comprehend how she could so intimately know and worship Someone she wasn't able to see. But now I understood because He was here with me. I felt His presence even in a muddy shower. Instinctively, I knew. He'd known my name all along, and He'd been biding His time, waiting for me to acknowledge His name, Jesus Christ.

It was suddenly as clear to me as the clean water running down my body.

I was as precious to Him as Bashir was to Gul, as Little Mac was to me.

The only proper response was worship.

It was what Sophie had been trying to tell me all along. I grabbed onto it like a lifeline with both my hands and held on.

King David worshiped when he'd lost his son. He'd stumbled onto a secret none of his servants understood. His relationship with God was the only assurance he needed that he would see his boy again.

Down at my feet, the remnant of dust turned to mud, swirled around, and disappeared down the drain. Little Mac and I were not alone that day in the chaos of my pickup truck. Jesus was with us, though I could not see or feel Him at the time. He felt my horror, heard my cries. He finally answered the pleading of my heart from so many months ago.

The night I sat alone in a car in a funeral home parking lot and begged a starless sky for forgiveness. He forgave me.

35

Days later, I was packing when I glanced in the scratched mirror taped to the shelves above my desk. I needed to get a haircut. It wouldn't do to see Sophie and look so scraggly.

Besides, I wanted to see Gul and Bashir one last time.

I pushed more T-shirts to the bottom of my duffle bag and closed it. I would finish packing after I got my haircut. I grabbed my backpack, stuffed my wallet in it, walked out of the tent, and down the path to the barbershop.

Walking the perimeter of Camp Paradise probably for the final time, I pushed open the door to Abdul's. I'd had my eye on two lapis lazuli stones in the window that looked like the night sky in Kandahar. I picked the stones up and turned them over in my hands. Weighty, they were cool to the touch, smooth like polished glass. The silver flecks of light covering each stone reminded me of the thousands of stars that littered the deep, blue-black Afghanistan sky. A streak of silver across the base of one looked like the shooting star I saw the night I learned Glenn's secret pain.

She wouldn't think it was the most romantic gift, but I couldn't think of a better thing to represent the country. They made me think of the hidden value in people and in countries.

When I'd arrived, I had ambitions to see a change in the situations of the local citizens. I'd hoped to see a strong police force develop and see people have the opportunity to govern themselves. But after being in-country, I saw my timeframe for all that happening was way off. I was still hopeful the people of Afghanistan would one day live in peace. In the meantime, I was happy that I was able to train some of the bravest law enforcement officers I'd ever met.

Abdul rang up my purchase and handed me the lapis lazuli in a plastic bag. I stuffed them down in my backpack, moving Little Mac's pinwheel to an outer pocket. The little fins were covered in tan dust. I wiped them clean with my finger until I could see the shiny blue plastic again.

It traveled all the way to Kandahar with me and would go home. At night, when I was alone in my tent, I'd pull the pinwheel out and watch it spin. It was the only thing I had left of Little Mac.

I hurried across the courtyard and over to the barbershop. I glanced at my watch. It was almost closing time, but I hoped Gul could work me in. I pushed the door to the barbershop open.

Gul looked up when I came in. Then, a broad smile stretched across his face, and he nodded hello. He was just finishing up a customer's haircut.

Bashir was there, perched on an empty barber chair. He ran across the floor when he saw me. Held his hand out. I patted my pockets in mock distress, held my bare hands out.

Bashir looked crestfallen. He turned to sit back in the barber's chair. I didn't have the heart to tease him further. "Bashir," I called.

He turned back, an expectant, shy smile on his face.

I dug in my backpack and produced a brand new

bag of pops. Sophie had come through for me.

I handed Bashir the entire bag. He had a look on his face as if he'd just won the lottery. He galloped to the chair, tore into the plastic bag, and shoved a cherry lollipop in his mouth. He cradled the open bag like treasure. I never thought I'd get so much satisfaction from watching a small child eat a sucker.

"Bashir, sit in that barber's chair with your bag of pops. I want to take a picture to send Sophie," I said.

"Who is Sophie?" Bashir asked. He rolled the sucker around in his mouth.

I turned the bag of pops around so I could photograph all the colors and straightened Bashir's shirt. "Sophie is my wife. Maybe one day you'll meet her."

"Is she pretty?"

I reached into my wallet and pulled out a photo of Sophie, the one I took at the fireworks show when she was pregnant with Little Mac. The same night I bought her the pinwheel for our baby boy.

"She is pretty!"

"The prettiest woman in the world," I said quietly and then to Bashir, "Sit up straight now, and I'll take your picture so Sophie can see what a great boy you are."

I backed up with my phone centered on Bashir's face. My finger was poised over the button. "Say Pumperni...say 'bread,'" I stammered, catching myself and changing the word at the last minute.

"Bread!" said Bashir. He smiled with the sucker stick poking through a gap where a baby tooth had been.

I snapped the photo and set my backpack on the floor. "Thank you, Bashir."

The ever-present smell of menthol enveloped the room. Fluorescent lights behind the barber's chairs gave off a tilted glow. It was a pleasant feeling now. The past had been cut away from the room.

I was up next, and I leaned back and closed my eyes as Gul took scissors and trimmed at my mass of unruly hair.

"Not too short this time, OK? I'm going home." Home, the word rang in my head, like a song that wouldn't go away.

"You want your beard shaved?"

I hadn't thought about it. I was getting rather fond of the beard. It had come to represent all I'd gone through, all I'd grown through. Every time I looked in the mirror I heard Travis's excited proclamation, "We'll have a Manliest Beard Contest!" and it made me laugh.

I ran my fingers through the red hair covering my chin. It was a great beard, no doubt, but for back home, it should probably be neater. "No, I'm going to keep it. Can you just trim it a little, shape it up?"

Gul nodded his approval. "A beard is a fine thing for a man."

"A very fine thing." I grinned then made myself sit still so he could finish trimming.

Gul finished his masterpiece, brushed loose hair from my neck, then applied talcum powder.

Out of the corner of my eye, I noticed Bashir get up from his barber's chair and wander over to my backpack. His gaze roved over the pockets. I was amused. He was probably looking for another bag of pops. He thought that magic black bag produced them. Bashir's eyes came alive. I watched his hand reach for a pocket in my backpack, and my heart pounded when I saw what it was he was after.

Little Mac's pinwheel.

Bashir's eyes looked pleadingly from the pinwheel to me and then back again.

No, not that. You can have anything but that. A familiar, clammy panic clawed its way up my back again. Would I ever be rid of it? This pinwheel was the last connection with my boy.

Thinking quickly, I motioned for Bashir to come over. He complied, but I could tell he was still focused on the prize he'd found in my backpack.

I yanked my survival bracelet roughly off my wrist. Made it myself from one continuous line of black five-fifty cord. I winced as the cord raked across the still fresh scratch marks on my palm. Marks from the gravel the day I'd rescued Bashir. If pulled loose at the right place the whole bracelet came unraveled. Like my life. That's how I felt when I saw Bashir looking at the pinwheel. I wadded the bracelet up and placed it in Bashir's tiny hand.

"There, nice, huh?" Who was I kidding? He'd probably seen a million of these. Every soldier who walked through the door had one. And, as I suspected, he was not placated. He humbly shook his head and pointed toward my pack.

I grabbed the backpack and ripped the pocket open, surprised at the violence of my own actions, but if I were to do it, I had to get it over with fast. My heart pounded in my ears. I found the stick, as smooth in my fingers as the day I'd placed it in Little Mac's. His face had beamed with joy, a little boy's laughter I would never erase from my memory.

I placed the toy in Bashir's outstretched hand, and it was done. My last link with Little Mac severed. He clutched the pinwheel to his chest as if it was a treasure. It felt like my heart tore inside me.

All that was left to me was a cold marble tombstone in Dogwood Hill Cemetery with a boy's name, date of birth, and date of death.

Bashir's face lit up. He ran circles, spinning the bright blue pinwheel. He laughed as the breeze made the little wheel spin, spin as it was created to.

Gul had been watching all this closely as he swept up shop. Every now and then when I looked up, I noticed his eyes studying us, Bashir and me. He seemed to be struggling with a thought. His brows were drawn together, and his whole being appeared to be weighed down with an invisible burden.

I was his last customer of the day.

"I would like to drink chai with you." He placed the broom and dustpan against the chipped tile wall.

"Now?" I'd really rather have left. That way I wouldn't have to watch the pinwheel spin around the room.

"Yes, I am done for the day. Please, do the honor of drinking with me." He carefully packed his barber tools away in the drawers of his stand. He meticulously placed each pair of scissors, each comb exactly where he wanted it. His life was orderly at camp. I bet he longed for the same order outside those walls. In Kandahar, life was unpredictable.

"Please wait while I change clothes." He emerged in a moment dressed in his native garb, the cream prayer cap perched solemnly on his head.

I didn't know what he was up to, but he was deep in thought.

We ordered at Green Bean's window.

"Two chai, please." I dug in my pack for my

wallet, but Gul waved me aside.

"I am paying today, please."

With a look from him, I knew I would insult him if I objected. He was so solemn. I had never seen Gul this way before. I knew he had a lot on his mind, but this was not the parable-quoting man who was so quick to laugh. I drank on Gul's tab.

We gathered our drinks and claimed a table facing the mountains. I loved those mountains. The bases were shrouded in fog, and the jagged tops gleamed most of the year, white with snow. I tried to memorize them. I'd leave them soon.

Bashir took his place at the table beside his father, mischief all over his face. I never knew what he was planning next. The next minute he was up, running circles around the patio, spinning his new toy in the wind.

"Bashir, come here," Gul called in Dari.

The boy immediately stopped at his father's side. For all his energy, Bashir was an obedient son. He never questioned Gul, just did as he was told. Such trust in his green eyes as he gazed up into his father's eyes, eyes that now filled with tears. What stirred up this emotion?

Gul took my right hand, his brown hand hard and sinewy from years of working barber's shears. Though he couldn't be much older than I was, in a way, Gul seemed ancient. Though I was a police officer and had seen and heard things that would age the average American, Gul lived in a land that had no pity on man, and his body was ravaged by it.

He took Bashir's hand and placed it on mine. He spoke to Bashir in Dari and then turned to me.

I swallowed down the question that came to my

lips because I knew he was not finished speaking. My head pounded. I was jittery. Before I could get the question out of my mouth, Gul turned to me.

"We can no longer stay in this country."

I knew the weight of his words because I knew that he loved this place. The mountains, the rose bushes blooming in such an unexpected place as a military camp.

Gul's face had aged significantly since the day we met. Lines crept around his mouth, and his eyes seemed sunken. He placed his hand over mine as I held Bashir's. "I told you many months ago, the dreams I had for my only son. The situation is such here that I fear he will never have the opportunity for the education I want for him."

Bashir grinned up at me, a gapped-tooth smile. His baby teeth were dropping away, his childhood with them.

"I am asking you, Mac McCann, to give us sponsorship once you are in the United States. I will see that he gets an education. One day he can return and help the people of his birth."

"You mean you want Sophie and I to sponsor your family?"

"Yes, that is what Sergeant Thorstad called it. I asked him for a way to make sure Bashir gets an education, and he said that we need a sponsor in America."

Sophie's instructions came back to me. I heard her in my mind the day she told me, "If there is anything else you stumble on that we can do for them, you already have my agreement, even if you can't get hold of me first."

I knew what she would tell me to do. She'd tell me

to say yes.

Our lives were about to change once again. For now, we would not only be the parents of a newborn, but we would also help a family navigate the waters of temporary residency. My throat was tight. For a moment, I couldn't speak. Then I grabbed Gul in a bear hug. I wanted to reassure him. I wanted to let him know how seriously I took this duty. Father to father.

A new light was in Gul's eyes, bright and profound.

I'd carved my name on a bench my first week in Afghanistan. Some would make a difference greater than a name on a bench.

Bashir Hadi would be such a one.

36

Thorstad refused to give up his ticket. I was only joking anyway. I put in my time and disembarked from my final flight.

I was almost home. The fifteen-hour flight from Dubai was again torturous, but I didn't mind. I was out of my seat as soon as they gave me the go-ahead. I grabbed my bag from the overhead, nearly missed hitting the passenger's head behind me.

Then they gave us the go, and I moved as rapidly as I could down the aisle, down that tunnel-vision corridor that wound until one felt as if one was lost in an awful dream. But I wasn't lost. I was almost home.

Everyone I passed I wanted to yell at that I was going to see my wife and my unborn child.

The smells and sights were familiar again.

I was moving, and my feet couldn't stand still. I was on the escalator and had second thoughts. I should have double-timed it down the stairs. Why did this thing move so slowly?

The airport was crowded. I scanned for Sophie. The crowd moved along so slowly. Too slowly.

Sophie, where are you?

My duffle bag was stuffed with last minute items. The strap cut into my shoulder, but I didn't care.

And then, I saw her, standing at the side of the crowd. She hadn't seen me yet.

No words. Just motion. Just momentum. I threw my bag to the floor and ran to grab Sophie, pulled her into my arms, and twirled her around. The surprised look on her face reminded me, and I set her down gently.

The waist of her thin cotton top was rounded, a little bump.

I bent, planted a kiss on her belly.

Sophie had tears running down her face. They dripped off her chin and mingled with mine as I pressed my lips to hers and pulled her in.

"I'm never leaving again." I kept saying it. "Never, Soph, never again."

She repeated my words until I muffled them with my lips.

I was just an awkward nineteen-year-old again, sitting in a foggy-windowed truck, kissing my girl for the first time. I pulled her as close to me as I could, and she buried her face in the crook of my neck. I kissed the top of her head, breathed in her blackberry-woodsy perfume.

~*~

The sun swept over Dogwood Hill Cemetery to the west. It dragged long shadows across the tombstones and set the carved words in even greater relief against the white stone.

We stood at Little Mac's grave. Grass covered the once-raw earth. Sophie carefully arranged flowers in the little urn attached to the headstone. Silhouetted against the sky, she bent low to see the name inscribed on the stone. She traced the letters with her finger. Sophie guided the pudgy fingers of our ten-month-old, the light of my life, my precious daughter. She had my reddish hair, curling in ringlets around her face, but her features were unmistakably her mother's. The same delicate forehead and pouty lips.

"See here?" I pointed so Maddie could see the letters. "That's your big brother's name."

Letters she didn't understand yet, but one day she would.

"Hmm," Maddie mumbled.

She was more interested in two brand new pinwheels she clutched in her tiny fist. One pink. One blue.

Sophie patted the ground next to the headstone. "Help Mommy put them here for your brother."

Together they bent down and planted the metallic pinwheels in the soft, warm earth.

I took Sophie's hand and squeezed it gently. She tilted her chin up and gave me one of the smiles I so lived for.

Our hardship had been a priceless gift in disguise.

A gift, bought with endless stretches of loneliness, paid for with tears, obtained at high cost through self-sacrifice.

The gift of appreciation was a gift I'd guard with my life.

A commotion from behind the headstone turned my head.

Licorice-headed, six-year-old Bashir emerged from behind Little Mac's headstone, and my heart felt as if it would burst with joy.

I could never have anticipated our halls would be full of toy cars once again, that our house would explode with a little boy's shouts. Gul managed to find an apartment only blocks from our home, and Bashir accumulated quite a collection of cars and track for them to roll along our living room floor. Sophie thought I spoiled him, but I didn't feel that way at all.

Bashir ran in circles, spinning a bright blue pinwheel. He ran over to Little Mac's headstone, and at my urging planted his next to the other two, then threw himself giggling into my arms.

He was already one of the top students in his class.

One day he'd return to Afghanistan, but for now, I'd enjoy his laughter.

A breeze kicked up, and three pinwheels spun comfortingly.

Spun as they were created to.

Thank you...

for purchasing this Harbourlight title. For other inspirational stories, please visit our on-line bookstore at www.pelicanbookgroup.com.

For questions or more information, contact us at customer@pelicanbookgroup.com.

Harbourlight Books
The Beacon in Christian Fiction™
an imprint of Pelican Book Group
www.pelicanbookgroup.com

Connect with Us
www.facebook.com/Pelicanbookgroup
www.twitter.com/pelicanbookgrp

To receive news and specials, subscribe to our bulletin
http://pelink.us/bulletin

May God's glory shine through
this inspirational work of fiction.

AMDG

You Can Help!

At Pelican Book Group it is our mission to entertain readers with fiction that uplifts the Gospel. It is our privilege to spend time with you awhile as you read our stories.

We believe you can help us to bring Christ into the lives of people across the globe. And you don't have to open your wallet or even leave your house!

Here are 3 simple things you can do to help us bring illuminating fiction™ to people everywhere.

1) If you enjoyed this book, write a positive review. Post it at online retailers and websites where readers gather. And share your review with us at reviews@pelicanbookgroup.com (this does give us permission to reprint your review in whole or in part.)

2) If you enjoyed this book, recommend it to a friend in person, at a book club or on social media.

3) If you have suggestions on how we can improve or expand our selection, let us know. We value your opinion. Use the contact form on our web site or e-mail us at customer@pelicanbookgroup.com

God Can Help!

Are you in need? The Almighty can do great things for you. Holy is His Name! He has mercy in every generation. He can lift up the lowly and accomplish all things. Reach out today.

Do not fear: I am with you; do not be anxious: I am your God. I will strengthen you, I will help you, I will uphold you with my victorious right hand.
~Isaiah 41:10 (NAB)

We pray daily, and we especially pray for everyone connected to Pelican Book Group—that includes you! If you have a specific need, we welcome the opportunity to pray for you. Share your needs or praise reports at <u>http://pelink.us/pray4us</u>

Free Book Offer

We're looking for booklovers like you to partner with us! Join our team of influencers today and periodically receive free eBooks and exclusive offers.

For more information
Visit http://pelicanbookgroup.com/booklovers